Mandy Byatt lives in Cheshire and has an MA in Creative Writing (Crime Fiction) from the University of East Anglia. She has been shortlisted in the Gransnet/HQ novel competition and *Woman & Home* short story competition, as well as longlisted in the HWA/Sharpe Books Unpublished Novel Award and Orange Pathé screenwriting competition. She was also a winner of a Radio 5 Live monologue competition. *Just Another Liar* is her debut novel.

D1334079

MANDY BYATT

JUST ANOTHER LIAR

avon.

Published by AVON
A division of HarperCollins*Publishers* Ltd
1 London Bridge Street
London SE1 9GF

www.harpercollins.co.uk

HarperCollins*Publishers*
1st Floor, Watermarque Building, Ringsend Road
Dublin 4, Ireland

A Paperback Original 2022
1
First published in Great Britain by HarperCollins*Publishers* 2022

A catalogue copy of this book is available from the British Library.

ISBN: 978-0-00-845991-8

Typeset in Sabon LT Std by Palimpsest Book Production Limited,
Falkirk, Stirlingshire

Printed and Bound in the UK using 100% Renewable Electricity
at CPI Group (UK) Ltd

MIX
Paper from
responsible sources
FSC™ C007454

This book is produced from independently certified FSC™ paper to ensure responsible forest management.

For more information visit: www.harpercollins.co.uk/green

For Mum, Dad and Nic – with love

The water is rushing into me, flooding my nostrils, bleeding through my eyelids, trying to prise open my lips. Plugging my ears with thunder. I don't know how much longer I can hold on, how much longer I want to.

And then the roaring stops. I'm floating, hands releasing their grip. Silence envelops me, shields me.

Until my hair is yanked, my neck snaps back, and I'm coughing, spluttering, retching, gasping, gasping, gasping for air. *You are cleansed. Saved.*

I take a deep breath and then I'm tumbling, plunging down, further and further, the water suffocating me. I am reborn.

CHAPTER 1

The silver heart of the necklace was cool between Anna's fingers. She wanted to slide it over her burning cheeks, press it to her eyelids. 'Right. Can we have a bit of quiet, please?'

The sixth formers ignored her, their chatter, giggles, beeping mobiles, filling both the room and her head.

She took a breath. She'd volunteered to accompany them on their visit to the local university but hadn't realised they'd be as excitable as a bunch of five-year-olds on their first visit to a zoo.

'I said: *quiet.*'

A group of girls at the back of the lecture theatre looked up, the pink 'O's of their lips showing their surprise at her raised voice. In the eleven weeks she'd been at St Edward's, she hadn't had cause to shout once. The independent school in a wealthy suburb of Manchester, with its fees of four thousand pounds per term, was worlds away from the comprehensive she'd taught at in Exeter.

'Can those at the back fill up some of the benches down here?'

She put her hand to her stomach as it groaned for the breakfast she'd been unable to eat. Her skin was clammy, a sheen on her face. The clock high on the wall said five past: was there time to go and flick some powder over her nose? Anna didn't want him to see her like this, had never let him see her when she was less than perfect – jumping out of bed, diving into the bathroom, brushing her teeth, showering, putting on make-up before he'd even opened his eyes.

Did he know she was here? Had he heard her name and thought it was merely a coincidence? Or was he rushing along the corridor now, anticipation doing the same dance through his veins as it was through hers?

And yet, this morning, instead of the buzz she'd been expecting to feel when the alarm had gone off, a sense of unease had taken its place.

She'd been tempted to call in sick, and it wouldn't even have been a lie – what earlier had been a dull throb behind her right eye was now like a hammer blow.

Crouching down, Anna dipped her hand into her bag, found a blister pack of paracetamol and popped the last two tablets out onto her palm. Her mouth was so dry she wasn't sure she'd be able to swallow them.

She straightened up and gave a reassuring smile, as much to convince herself as her students. No response: they were caught up in their own dramas.

So many times, she'd been tempted to step out in

4

front of Robbo. Last Saturday she'd followed his car, as she had every Saturday for the past few months, sunglasses on despite the rain, hair bundled into a cap. He would park at Sainsbury's, walk into town. Each step he took or window he looked in, the ten minutes or so spent in the bank, the quick browse around the farmers' market – she knew it all. It would have been so easy to walk into his path and feign surprise at seeing him. But so far, her cowardice had outweighed both the longing to speak to him and the need to make him realise she didn't want to give up on them. That she wouldn't.

She tipped the tablets into her mouth.

'You okay, miss?' A sandy-haired boy, with freckles to match – Tyler or Taylor or something like that – waved from the front row. The students around him nudged each other.

The bitter chalk of the tablets clung to the back of her throat. 'Sorry. Right. Where were we?' Reaching for her necklace again, she rolled it between thumb and forefinger, glanced at the door. In a minute, seconds even, he would be coming through it. She fought the urge to slip the silver heart into her mouth; he used to do that, pushing it between her lips, his tongue following, chasing it around.

Anna blinked, brought herself back to the present. 'So, remember what I said: ask questions, be inquisitive, soak up the atmosphere of the place. I know some of you won't be applying to come here but it's a good chance to get a feel for university life.'

The chatter continued, snippets floating across the room towards her: gossip about a celebrity, the latest series they were binge-watching on Netflix.

What would he say when he saw her? Ever since she'd made the decision to move to the town where he lived, she'd imagined the look of surprise, and then of delight on his face.

And yet her legs were trembling. Lack of food, low blood sugar probably. Certainly not nerves. How could she be nervous about meeting him?

She headed towards the lectern, clutching it with both hands when she reached it.

The glass door creaked and Anna's eyes swivelled towards it. Her heart was thudding, its beat filling her ears.

It wasn't him.

A small woman in flat, ugly shoes scurried across the floor towards her. The secretary.

'Miss Farrow?'

Anna nodded.

'So sorry for the delay. Some crisis in the lab. Professor…' Before she had a chance to get the words out, the door creaked again and the secretary turned. Anna didn't.

Instead she stared at the students, her white knuckles, at the sparkly Alice band that was attempting to hold the secretary's candyfloss hair in place.

'I'll leave you in his capable hands.' A touch on the arm and she was gone.

And Anna finally looked over.

At him.

Robbo.

He hadn't seen her, heading straight for the students, welcoming them to the department, explaining who he was. And then his head twisted towards her. His face lit up, briefly, before the smile left his lips. Anna told herself it was shock, that was all, he hadn't been expecting to see her, not here, not like this.

He turned back to the students, clapped his hands. 'Okay, everyone. We'll be splitting you up into two groups and we'll meet back here after the tour for questions.'

The babble of chatter filled the room again.

Unhooking her fingers from the lectern, Anna started walking towards him, legs heavy, every step like she was wading upstream through a river.

He was waiting for her. He stared at her outstretched hand as if he didn't know what he should do with it. But then his hand was on hers, warm, familiar, and she didn't want him to ever let it go.

'What...?' He shook his head and then dropped her fingers as if he'd been burnt.

The door creaked. A girl with blue hair swept in.

'Ah, here's Millie, everyone.' Robbo moved towards the students. 'She's going to take you on a tour of the laboratories.'

'Hurry up. Haven't got all day,' Millie said, bouncing up and down on her Doc Martens.

Robbo said something to the girl and she let out a squeal of laughter before slapping him on the arm.

Planting her feet firmly on the ground to stop herself from moving, Anna glared at her, wondering how it would feel to yank her by that ridiculous blue hair and drag her away from Robbo. She wouldn't be laughing then.

Anna lost sight of them as the students filed towards the door.

'Are you not coming, miss?' Tyler – that was it, she remembered now – was holding the door open for her, the last to leave.

'Be right with you.' She picked up her handbag, rummaging through the contents, pretending she was searching for something.

He hesitated.

'Go on.' She flicked her hand in the direction of the other students. 'You'll lose them.'

The door swung to with a bang as he left.

Anna had pictured many things, built up scenarios in her head of what Robbo would say when they met, but this, what had just happened, had not been one of them. The look on his face when he'd seen her... it had stamped on the hope she'd been kindling. But maybe she'd imagined it? Perhaps it was just shock after all?

The door creaked.

Robbo.

No, she hadn't imagined it: something much darker than shock was written over his face.

And yet, as he walked across the room, she convinced herself it would be all right, he'd pull her towards him, put his lips on hers.

He stopped three feet away from her, just out of reach but close enough for her to smell the spice of his aftershave. There was a blue hair on the collar of his corduroy jacket. She fought the urge to brush it away.

'What are you doing here?' He ran his hand through his hair, a gesture so familiar she had to dig her nails into her palms to stop herself from crying out.

'I work at St Edward's.'

'You work in Exeter.'

'I fancied a change.' The lie sounded flat, hollow.

'But you know *I* live here, work here.'

Anna unclenched her fists, flicked her hair back over her shoulder. She knew it looked good: one hundred and twenty pounds spent on honey-blonde balayage highlights had seen to that.

'I was headhunted.' Another lie. 'It was too good an opportunity to turn down. Head of department.' At least that was the truth. She was gabbling, trying to fill the silence with words to prove she hadn't taken the job because of him. Because of what they'd had.

But it was too late: his chocolate-brown eyes darkened, his head shook back and forth. The lips she'd liked to trace with her tongue settled into a thin line. He didn't want her. Her throat tightened. She tried to swallow but her mouth was still too dry, the residue of the paracetamol acrid, the taste filling her mouth. What had she done? How could she have been so stupid?

Wrapping her arms around herself, she took a deep

breath, stuck her chin out. 'It's not a problem, is it? We're grown-ups. Just because we had a... a fling, that doesn't mean anything, does it? For God's sake, Robbo. It's more money. Better prospects. You're not going to begrudge me that, are you?' The words *after everything else* hung in the air between them.

'Oh, Anna.' He scuffed the toe of his shoe on the parquet floor, back and forth. Tan, a soft leather; she'd never seen them before. 'I won't change my mind.'

'Did I say I wanted you to?'

He had the good grace to blush. 'You need to move on.'

'I have done. I was headhunted, Robbo. Get it? The world doesn't revolve around you, you know.'

He held up his hands in an apology. 'Sorry, it's just a shock, seeing you here like this. And I'm glad you've moved on. Any bloke would be lucky to have you. Is there anyone?'

Was there a hopeful note to the question? A *yes* would show she was over him, hadn't taken the job because of him. The urge to say it itched away at her: would the jealousy still be there, the jealousy that caused him to snap, sulk? To hit. Not her, of course, never her, but years ago, he had punched a guy who had slapped her bum in the college bar. Robbo's ferocity had frightened her at the time – how she wished he would show that same ferocity now. But if there was a chance, just a chance he might reconsider... if it was just shock that was making him act this way, say these things...

'No.' She shook her head. 'No, there isn't.'

His chest was rising and before he had the chance to let out the sigh she could sense building up in him, she said: 'But I'm online dating. Playing the field. Meeting some interesting men. Very interesting. Very...' Her words petered out.

'That's great, Anna. Really, it is.'

'Yes.' She nodded. 'Yes.'

He stepped forward and, for a second, she thought he was going to kiss her, but he simply lifted his thumb to her cheek. His hand lingered for a moment before he snatched it back.

'You shouldn't have come here, Anna.'

His voice was so quiet she could hardly make out his words.

'Robbo?'

'I mean it, Anna. Stay away from me. It's over.'

The smell of chicken chow mein filled the room but, instead of fishing the ready meal out of the microwave, Anna headed straight for the fridge. She was going to finish off last night's bottle.

Her mobile beeped. She allowed herself a moment of believing Robbo might have texted her, excitement making her snatch up the phone.

It wasn't him. Of course it wasn't. He probably didn't have her number now. She certainly didn't have his; he had changed it, no doubt fed up with the constant calls she'd made when he'd dumped her last November. *Over.* That's what he'd said to her then, the same word he'd used this morning. No explanation for why one day he loved her and the next he didn't.

She opened the message. Lisa.

You'll never guess... Her sister always liked to build the tension in any situation.

Waiting for the photo to load, Anna took a large gulp from her glass, the wine like acid in her mouth. Of course she could guess – she knew love when she saw it, in others at least. And Joe had whisked Lisa off to Paris to celebrate their year anniversary. After meeting on an online dating site, the pair had been infatuated with each other ever since. They liked the same bands, food, films, laughed at the same things. Lisa, who had forged a sick note nearly every week to get out of PE when they'd been teenagers, had taken up running, saying it was important to have a hobby they could share. They pounded the streets. He massaged her feet afterwards. She washed his running gear. A perfect couple.

Anna took another swig of wine. A solitaire diamond, shaped like a raindrop, filled the screen. She'd pointed out a similar one to Robbo last June when they'd gone to Lyme Regis for the weekend. He'd laughed, tugging her away from the window, said he'd buy her a crab sandwich instead.

Congrats! She added some emojis, a love heart and a bride, a couple of champagne flutes.

Will you come wedding dress shopping with me?

Of course I will. There was no one else to do it, after all. Their stepmother wasn't the motherly type, even

12

though she'd been in their lives since their mother had died when Anna was six and Lisa was four. And her father... he probably wouldn't go to the wedding if it wasn't in a church, which Anna was sure it wouldn't be: after having religion shoved down their throats throughout their childhood, both she and Lisa had turned away from it as soon as they'd left home.

What you up to? The reply came back almost immediately.

Just chilling at home.

Home. Anna sighed. This wasn't home. A rented ground-floor flat in a block near the hospital, it was a box with three rooms: a kitchen-cum-living area with patio doors that opened onto a patch of sunless lawn bordering the road; a bedroom with a double bed pushed up against one wall, fighting for space with a single wardrobe and a lop-sided chest of drawers; and a tiny bathroom with a bath so short she couldn't lie back in it. So unlike her flat in Exeter, with the airy rooms framed by Georgian windows, the high ceilings. The sofa she'd saved up three months' salary for. The huge brass bedstead dressed with white linen and pale blue cushions. Her dressing table, her cosmetics piled high on it, fairy lights around the mirror. That was home. Especially when Robbo was there with her.

The headache she'd had all day was still lingering over her right eye. The flat was unbearably hot; the boiler seemed to have a mind of its own, pumping out heat, regardless of what the thermostat said. Levering

13

herself up, she went over to the patio windows and opened the doors, breathing in the frosty air. She looked up. Snow had been forecast even though it was nearly the end of March. A child on a bike wobbled past on the other side of the street, illuminated by a lamp post, a couple following, their fingers laced together, arms swinging as they walked.

It had been a mistake to come here. What had she been thinking? That he would just sweep her back into his arms, tell her he should never have let her go? She was an idiot. Lisa had said as much when she'd found out Anna was moving to be near to him. Her sister's words had stung: 'How many more times has he got to let you down before you finally get the message?'

Anna could almost forgive him for dumping her after uni. They were young, after all, and he was off to the US to do a master's. Vague talk of her going with him petered out when she signed up for a postgrad in teacher training at Exeter. Promises to keep in touch were made and kept from her side, but his messages grew fewer and fewer, until one day she gave up waiting for the phone to ring.

And so, bit by bit, she had wiped him from her mind, immersed herself in her career, had fun with her friends and met new men. Nice men. Rich men. Men who made her laugh. Men who were great in bed. She'd convinced herself she was okay, that Robbo was her past.

She walked over to the kitchen area: she needed another glass of wine.

March 25th. The calendar stuck to the fridge door caught her eye. Today's date had hearts drawn around it. How pathetic it now seemed; something her students would do. A year ago today. It was Fate, that's what she'd told herself when she'd been asked to stand in for the head of sixth form: she was going to meet Robbo on the very day it had all started again last year.

She'd been helping Lisa out at a conference, a last-minute favour as her sister's business partner had dislocated her shoulder, skiing in Andorra. And luckily for Anna, the heating had broken at her school for the second time that winter, which meant it was closed. A swarm of delegates at the reception desk had distracted her so when she shouted, 'Next' and he'd said his name, she hadn't looked up immediately. But then, catching the familiar scent of his aftershave, she'd lifted her eyes. Her fingers grazed Robbo's palm as she handed him his badge. He dropped it. Coughed. Blushed. Ran his fingers through his hair.

It was only natural they would end up going out for dinner, despite Lisa's tutting; after all, they were old friends, weren't they?

And only natural they would end up in bed. Fifteen years apart and their bodies hadn't forgotten they fitted together.

The next morning, her arm draped over his hips, Anna knew she wouldn't let him go again.

Nearly eight months it lasted, eight months of calls, texts, of him travelling down to Exeter to see her when his job would allow.

And then, almost as quickly as it started, it was over. Her mobile had beeped on a damp November day when she was rushing from one class to the next: I can't do this anymore.

She had begged. Cajoled. Cried. The students had milled around, oblivious to the fact that her world had suddenly tipped sideways. Why, Robbo? Please, I love you. Why? There must be a reason. Her pleading had been met by silence.

A couple of weeks later, she'd had the phone call from St Edward's: they were very impressed with her application and could she come for an interview? A moment's hesitation and then the 'Yes' was out of her mouth. Why not? If she could get the job, be nearer to Robbo, surely he would see sense?

Her mobile buzzed again. Lisa. What's happening with Robbo?

Nothing. She stared at the word.

Bastard.

Anna smiled; it wasn't the first time her sister had called Robbo that. Her phone beeped again.

Get yourself on online dating. Might meet the man of your dreams?

A snort escaped Anna's nose. Can't all be as lucky as you! Now get back to your fiancé, she typed, adding a smiley face and three kisses, before putting her phone on silent.

Emptying the last of the bottle into her glass, she went back to the open doors.

A flurry of snowflakes cascaded and swirled in the

16

air. Anna stuck her hand out, marvelling at how quickly the heat from her palm dissolved them. She'd got Robbo so wrong. She'd believed his words of love, the future she'd spun around them. Was it all just in her imagination? Had she fed a fairy-tale ending to herself over the years, built him up into the man she was destined to be with? Never given anyone else a chance because her head was filled with Robbo?

She had to let him go. Life was so ephemeral; a touch here, a word spoken there, and it was gone in an instant. The years were passing and she was alone, the family she craved as elusive as the snowflakes she was trying to catch. And it was all her fault. 'Over.' She said the word out loud, quietly at first, and then shouted it out into the swirling snow.

Was it snowing in Paris? Were her sister and Joe sitting in a dimly lit restaurant staring out at the wintry evening? She could taste their happiness, wanted it for herself. She had to move on. Robbo was right.

She took a long drink. Men were attracted to her. Always had been. The problem was finding one she was attracted to, someone who made her light up inside when she caught sight of him. A man who would make her stomach flip like Robbo did. But someone who wouldn't let her down like he had.

Anna shut the patio doors and went back to the sofa. She picked up her tablet, opened the dating site Lisa had used and clicked *new profile*. It took ten minutes to tap in her details, to choose a photo from a holiday a couple of years ago, describe herself in one hundred words, enter her card details. Done. It would probably come to nothing, but what did she have to lose?

She put the tablet down. No good staring at it, waiting. It could be days before anyone sent her a message, weeks perhaps. And even then, they would probably not be her type; Lisa said she was choosy. Too choosy. Anna flicked on the TV, found an episode of *Real Housewives* she hadn't seen before, propped a cushion behind her head and let herself get sucked into the bitching and preening.

Her neck was stiff when she woke. She rubbed at her eyes, staring at the clock on the mantelpiece. Gone midnight. She should go to bed. Anna pushed herself off the sofa, switched off the TV and picked up her tablet. After three attempts at her password, she was back on the site. A number on the dashboard showed she'd received one message.

Hey Anna, just thought I'd say hello. I'm new to this site too. Must be Fate? Would be lovely to chat to you. David x

Anna clicked on the profile, smiled. He was an attractive guy, in his late thirties. He had the same dark hair as Robbo, the same glint in his eye. She flicked through his photos. He could almost be his brother, could almost be Robbo himself if you squinted.

A scuffling noise in the garden made her look up. It was probably just a cat. Why hadn't the security light come on, though? It had interrupted her sleep nearly every night since she'd moved here, the glare pushing through the flimsy curtains. The bulb must have gone; she would speak to the landlord about replacing it.

She yanked the curtains shut and returned to the sofa.

Another message was waiting for her on her tablet.

Hey, just thought I'd point out I'm not just after a bit of 'fun' (if you get my drift!). I'm hoping to find someone who wants to float off into the sunset with me... David x

Anna smiled. It was a cheesy line, one she was sure he'd said to a lot of women. She studied his profile again. Definitely a charmer. And very cute. More attractive even than Robbo. She drained the last dregs of her wine, imagining Robbo's face if he saw her in town with this vision of a man. Would he be pleased for her, happy she was moving on? Or would jealousy flash across his face, make him shake David's hand a bit too vigorously, his grip a little too tight?

She slapped herself on the forehead. She was doing it again. This wasn't about Robbo. This was about her. She was nearly thirty-seven. The dreams of having a husband, a home, a brood of children, were disappearing with every school term. She had to do something. Start somewhere. Open herself up to the possibility of falling in love with someone else.

Tomorrow was Saturday. Before, she would have filled the day with following Robbo, but what was the point now? She thought of his face when he'd seen her this morning, how he'd told her to stay away from him. Lisa was right. He was a bastard, filling her head with his lies. He didn't deserve her. She reached under her hair, her acrylic nails struggling with the clasp of the necklace. The silver heart fell into her lap, the chain snaking after it.

'Fuck you, Robbo,' she spat into the emptiness of her flat, snatching up the necklace and flinging it across the room, before opening David's message and typing her reply.

CHAPTER 2

'It's only me.'

Denise closed the lid of her laptop and stood up, fixing a smile onto her face. The remnants of dinner were scattered everywhere: pots and pans obscured the worktops, her gravy-encrusted plate and Mother's bowl stacked on top of them. The smell of burnt meat hung in the air.

'Not disturbing you, am I?' Laurence said, as she bustled around, running the hot water tap, squirting too much washing-up liquid into the sink, plunging her hands into the tepid water.

'No, of course not.' The white lie was masked by her smile. The little chats she felt obliged to have with him when he called to see Mother were a small price to pay for the couple of hours' freedom his visits afforded her.

He nodded at the laptop. 'How's it going?'

'Fine if you're interested in axe-murderers. Or men who could pass for axe-murderers at least. Or men who look like they've been dropped on their heads at birth or—'

'You're too picky.' He plonked himself down in the chair Denise had vacated. 'Let's have a gander.'

Before he could open the laptop, Denise whisked it away with suds-covered hands and wedged it under her arm. 'No point,' she said. 'Waste of time. Waste of money too. Do you know how much—'

'You told me,' Laurence said. 'I'm sure I could find you a nice chap though.'

'Are there any left out there?'

He clutched at his left breast. 'Denise. How could you? I take that personally.'

He was joking, of course, poking fun at her. He was probably trying to elicit a compliment and yet a flush came to her cheeks. She didn't want to offend him. He was very good to Mother, there was no doubt about that.

'I didn't mean you, Laurence.' She raised her eyes towards the ceiling. 'Go on, she'll be waiting for you.'

She waited until he'd left the kitchen before putting down the laptop. She should never have confided in him about the online dating. It was her own fault for leaving her laptop open yesterday when she'd gone to the loo. She'd thought he was upstairs with Mother but when she'd returned to the kitchen, Laurence had been at the table, scrutinising the men who had popped up in her search results. It seemed daft to deny she was giving it a go and, anyway, what did it matter? And Denise did feel better for telling someone. Even if that someone was Laurence.

22

He'd clapped his liver-spotted hands together and declared it 'a grand idea', saying she needed her own life, deserved to find someone special, someone who would look after her for a change. She'd made him promise not to tell Mother what she was doing: she couldn't face the smirk that would spread across her face, the joy she would take in the rejections that were bound to come in.

Denise lifted the laptop lid. She had time. Laurence would be with Mother for an hour at least, maybe two, if she insisted on embroiling him in one of her diatribes on the state of the country. As an avid news-watcher, she could bore anyone silly on the NHS, politics, the state of education, the nation's diet. Her one good hand allowed her to surf the internet on her iPad, the TV on in the background, BBC News presenters chattering away to her like old friends.

Denise cast a quick glance towards the hallway before navigating to the dating website.

Raise your expectations. She had read that in one of the self-help books she'd picked up at the library. She was getting what she got because that's what she was expecting. Aiming too low, that's what she'd been doing. The men she'd emailed so far had been on her level, a three out of ten if she was feeling generous: slightly overweight, plain-looking veering towards odd, jobs rather than careers, never married, no prospects.

Finding the advanced search page, she began to click through the options. Anyone over fifty was out, arrogant prats after a slim woman, anyone more than two inches shorter than her. She pressed *enter*. Waited. Zipped up her fleece and stared out of the window at the snow swirling through the inky-black sky. Thirty-three results in a twenty-five-mile radius. After deleting those men she didn't like the look of, she was left with just seven profiles. Maybe she'd raised her expectations too much?

She clicked on the first. Hmm, he was into classical music. Liked fine wine. Neither of these scored highly with Denise. She opened the next profile. A linguist. *A cunning linguist*, he'd written. He liked experimentation. She blocked the man from appearing in her search results. She sighed. The next three were no better: one wanted someone who was good at cooking, another was just up for fun, rather than a long-term relation-ship, and one said he swung both ways.

She opened the last profile. A gasp escaped her lips as the photo expanded in front of her: he was gorgeous. She read his words, read them again. He was a doctor. A doctor! Hushed voice. Soothing words. Comforting hands. A strange feeling surged through Denise's body, a feeling so alien to her that at first she couldn't place it. And then she realised what it was: lust. As heat rose up her chest, she picked up a stray takeaway leaflet from the table and fanned herself with it. She studied his photos, licked her lips. He was on a mountain in one image, skis in hand, all sunglasses and stubble. In another he was sitting by a pool, a bottle of beer held aloft. Denise imagined running her hand over his biceps, down his chest, down to his...

'She wants tea.' Laurence was standing in the doorway, Mother's plastic cup in his hand.

'Right, right.' Banging shut the laptop lid, Denise pushed herself out of the chair, picked up the kettle and went to the sink. The water burst out of the tap as she turned it on, soaking her fleece. Her bosom was heaving, hands shaking, a smile twitching at the corners of her mouth.

She smelt him before she realised he was behind her: his aftershave, pine that reminded her of cheap toilet cleaner, and, mixed with it, the sourness of alcohol. A golfer, Laurence favoured the nineteenth hole over the others.

'Here, let me.' He prised the kettle out of her hand. 'Sit down, sit down.'

'I...' She sat, not knowing what else to do. Yesterday's newspaper was flung across a chair. Picking it up, she pretended to scour the front-page story: a woman had drowned in the canal. Denise shuddered; she couldn't imagine a worse death than drowning.

'Found anyone?'

'Hmm?'

'On the internet?'

She turned the page of the newspaper. 'I was just doing some work. Which reminds me,' she said, 'you were going to send me the receipts from the fete.'

'Sorry. Completely forgot. Made over a thousand pounds. Smashing day. You should have come.'

'Great,' she said. 'That'll pay for a cow.'

'Yes, Reverend Muthui will be pleased. That's five

we've managed to buy in the last year. People are so generous, aren't they?'

She finally looked up. Laurence was spooning three teaspoons of sugar into Mother's cup.

'It's not just the money,' he continued. 'We couldn't run the charity if it weren't for people giving their time too.' He beamed at her.

'Oh, it's nothing,' Denise said. It actually wasn't nothing. Sometimes the books she did for the charity took more time than those of her paying customers. Still, it was all for a good cause.

'I'm off out to Kenya again later in the year. You should come.' The kettle clicked off, the noise of the water whistling to a crescendo before dying down. 'You could help out in the school. Teach maths?' He filled the plastic cup, splashed plenty of milk into it and pressed the lid on.

'I can't get away, can I?' Denise nodded at the ceiling. That was one thing she could thank Mother for – she came in handy as an excuse. A five-minute chat with Laurence she could just about manage, but a fortnight cooped up with him? No way.

'Respite care.'

'Sorry?'

'You could put her into respite care.'

'No.' The word came out more forcefully than she'd intended it to. 'Sorry,' she said, looking back down at the newspaper.

'You do too much, darling.' Laurence sighed, squeezing her shoulder as he walked past her. 'You've got your own life to lead too.'

26

Darling? Where had that come from? She waited until she heard the creak of the top stair before she pushed the newspaper to one side and opened her laptop again. Her finger jabbed at the *enter* button, bringing the screen back to life. David gazed back at her: Mr Gorgeous.

Yes, she did have her own life to lead, and she was going to have one last attempt at living it.

'She wants you.'

Denise jumped. She'd been staring at the message box on the dating site for the past half hour. There had been no reply from David, despite the fact she'd composed what she thought was a witty message, and updated her profile to make herself sound more interesting than she really was. Being into skiing and fine dining sounded so much better than being into self-help books and chocolate. She'd changed her photo too, choosing one that was over seven years old, when she was slimmer. She looked happy in it, radiant even. It had been taken at her and Ian's engagement party. And she *had* been happy: they were to marry six months later, then there would be the move to the house they were renovating and, following that, and most important of all, there would be the baby they both longed for. But none of it had worked out. Mother's stroke just two weeks after the photo had been taken had seen Denise moving back from Scotland to care for her. Ian followed when he found a job in the area. But it hadn't worked, and he had given her an ultimatum.

Laurence pulled out a chair at the kitchen table. 'I could do with a strong drink. I've had the latest on Europe, the immigration problem and the demise of the state pension.'

Denise smiled. He had the patience of a saint. She shut down her laptop. 'I'd better go and see what she wants.'

She hovered by the kitchen door, waiting for Laurence to get the hint.

'Right, I'll say goodnight then. See you tomorrow.'

'Night.' Denise heard the click of the back door as she trudged up the stairs.

'Denise, is that you?'

'I'm here.' Mother's bedroom was immaculate. The huge wooden bed sat on a thick burgundy carpet, while ornaments amassed over the years were neatly displayed, the smell of lavender furniture polish hanging in the air. Mother liked everything shipshape. She'd go mad if she ever saw what the rest of the house was like – Denise only tidied up downstairs the day before hospital visits, when Mother had to leave her bedroom.

'Pass me my iPad.'

No please or thank you. Denise was used to it. 'Isn't it a bit late…'

'I'm not a bloody child, Denise.'

Denise picked up the iPad from her mother's bedside cabinet and plugged it into the stand on the overbed table. A scandal about a politician, something involving a dungeon and whipped cream, had broken earlier; she'd be wanting to catch up on that. The stroke had taken everything away from Mother, everything except her left arm, her brain and her thirst for news and gossip.

Mother clutched at Denise's hand as she removed the empty cup from the bedside table, yellow fingernails digging into her palm. 'Laurence comes to see me, not you,' she hissed.

Denise tried to pull her hand away. 'Mother, you're hurting me.'

'I'm watching you.' The pressure of her grip increased before she suddenly let go.

Denise looked down at her hand, blood threatening to break the surface of the four red marks on her palm.

And then her mother started to laugh, tears pooling in her eyes, spilling over. Denise shook her head, wondering what was so funny. That was how Mother was: dark one moment, full of light the next.

'What is it?' Denise took a tissue out of the box on the bedside cabinet and dabbed at Mother's cheeks.

As quickly as she'd started laughing, she stopped, pushing Denise's hand away. 'That anyone could find a fat cow like you attractive. Really, sometimes, I think my mind is going the same way as this useless body.'

Denise went straight to her laptop, even though she knew there would be no message from David. And yet, and yet... she still allowed herself a small glimmer of hope: she needed something to stop her sinking down to the depths into which Mother was trying to drag her. She wished she could blame Mother's attitude on the stroke, but it wasn't that. Denise couldn't remember a time when she had been any different with her. It was like she was two people: an arm squeezing her shoulder and a kiss on the top of her head one minute, and a slap around the face telling her she was useless the next.

She pressed the *on* button, woke up the laptop and closed her eyes as she waited for the dating site to load. Praying to a God she'd long since stopped believing in, she opened her profile. A number *1* winked on her inbox icon. She had a message!

This called for a glass of something to celebrate – and to calm her nerves. But there was nothing in the house. A couple of years ago, after one too many nights staring at yet another empty bottle of wine, Denise had stopped drinking. While the alcohol had numbed the loneliness, put a haze over the grief of losing Ian, ultimately it had made her feel worse, not better. Tired, sluggish. Depressed even. Now her comfort of choice was a piece or two of chocolate. Sugar put a smile on her face. Gave her the energy to get up every morning. Was it any wonder she'd put on weight? The scales said half a stone, but the scales were old and probably broken. The mirror, now that couldn't lie, and it told her more than half a stone. Alcohol was fattening, she knew that, but she'd been good all day, only having two Rich Tea biscuits and, anyway, she wanted a drink. She stood up. Wasn't there a bottle of sherry under the sink? Bought three Christmases ago when her sister, Karen, her husband and their three kids had visited from South Africa? Bending down, Denise's hand reached past bottles of bleach, furniture polish, fabric conditioner. There was.

The sweetness was familiar, but the alcohol was not. Its warmth filled her mouth, slipping down her throat, her chest aflame. Another sip and the heat flooded her face. A fuzziness filled her head, a feeling she liked, had missed.

Denise sat down in front of her laptop, took a deep breath, another sip of sherry, and clicked on the icon to open her messages. Were things finally starting to go her way?

No.

The message wasn't from David. She slumped back in the chair, drank down half of the contents of the glass in one gulp. Still, maybe this – she peered at the name – Pete1983 would be just as dishy as David was?

He wasn't. Even when she squinted. He reminded her of the wrestlers she'd seen on TV when she was little, fat rather than muscly, bald head, pinpricks of eyes sitting above acne-pocked cheeks. She didn't even bother opening the message, just pressed *delete* and watched it disappear.

The sherry bottle was where she'd left it. As she poured herself another large measure she heard a tapping at the back door.

The outline of a figure, one that looked suspiciously like Laurence, was visible through the frosted glass.

'Have I left my glasses here?' he whispered, when she opened the door an inch. 'Sorry, didn't want to wake Veronica by banging too loudly.'

'She'll be asleep by now.' Within five minutes of picking up her iPad, Mother's eyelids would have started to droop.

'Did I leave them on the kitchen table?' Laurence pushed past her, bringing a draught of icy air with him.

'Haven't seen them.' She turned. He had a bottle in his hand.

'What's that?'

He held it aloft. 'Wine?'

'I meant, what's it for?'

'You looked like you could use a drink when I left.' He pointed at the sherry bottle on the side. 'See, I was right. Wouldn't you prefer a nice glass of Pinot Noir rather than that old thing?'

Denise wavered. She would, but she didn't really want to drink with Laurence. And Mother might be asleep and might never find out but it wouldn't look good if she did. The red marks on her hand were starting to sting. No, Mother wouldn't like it at all. But it was just before ten on a Friday night and she had nothing better to do. And, anyway, what harm could it do? A drink was a drink. She wasn't planning on sailing off into the sunset with him.

'Go on then.'

'Glasses?' Laurence said.

She smiled. 'They're on your head.'

He smacked himself on the forehead, chuckled.

Denise hunted around in the cutlery drawer, unearthed the corkscrew and passed it to him. Laurence was still chuckling. A giggle bubbled up inside her; he wasn't so bad. She found some glasses and rinsed them as he stabbed at the cork, twisting the handle, pushing down the levers until it popped out. Of course, there were times when she wished Laurence hadn't moved next door to them, on days when he was constantly in and out of the house. Though having him as a neighbour was at least preferable to his original idea: after Mother's second stroke, he'd wanted to move in, to help out. Karen had thought it was a great plan, declaring it testament to his devotion. *What about my devotion?* Denise had wanted to scream at her sister. *You're living the sun-kissed life in South Africa, while I'm dealing with all this.* But she hadn't. *He should find someone else*, was what she'd said instead. *Leave us to get on with it.*

As he poured her a glass of wine, she had to admit that, on balance, she was glad Laurence had stuck around: he was a friend to her of sorts. She had always thought his allegiance lay with Mother but, when she looked at it objectively, he was just as supportive to her, always asking how she was, running errands, taking Mother to hospital appointments to give her a break. He was someone she could rely on, was there on those days when she'd almost forgotten what it was like to hear another person's voice – one that wasn't screaming at her, anyway. After all, if Mother had agreed to marry him, all those years ago before she took ill, he would be her stepfather now. But she had flatly refused to tie the knot again, having never quite got over being left by Denise's father. She'd had other boyfriends, of course,

33

before Laurence. Too many to remember in fact. Apart from one. Terry. Denise shuddered. A religious education teacher, he'd been the most un-Christian person Denise had ever met: he'd once come up behind her and forced her head into the bathroom sink when she'd been washing her hair. She'd thought she was going to die. Even now she couldn't stand to get water on her face.

Laurence handed her a glass. 'Any luck?' He nodded at the laptop.

She shook her head. 'I've given up.'

'Never give up, Denise. Look at your mother.'

Denise peered into her wine glass, scared the expression on her face would give her away, that it would show there were times, times that were becoming all too frequent, when she hoped Mother *would* give up. She lifted the glass to her lips, gulping at the wine, savouring the sweet taste of cherries as she rolled it around her mouth. It was certainly better than the fusty sherry. Why had she stopped drinking? It put a haze over everything, softened the edges of her life, made it seem almost bearable.

'There's someone out there for you, Denise. You just have to open your eyes, your mind.'

She let out a long sigh. She had opened her mind and look where it had got her – nowhere.

'Top-up?'

Denise stared at her empty glass. He'd only been here five minutes. And while she enjoyed the feeling the alcohol gave her, the sense that she wasn't really there, all sights and sounds muffled, she was sure to have a hangover in the morning. Nonetheless, she held out her glass.

'You need to lighten up a bit.' Laurence poured her some more wine before standing up and crossing the kitchen. She turned her head to find he was hovering behind her. 'You're very tense.'

She went to get up but he pushed her slowly back down, the warmth from his fingers penetrating her fleece. And then he was scooping her hair to one side, his hands on her neck, kneading, fingers and thumbs working their way down, under her blouse, to the tight muscles either side of her spine.

'Come on, relax, darling. Let your shoulders drop.'

She wanted to pull away and yet found she couldn't – how long had it been since someone had touched her?

'There, that's better, isn't it?'

Denise buried her nose in her wine glass, her face aflame.

'I've got a bit of a stiff neck myself.' Laurence lowered himself down on the chair next to her. 'All this golf, you know.' He rocked his head from side to side, up and down.

The clock ticked; a car backfired in the next street. Denise knew what he wanted and yet she didn't know if she could touch him. She lifted her glass to her lips and knocked back the wine as if it were water.

Standing up, she moved behind him, her eyes taking in his bald patch, the dark spots the sun had scorched. She placed her fingers on his beige jumper, grimacing at her bitten nails. She used to have lovely nails, long, clear polish, would drag them down Ian's back when they made love. She took a deep breath. The folds of Laurence's neck hung over the back of his collar; she couldn't touch his skin, she wouldn't.

'When you're ready,' Laurence said.

Slowly, lightly, she began to massage his shoulders. She focused on the cactus plant on top of the fridge, thinking of the photos of David on the dating site and trying to imagine it was him she was touching, his tanned skin, his tight muscles. But her imagination deserted her, swept away by the pine stink of Laurence's aftershave.

She took a deep breath and decided she would count to one hundred and then stop. Would feign a headache, not much of a lie as her head was heavy, muzzy.

She was almost at ninety-six when he put his hand up and caught her fingers. Swung himself around on the chair. Pulled her down towards him. Put his other hand on her face. And before she could cry out, move her head, his lips were on hers, his fat tongue, dry from the wine, invading her mouth. Her lungs gasped for air. She tried to push at him, to close her lips, but his arms, his lust, were too strong for her.

And then a strange thing happened: while her mind was saying *no*, her body began to say *yes*. She willed herself to stop but it was too late: her tongue was moving in rhythm with his, her hands were tugging his jumper up, trouser zip down. No, no, this wasn't right. This was Laurence for God's sake. And yet, although the rational side of her was still screaming *no*, the animalistic side of her, that innate feeling to be wanted, was telling her *yes*, was pulling him to the floor, pushing her pants down, taking him in one hand, guiding him towards her.

It was over in a matter of minutes. He rolled away from her, stood up, his hands doing the opposite of what Denise's had done: jumper down, zip up. He opened his mouth but no words came out.

Denise lay there, watched him leave, could hear his footsteps receding. The clock on the wall said ten thirty. She moved her gaze to the side. There was a potato peeling on the lino, a splash of water, crumbs, the top from a milk carton, a ball of dust, an earwig.

She stood up, ripped off her pants, threw them in the bin. Emptying the cold water out of the sink, piling the crockery on the side, she turned on the hot tap, squeezing washing-up liquid into the gushing flow, watching as the bubbles rose. She cleaned herself first, scrubbing and scrubbing with a wet tea towel, and then she washed everything that was not in a cupboard, ignoring the pain searing her scratched hand every time she plunged it into the water. She spritzed the sides with antibacterial spray, wiping them over and over. And then she filled a bucket, squirting nearly half a bottle of bleach into it. With a dustpan and brush she swept up what she could of the dirt on the floor. And then she put a mop into the bucket, and started to disinfect the floor, her arms like a pendulum, but getting faster and faster.

It was only when she'd finished, an hour later, that

she sat down. She leant forward, placing her arms on the kitchen table and dropping her head on top of them. This stupid idea of finding someone to love had sent her giddy, mad even. It had awakened something in her she should have kept buried. It had been her own stupid fault, all of it, thinking she would find someone, that she could have a relationship, was entitled to one. She would forget men, delete her profile, concentrate on Mother and on her book-keeping. Sitting up, she hauled her laptop towards her and switched it on.

An image of Laurence's face, his bushy eyebrows, the mole protruding from his chin, flashed into her mind. He was Mother's boyfriend, for God's sake! How could she ever look him in the eye again? What had she done? Would he tell Mother? No, surely not. But maybe she would guess. Denise glanced at the marks on her hand. Mother had warned her and she had paid no attention, thought she knew better. She tried to swallow. She would blame it on the wine, convince herself that loneliness, her need to feel wanted, had nothing to do with it. David. Why couldn't he have replied? Just a word from him and she wouldn't have needed to be held by someone else. Certainly not by Laurence.

A number one was winking next to her inbox. Her finger hovered over the *delete your profile* button. She didn't want any of this. It was madness. Nobody wanted her, except men who looked like nutters. And Laurence.

She should press *delete*, forget the whole thing. Forget tonight especially.

And yet… Tears filled her eyes, ran over her cheeks.

She was crying at her foolishness, at the glimmer of hope that refused to be extinguished, even though it was pointless. Pointless searching, hoping, trying to *raise her expectations*. Her whole life was pointless.

Denise clicked the message. Blinked. It couldn't be, could it? She rubbed the back of her hand across her face, reaching for the tea towel to wipe away the snot from her top lip, edged forward, peered at the screen.

David had replied. At 10.23. At the exact moment Laurence had been on top of her, grinding away.

CHAPTER 3

Great to hear from you. I'm new to all this too. Scary, isn't it? You don't know who you're going to meet.

You're right, we do seem to have very similar interests. Great to hear you love walking, especially when there's a good Sunday roast at the end of it. Where do you like to walk?

Can't believe Paul Simon is your favourite singer too. 'Hearts and Bones'... what's not to like in a song like that? Did you see him when he toured last year?

Hope to hear from you soon x

Petra's leg jerked so violently that the mug resting on her knee jumped, causing the lukewarm chamomile tea to crash out of it like a wave onto the wooden floor. It was what, only five minutes since she'd sent the last message? She put the mug onto a coaster on the coffee table and dashed into the kitchen. The clock on the oven blinked ten minutes past midnight. There wasn't time to wipe up spilt tea but, if she ignored it, the thought of the puddle lying there, soaking into the oak floorboard, would hover at the back of her mind and then she wouldn't be able to concentrate. And that was the one thing she needed to do. She picked up a cloth and ran back to the living room.

Her hand scrubbed back and forth, her eyes fixed to the screen. No, it hadn't been a figment of her imagination. The message was still there. And signed off with a kiss.

The grandfather clock boomed quarter past. She had to hurry. Bolting back into the kitchen, she chucked the cloth into the bin, pumped antibacterial handwash onto both palms and rubbed it around her fingers, hands, wrists, all the way up to her elbows, savouring the smell of antiseptic as she headed back into the living room.

Careful to avoid the damp patch on the floor, she positioned herself on the sofa and rested the laptop on her knees, fiddling with the end of her plait. With a few clicks he was there, sea-green eyes staring at her, a grinning mouth. She had to admit he was attractive. Dark, curly hair, a hint of stubble, white, even teeth. Who could resist that? Who wanted to? He was perfect. And he was a doctor for Christ's sake! A doctor. Someone who cared for people, listened to them. Someone who had given his life to helping others. Someone who could help her.

Another click and she was back to the message, scanning every word, every punctuation mark, for meaning. Her gaze fixed on the kiss: was it flirty or was it just what people did these days? Her finger rested on the *reply* button, her knee jumping. She slammed her hand down on top of it but could still feel it twitching underneath. Should she do it? Did she dare? Was this really what she wanted?

Whatever she wanted, there was something she needed: it clawed at her stomach, made her mouth water, filled her head so she had little room for anything else. Vodka. But there was no alcohol in the house, hadn't been for nearly five months. That's what she told herself, told others. Promised them. But of course there was; she only had to pull the bottom drawer of her bedside cabinet all the way out and there it would be, nestling on the carpet – her emergency supply. For when things got bad.

Images of what had happened earlier tripped through her mind, bringing back the pain that made her want to howl like an injured animal. And the words, worse than any physical injury; words wormed their way into your brain.

More chamomile tea, that was the answer, not vodka. Something calming. Something to stop the thoughts whizzing around her head. That's what they all drank at work – they needed to, given the suffering they saw. The cat today had been hit by a car, its left leg hanging, useless. Petra had stroked its tiny head, willing it on as the vet amputated the limb. Had carried on stroking, long after it had gone. She looked over at Jude, the greyhound she'd brought home from the rescue centre five years ago. If anything should happen to him, she wouldn't be able to bear it.

43

She put the laptop to one side. She would make a fresh cup. The kitchen was to the left, but she turned right, towards the stairs, putting her hand on the banister, squinting up into the darkness. *Tea, tea*, she repeated, willing herself to turn around. Her hand moved but, instead of pushing her backwards, it levered her up the first step, and then her legs took over, propelling her forwards, two steps at a time.

And then she was outside the bedroom door, nudging it open an inch, her leg twitching to move, the rest of her wanting to stay where it was. Even through the small gap she could taste the misery that hung in the room. It permeated everything, tainting the soft periwinkle walls, the floral curtains and matching bedding, the thick cream carpet. The room had been redecorated before Christmas. A new beginning. But it hadn't been. Petra hated the hours spent awake, listening to his breathing, being drawn to the warmth of his body but not letting herself move towards him.

She thrust her hand through the doorway, feeling for the light switch on the right. Her knee jerked and the door swung open. As she stepped into the room, the smell came at her. A mustiness, as if something had died in there. A smell he said was in her imagination. Petra lunged for the bedside cabinet, sinking to her knees and yanking the drawer out. It was still there. Why wouldn't it be? She unscrewed it, smacked the top of the bottle to her lips and tipped her head back. Alcohol rushed through her bloodstream, reaching her head where it dissolved the thoughts clattering around her mind – of the row and what it had made her do.

The slam of a car door, the crunch of footsteps on gravel made her stop mid-gulp. Sam.

Coughing, spluttering, she screwed the top on again, flung the bottle back and rammed the drawer into place.

She had just made it to the top of the stairs when the front door opened slowly, quiet footsteps coming into the hall.

Her husband stared up at her. 'I'm sorry, Pet.'

Petra didn't answer. The laptop. It was lying open on the sofa. She imagined Sam looking at the screen, the confusion on his face when he saw what she'd been up to. Disbelief, perhaps? Or would he shrug and admit it was inevitable, that it was bound to come to this? That he couldn't give her what she wanted, and so she would find someone who could. She couldn't let him see what she'd been doing; he would never believe she was doing it *for them*. She flew down the stairs as fast as her jerking leg would allow, scooted around him as his hand reached out for her.

Hurtling into the living room, she slammed down the lid on the laptop, picked it up and thrust it under her arm. Jude looked up from his basket and sprang up onto tired legs, before darting past Sam as he came into the room.

'Sorry.'

She turned at the sound of his voice, her gaze searching for something to focus on, anything but his face: there was a hole in his left sock. His big toe was protruding through it, grotesque.

He stepped towards her. 'Really. I am.'

She took a step backwards. Then another.

He nodded at the laptop. 'What've you been up to?'

Did he know? Was it written on her face? She shivered, even though the log burner was still blasting out heat, the chill starting on the top of her head, working its way down her body, as if she'd been frozen. She couldn't move, even her leg was still. Every part of her was brittle; one push and she would fall over, crack into tiny shards of ice.

She forced herself to open her mouth: 'I was going to ask you the same question.'

'I met up with Jacko.'

'It's gone midnight.' She pushed past him and went into the kitchen.

'We went to the Spice Lounge.' He followed her. 'You know Jacko, always likes to finish off a night with a vindaloo.'

Oh, she did. She knew Sam's half-brother only too well.

At odds with the rest of her, her mouth was on fire. She eyed the tap, picturing the ice-cold water that would gush out as soon as she turned it on. And yet, despite her thirst, despite her legs itching to move, her feet stayed rooted to the cool tiles; she didn't want to risk putting the laptop down until he was safely out of the room. Why couldn't he just go to bed and leave her alone?

He went to the fridge, took out some juice and reached for a glass off the shelf. 'Want one?'

She shook her head.

'Miranda's booked a villa in Italy for May half-term. Jacko showed me some photos. Looks amazing. He said we could join them if we wanted to.'

She shook her head again.

'Put the laptop down,' he said.

She clutched it tighter. He knew. He knew. The iciness clung to her skin. The tremor in her leg started, reverberated through her body.

Sam drained the juice in one go and placed his glass on the side. He stepped towards her and reached for the laptop, his hand grasping, trying to tug it away from her. The strength seeped out of her arms. She held her breath as he took it from her, knowing that if he discovered what she'd been doing, it would all be over. But he didn't open it, he simply placed it on the side, next to the glass.

He must have mistaken the relief she was certain was etched on her face for something else, for he pulled her towards him, his arms surrounding her. Her body was rigid, from the cold, the fear, from the fact that she didn't want him to think a hug would make everything all right. She breathed in the smell of him, his aftershave, the lemon fabric conditioner, the reek of curry seeping from his pores. The alcohol.

He squeezed her tighter, his arms trapping her plait, making her want to cry out. 'Am I forgiven?'

The word *yes* was buried somewhere inside her. All

she had to do was find it, force it out, let it escape her lips, then everything would be okay. She could ignore the message, delete her profile, pretend it had never happened. *Yes*. Just three letters. One syllable. A murmur would do. She could surely say it, even if she didn't mean it?

'Petra?'

It had been months since she'd let him hold her like this. Her nose squashed against the cotton of his shirt, she felt as if she were suffocating, her mouth trying to suck the air in as his arms crushed her. She squeezed him back, a short sharp pressure, hoped it would do, hoped he would let her go. A kiss on the top of her head and then he slowly released her.

'Shall we go to bed?' Sleep wasn't on his mind, of course not. The need to be with him, to have him inside her, was overwhelming; it clogged her mind, even crowding out the craving for the bottle under her bedside cabinet. And yet… And yet, she couldn't. She wasn't ready.

'The consultant said…'

He ran his fingers through his hair. Three words were enough. 'Of course. Yes. Sorry. I'll head on up then.' He gave her a reassuring smile, a smile that said, *don't worry, I understand*. He didn't though. No one did.

She glared at his back as he walked out of the room, heard his footsteps heavy up the stairs. 'Peanut', that was his name for it. She had laughed when he'd said it, teasing him, asked him if he'd call it that when it was born. But, of course, there never was a birth, just a void inside her, an emptiness where the baby should have been.

He wanted to keep trying, had brought it up this evening: 'We aren't the only couple to fall pregnant naturally after IVF not working. And if it happened once, it can again.'

'Miracles only happen once,' she'd replied. She'd regretted saying it as soon as the words were out of her mouth, but she'd wanted him to hurt as much as she was hurting. She imagined him with a daughter on his knee, his arm around her, reading to her perhaps, kissing blonde curls. The icy feeling rushed back through her. A baby. A baby would make everything all right.

'You won't be long, will you?' His words carried down the stairs.

She didn't bother answering. He would be asleep as soon as his eyes closed, as he was every night, snoring gently on and off throughout the long hours, kicking the duvet off at some point, while she lay there on her side, shivering, googling private clinics that offered IVF via a sperm donor, deleting her history afterwards so Sam wouldn't find out.

Turning on the tap, she filled a glass with water, gulping it down, the liquid trickling out of the corner of her mouth and over her chin. She lifted the laptop lid and the screen sprang to life. The message was still there. She moved the cursor until it hovered on the *delete* button. One click. That was all it would take. Just one click. But then she thought back to what had happened earlier, to the pain that had seared through her, Jude slinking behind the sofa, his whimpers drowned out by the shouting and the slam of the front door as Sam had stormed out. Things had to change. And maybe, just maybe, Doctor David was the answer to their problems, would save their marriage.

Her fingers were so cold she could hardly type, yet the vodka still warmed the emptiness in her belly, spurred her on. She read through what she'd written and pressed *send*. And then she sat in the dark, waiting for a reply, her knee jerking in time with her husband's snores as they floated down the stairs and into the empty room.

CHAPTER 4

Ten weeks later – early June

Anna glanced at her watch. Right on time: ten minutes late. Silly really, to keep him waiting, to leave him wondering if she was going to turn up. But, if he felt anything like she did, the anticipation fizzing away inside him would be delicious. Ten weeks. Seventy days of longing, of texts, late-night phone calls, long emails in which they'd got to know each other.

The cavernous room was filled with the babble of Friday-night drinkers. A former bank, it was devoid of windows and empty of much artificial light as well, with low-energy bulbs hanging from wall lights emitting a faint haze. Anna blinked, her eyes getting used to the dimness after the glare outside: seven thirty and the sun was as relentless as it had been for the past month. Had he spotted her, illuminated by the light from the open door? She flicked her hair back over her shoulder.

Was he watching her now? She swallowed, her mouth dry, and strode to the bar.

Pushing her way to the front, she edged in between a woman in a floral dress, the heady scent of cheap body spray emanating from her, and a guy in a garish blue shirt.

Anna placed her arm on the bar, next to the white arm of the woman. Had she been inside all summer? Thanks to the heatwave, Anna's skin was as brown as if she'd been to the Caribbean for a month. The woman must have seen her looking, for she pulled her arm quickly away.

'Next!'

The man to her side started reeling off his order but the barman ignored him, directing his gaze at Anna instead.

At first, she couldn't place him; he was so out of his normal surroundings. And then it came to her. Sandy hair. Freckles.

'Tyler. What are you doing here?'

'Working?' He used the same tone she used with students who asked obvious questions.

'You should be studying,' she shot back.

'It's only Friday and Saturday.' He shrugged. 'I need the money.'

'Excuse me.' Blue shirt guy waved his hand between them. 'Two bottles of Bud, a white—'

'What can I get you?' Tyler asked Anna.

Anna hesitated. He was in the lower-sixth, seventeen, maybe even sixteen, not old enough to work in a bar.

Even if he had been of age, the school didn't approve of part-time jobs, preferring the students to concentrate on getting A stars in their exams. And although Benson, the head, admitted a job could be useful for a CV, he railed against students taking one for financial reasons. These pupils had wealthy parents was his argument, what did they need a job for?

'Two bottles of Bud.' The guy waved a twenty-pound note in front of Tyler's face.

'Anna?'

She did a double-take at her name. Blue shirt man's head swivelled towards her.

Tyler grinned at her. 'I can hardly call you "Miss", can I?'

'Sauvignon.'

'Large?'

'Medium.'

'Sure?'

'Sure.'

'Let me get you that.' The man next to her put his hand on top of hers. 'On your own?'

Anna pulled her fingers out from under his. The cheek of him; he had to be a player, wearing a shirt like that.

'Can't blame me for trying.'

Tyler got a bottle of wine out of the chiller, selected a measure, topped it up and then tipped its contents into a glass. She fiddled with the heart on her necklace; after ten weeks of banishing it to the bottom of her jewellery box, she had finally dug it out, knowing it went well with her dress. So what if Robbo had bought it for her? It was only a necklace, and Robbo was part of her past now. Maybe David would buy her a new one?

'Here you go.' Tyler placed the glass onto a napkin, his fingers lingering on its stem.

Anna already had her purse out. She unzipped it, pulled out a ten-pound note, offered it to him.

He waved her hand away, put his fingers to his lips in a shushing movement, winked and then nodded at the man next to her.

The place was even fuller now than when she'd arrived. She forced her way through groups of chattering drinkers, all the time her eyes darting from one table to the next. But there was no man sitting on his own. No David.

Finding an empty table, albeit one with dirty glasses and crisp packets strewn over it, she sat down. Taking a sip of her wine, she scanned the room. No one else was on their own, apart from the woman at the bar, who was now bustling past people, her eyes darting this way and that. Was she on a first date too? Perhaps not. The dress she was wearing looked like something out of the 70s and not in a fashionable boho sort of way. Anna ran her hand across her dress: Miu Miu. It had cost a bomb but it fitted her perfectly.

The slim silver watch on Anna's wrist said twenty past. Where was he? She hadn't expected him to be late, had imagined him arriving a good half an hour early, as eager to see her as she was him. She fished inside her bag for her phone and swiped the screen to unlock it. Nothing. Well, nothing from David. There was a message from her sister. So? Lisa was short and to the point, as ever. She ignored it and typed out a quick message, cursing as her newly done nails made the job twice as long. Are you here yet? Placing the phone on the table where she could see it, she picked up her wine glass and took a large swig.

'Anna.'

Relief flooded through her; so, he had been watching her. Taking her time, she took another mouthful of wine, before looking up.

'I thought it was you.'

Great. That was all she needed. Richard Leek, head of geography, loomed over her. 'Are you waiting for someone?' Plonking himself down in the chair next to her, he didn't wait for an answer. His knee touched hers under the table. She pulled her leg back and frowned.

'That seat's taken.'

'Who by? The invisible man?' His hawking laugh drowned out the chatter around them. People standing nearby turned to stare.

Raising his glass to his mouth, he downed nearly a quarter of his pint before slamming it down on the table, his lips making a smacking sound. Anna's fingers curled, her nails digging into her palms; in the absence of a personality, Richard courted attention by being loud.

'You're looking very lovely tonight. You always do, though. Where do you shop? I'm guessing you go into Manchester. Those independent boutiques. Am I right?'

The muscles in Anna's stomach clenched. He was a

trier, she'd give him that. He was always sidling up to her in the staffroom, two mugs of thick black coffee in his hands. And he always left work at the same time as her, loitering by his car, fumbling with his keys: would she like to join him for a much-deserved drink?

She took a small sip of her wine. She had to get rid of him. How would it look when David arrived and saw she was with another man? And someone like Richard to boot.

Hoisting the strap of her bag over her shoulder, she grabbed her wine glass, stood up.

'Going already?'

'I'm meeting someone.'

'Oh, yes, Siobhan said you'd got a date.' He licked his lips, his tongue like a viper's, flicking in and out. 'To be honest, I didn't have you down as the internet-dating type. A gorgeous woman like you. Bet you have your pick of men.'

Anna swallowed. She'd kill Siobhan. They'd become good friends in the five months she'd been at St Edward's. They often spent Saturday afternoons heading into the city centre, going around those independent boutiques Richard had mentioned, having one too many cocktails before catching the tram back. Tuesday night was Pilates night, Thursday a swim and sauna at the local health club. Anna had even covered for Siobhan when she'd overslept one day.

'Hasn't turned up then?'

'He's running late.'

'Got a photo of him?'

She glanced down; her phone was on the table. Before she could pick it up, Richard had grabbed it.

Her heartbeat thundered, roaring in her ears. She snatched it out of his hand, wiping her fingers on the back of the chair, trying to remove all traces of his sweaty palm. She had to get out of here. If he'd seen what was on there...

'Just thought I'd check him out for you. There are a lot of nutters out there, you know.'

'There are a lot of nutters in here.'

He grinned. 'Touché. But, honestly, I'm quite harmless. Quite a good catch. Got my own hair, teeth, house, job.' He started to count off each item on his thin fingers.

Don't forget your arrogance, your vanity, your inclination to turn everything you say into sexual innuendo, she wanted to say, but didn't. Richard was well liked by the head. It wouldn't do to get on the wrong side of him.

'Nice seeing you, Richard, but I really have to go.' Her phone buzzed. 'That'll be him now.'

'Have fun, sweetheart.' He wiggled his fingers at her. 'Don't get up to anything I wouldn't.'

Sweetheart? Who did he think he was? She walked away from him, heading towards the beer garden.

After the cold draught of the air conditioning, the warmth outside was a relief. She put her wine glass onto the edge of a bench, smiling her thanks at the group of men who were squashed onto it, and opened the message.

Hey, how's it going? I want all the juicy details.

Siobhan. Anna's fingers gripped the phone. She'd been wrong to trust her. To tell her everything. She'd confided in her about how she'd ended up at St Edward's, in this town, had told her the whole sorry tale about Robbo. And they'd picked through every bit of her relationship with David, discussing him endlessly, scrutinising his messages. Anna had even shown her the photos she'd sent him. What if Siobhan had told everyone about them? Was that what was spurring Richard on, the thought of Anna, naked, on show?

Anna greedily breathed in the cigarette smoke that hung in the air, catching the eye of the smoker at the table. As he held out his packet towards her, grinning, she realised it was the man from the bar, the guy in the blue shirt. In daylight, he wasn't so bad-looking, despite the beard. She shook her head, returned the grin. She wanted nothing more than to suck that hot tar into her mouth, down into her lungs, to feel the light-headedness from the first drag. But she didn't want to be kissing David with fag-ash breath. And she was sure they would be kissing. Sure they would be doing a whole lot more.

Seven thirty. Where was he? She'd been so looking forward to this night, to finally meeting him. She knew his mind, now she wanted to know his body. But it was much more than carnal longings that consumed her. After Robbo, she thought she'd never find someone who got her the way he had, had thought she didn't want to, but how wrong she'd been. From their first tentative messages on the dating site to the flirty texts, the soul-baring emails typed in the free periods when she was supposed to be planning lessons, she dared to hope she'd finally found the one for her. And, what had been more surprising to her, David felt the same. She'd asked Siobhan if it was crazy to fall for someone she'd never even met. Her friend had shaken her head, said they'd probably talked more intimately than many people who had been dating for a year. And it was true: Anna had told David more about herself than she'd told anyone. Even Robbo. They'd shared their minds without their bodies getting in the way. She'd even confided in him about Robbo. And he'd understood. 'Let it out,' he'd said. 'Let it out and let it go. He doesn't deserve you.' She took a long drink. Robbo had done her a favour by telling her to move on. David Kingfisher was perfect for her.

Lisa had been smug, had not refrained from saying, 'I told you so.' High on planning her wedding, her sister couldn't laud the joys of internet dating enough. And she couldn't wait to meet David. 'I'll give you a month to acquaint yourself with him,' she'd said, laughing, 'and then I'll be booking my train ticket.'

It had been as much Anna's fault as David's that, ten weeks down the line, they still hadn't met. He went away to a lot of conferences – perks of the job, he said – or he was often called into work at short notice. And she'd had to cancel a couple of their dates, thanks to a meeting the head called last minute and, before that, a tummy bug, a twenty-four-hour thing.

That's when she'd sent the photos, the night of the meeting. She'd picked up a ready meal and a bottle of wine on the way home from school. He had phoned her when she was three-quarters of the way down the bottle, said he was missing her, couldn't wait to be with her, to hold her. She couldn't remember who had suggested the photos, hadn't cared as she'd donned a basque from Agent Provocateur, giggling as she tried to lace it up, and giggling as she posed, even though she knew she looked good, her arm stretched out, her body angled this way, that. And then she'd taken it off, taken everything off, and posed again.

The men at the bench downed their pints, moved off, the smoker throwing her a wink. She smiled at him, thinking he was the sort of guy she'd go for if she wasn't in love with David. Anna sat down. Love. Was that what this was? She couldn't deny it, the delicious feeling whenever she thought of him, the throb between her legs when he whispered to her down the phone. Ten weeks. It seemed no time at all and yet forever. But tonight. Tonight they were finally going to meet.

She swiped her phone. Nothing. Where was he? Should she ring him? But it would be pointless if he were still at the hospital – his phone would be in his locker or stuffed in his desk drawer.

The weight of the bench shifted as someone sat down to the side of her. Her fingers clenched around her wine glass. Finally. She turned her head. It wasn't him.

'He must be mad.'

'Who?'

'The guy who's stood you up.' Tyler crinkled his eyes against the sun as he looked at her.

Was he flirting with her? She pursed her lips. 'Shouldn't you be working?'

'You're not going to grass me up to Benny Boy, are you?'

Anna swirled the wine in her wine glass. 'That depends.'

'On?'

'On whether you're going to tell the rest of the sixth form I've been stood up. Not that I have.'

He laughed and she couldn't help but do the same.

'Deal.' He held out his hand and she grasped his fingers, noticing how delicate they were in her palm. Boy's fingers. Boy's hands. A skinniness to them, to him. Despite being tall, probably six foot, Tyler wasn't yet a man.

'Mr Leek's in here though.' She looked around as if Richard might have followed her outside. She wouldn't put it past him.

'He won't tell Benson. I always give him free drinks.'

'Can't fault your initiative.' Anna laughed. 'How did you swing it though? Aren't you supposed to be eighteen to work behind a bar?'

'Fake ID.'

She shook her head. It was no different to what she'd done when she was a teenager.

'What do you need the money for?'

His pale blue eyes clouded over. He stood up, dipping his slim fingers into abandoned pint glasses, clutching them in a pincer movement. 'Just this and that. Clothes, stuff, you know.'

'Right.' It was probably to do with a girl. Adolescent love, there was nothing like it. The innocence of thinking you'd met the one, that you were going to be together forever. And then life slammed into you, took all of it away. Until. Until you met someone who made you feel like a teenager again. She peered at her watch: where was David?

'You should go,' Tyler said. 'Tell him he's missed his chance.' He didn't wait for a reply. He loped off, weaving in between groups of people, around benches, back to the coolness of the bar.

He was right, of course. What was she doing, sitting waiting for David? Had he stood her up? But he'd been texting all day, saying he couldn't wait to see her, to hold her. There would be a problem at the hospital, something like that; he wouldn't let her down.

Her stomach flipped as she felt a hand on her shoulder. She looked up. The man who had offered her a cigarette earlier stood in front of her.

'Need a top-up?' He nodded towards her glass. 'Sauvignon, is it?'

She shook her head.

Her phone buzzed. Her hand moved so quickly it knocked her glass, sending it flying off the table and crashing to the ground. A cheer went up from those around her.

She opened the message, deaf to the laughter. At last.

'You're smiling like you've won the lottery?'

'What?'

'Looks like I missed my chance.' He pointed at her phone.

'Sorry.'

She tapped out a reply to David, assuring him it was no problem, she understood: when he was needed at the hospital, he had to go.

Anna's phone pinged again. A row of hearts and kisses, followed by sorry, sorry, sorry.

'Don't stand a chance, do I?' the man in the blue shirt said.

Anna shook her head. No one stood a chance against David. Not even Robbo.

CHAPTER 5

Denise recognised the perfume. Chanel No. 5. Ian's favourite. He would pull her towards him, nuzzling her neck, saying that if she never wore anything else for the rest of her life, he would be a happy man. She hadn't worn it since the day he'd left. The bottle he'd bought for her thirtieth birthday sat on her dressing table, dusty, a reminder of the person she'd once been. Earlier, as she'd put on a slick of lipstick and smudged blue powder across her eyelids, the bottle had caught her eye: had the scent lasted or would it now bear the stench of decay that covered everything? Maybe it was time to throw the bottle away. She'd picked up a thin can of Impulse, sprayed herself from head to toe. Time to move on.

And now the woman next to her had brought it all back, just by wearing that perfume. If she hadn't been so keen not to lose her place at the bar, Denise would have moved further along, away from the fragrance, the memories.

The woman's arm lay on the bar next to hers. Brown, soft skin, a sheen of pale hairs, the opposite to hers. Pulling her arm away, Denise put it down by her side, trying not to touch the other woman, not wanting to let the scent linger on her. Why hadn't she put on a longer-sleeved cardigan, something that reached all the way down to her wrists? Her hands weren't bad, slim fingers. Ian had always held her hand wherever they went, entwining his fingers with hers. A buzz of nerves fluttered under her ribs. Would David do the same?

The woman moved away, taking her perfume with her. The barman, a slip of a boy who didn't seem old enough to be in a pub, never mind serving behind the bar, nodded at the man next to her. It should have been her turn. But she didn't mind waiting, she had been enjoying the last few minutes of anticipation. Funny really, ten weeks of waiting and still she wanted to stretch it out, enjoy the fantasies she'd conjured up, of what he would look like in the flesh, the sound of his voice unadulterated by a crackly phone line. The feel of his palm on her back, the softness of his lips, his arms around her. The clock over the bar said twenty past: ten minutes to go. She'd made sure to arrive good and early, wanting to be seated, lounging in a chair, a drink in her hand when he got there.

'A Coke, please.'

'Anything else?'

She hesitated. A glass of wine might calm her down. But look what had happened last time she'd had a drink. She tried to block the thought; she didn't want anything to spoil this night, but the memory of Laurence seemed to be etched onto her brain. It would pop into her mind when she was sitting on the loo, or brushing Mother's hair. And was she imagining it or was Mother looking at her differently since that night too? Or was her behaviour over the past ten weeks only as vile as the previous ten and the ten before that?

'Ice and a slice?'

As the barman scooped some ice out of a black bucket, Denise wished he would just upend the whole lot over her. A droplet of sweat trickled down the back of one thigh. She'd have been all right if she hadn't got the bus, hadn't had to walk the fifteen minutes to the stop and the five minutes when she got off, fighting her way through the heat. Hotter than the Med, that's what the forecasters were saying. Record temperatures.

'Two pounds twenty.'

Denise already had her hand in her purse, her fingers scrabbling for change. She picked up her drink, enjoying the coolness of the glass against her palm, longing to dip her fingers into it, pat water onto her reddening cheeks. She needed to sit down, gather herself, before David arrived.

The pub was packed, people taking refuge in its cool interior. 'Excuse me, sorry, sorry.' She headed for the door; that way she could see him when he arrived. And, more importantly, he would see her. Spotting two empty tub chairs next to the window, she walked as quickly as she could over to them, hoping they weren't too narrow. She lowered herself slowly into a chair. It was fine, it must have been bigger than it looked.

She should have lost weight. There had been plenty of time, after all. David's mother had been ill and then there'd been his trip to Nice for a conference. All those weeks when she could have been eating salads and going for a daily walk. But the longing for him had pushed her firmly in the direction of chocolate. Would he be disappointed when he saw her? A man like him could have his pick of women. She should have fore-warned him. She had hinted at it, admitting that the photo she'd used on the dating site was a few years old. His response was just what she wanted to hear: he loved people for what was on the inside, not the outside.

She took another sip of her drink, careful not to have too much. If she needed the loo, then she might miss him. And, thanks to the dim lighting and the crowds of people in the pub, she didn't rate her chances of finding him if she did.

Sweat had plastered her frizzy hair to her head. She had debated tying it back but she didn't have the neces-sary skills to tame it into a chic bun and, anyway, David had said he loved her hair. The familiar tingle of longing shook her body. He'd said he couldn't wait to run his hands through it, to touch her...

'Excuse me.'

Sucking her stomach in, she looked up. A man in a shiny blue shirt was staring at her.

'David?' He seemed different than he did in his photos

– his curls were all gone and he had a beard – but perhaps the photos on his profile were old ones.

'Sorry?'

'David Kingfisher? I'm Denise.' She held out her hand, a silly thing to do, seeing how intimately they'd chatted over the past ten weeks. Shyness made her face glow.

He took her hand, shook it, a smile playing on his lips.

'This is all very formal, isn't it?' he said.

Why wasn't he sitting down? Was he waiting for her to get up? Were they going on somewhere? Maybe he'd booked a table at Picasso's? Denise had always wanted to go there since she'd seen a review in the local paper. It had scored five out of five stars in every category.

'Is this free?'

'Yes, of course, I was saving it for you.'

'You were? How kind.'

She returned his smile. As his texts and messages had confirmed, he was the perfect gentleman.

His hands moved towards the chair. And then he picked it up and carried it over to a table a few feet behind her.

The heat rose in her cheeks. What an idiot! She imagined the pitying looks his friends were throwing her. They probably thought she'd been stood up. She stared at her watch. Maybe she had.

Straightening herself up in the chair as best she could, she replayed the fantasy she'd been going over in her mind the past couple of days, the one where everything went exactly as she wanted it to. Hadn't he said he couldn't wait to meet her, that there was a connection between them, something he'd never experienced before? And she'd felt it too: there was something about this man, something that was going to change her life. He would show up.

She reached into her bag, rummaging for her phone, panicking when she couldn't find it and then remembering she'd left it charging on her bedside table. How stupid could she be? Of all the times to forget it.

Finding a pear drop nestling at the bottom of her bag, she popped it into her mouth. He must have been held up but now he had no way of letting her know. She looked out onto the street. It was going to be okay. By the time twenty cars had passed, he would be here.

Twenty cars passed. Twenty red cars, that's what she should have said. She started counting again and moments later one flashed past before screeching to a halt. She leant forward, craning her neck. A red Mercedes had parked at the bus stop. The driver would get a ticket for sure. It was the same make Laurence had, a show-off sports car, sleek, shiny. The same shade of red, even.

As the door of the car opened, a gasp caught in her throat. Laurence. What was he doing here? Why wasn't he with Mother? Had something happened? Had he followed her? She imagined him striding into the pub, demanding to know who David was, asking him what his intentions were, making a scene.

She levered herself out of the chair. The heat hit her in the face as she opened the door to the street, sucking the breath out of her so that her shout came out as a whisper. 'Laurence.'

He hadn't heard her, was peering through the window of Picasso's, poking his head through the door of the Golden Lion.

'Laurence,' she tried again, but it was no use, he was too far away.

She started off down the high street – if she kept turning around, she would spot David as he went into The Vaults.

'Laurence.'

This time he heard her.

He waved and came sauntering towards her. She tried not to notice his man boobs bouncing under his polo shirt.

'Is it Mother?' She wanted it to be. Anything rather than the fact that he had followed her.

'Nothing serious.' He put an arm around her shoulder.

She stiffened at his touch but her need to know what was wrong stopped her from moving away. Panic started to bubble in her chest. 'What is it?'

'Can't find her tablets and you know how she can't sleep without them.'

Denise unhooked herself from under his arm. The air she'd been holding in her lungs escaped. She turned to look back at the bar. Had she missed David?

'But they're on the bedside cabinet, where they always are.'

Laurence shook his head. 'Searched everywhere. Been on my hands and knees under the bed.'

'Have they dropped into the drawer?'

'I don't know. She wouldn't let me rummage in there.'

Denise looked towards The Vaults. A man, tall, with dark curls, was going in. David.

'I'll have to come back.' She bit her bottom lip as tears clogged the back of her throat.

'What about your…'

The word 'date' hung in the air between them. She hadn't told Laurence she was going on a date. She didn't tell Laurence much these days. Not since that night. He'd thought what had happened meant the start of something beautiful between them but the very next night he'd come up behind her when she was washing up, and she'd jabbed him away with an elbow and a firm 'No.'

'You didn't say "No" last night,' he'd said.

'You're engaged to Mother.'

'Exactly.'

She wanted to ask what he meant by that, but the intimation was obvious: she was a trollop for sleeping with Mother's boyfriend. Would he tell her? Denise had a horrible feeling that, if she'd asked him, Laurence might have said, *That depends*, so she'd just kept her mouth shut and turned back to the washing up.

The town hall clock chimed eight.

'I'll just go and tell my friends I've got to go,' she said, moving away from him.

She strode off along the street, hoping he would get a parking ticket. Reaching the bar door, she pushed her way inside. It was hopeless: if David was here, she

72

wouldn't find him. She could send him a text. But, of course, her mobile was at home. She would send him one as soon as she got back, as soon as she'd found Mother's pills.

Laurence's car was pulling up at the kerb as she backed out of the bar. With a sigh and a last glance through the pub window, she opened the car door and manoeuvred herself into the tiny space.

'I hope I haven't spoilt your evening.' Laurence's hand brushed against her knee as it moved towards the gear-stick.

She shook her head, tears stinging the back of her eyes.

'Poor Denise.' He patted her knee, letting his hand rest there. 'Don't worry, darling, the night's still young.'

enough though her. She could trust him, trust her . . . [illegible] . . . for the hundredth . . . [illegible]. She would [illegible] . . . not . . . [illegible] . . . there . . . [illegible] . . . as the waited . . . [illegible] . . . simple truths.

[illegible] . . . a revelation that this . . . [illegible] . . . she led out of the park. With a snap and a hiss, taking [illegible] the path window, the way out the way out, and [illegible] . . . all out, the way out . . .

[illegible] . . . and not handle . . . [illegible] . . . tended that the power [illegible]

[illegible] . . . hand leans through the back . . . [illegible]

[illegible] . . . on their interest . . . [illegible] . . . being her loss [illegible] . . . don't worry, he has the fingers all wrong . . .

CHAPTER 6

Can't wait till tonight x

Petra read the message again. Her leg jerked; she put both hands on her knee to steady it. Nerves, that was all. Anticipation. Excitement maybe. It was good to be romanced, to feel wanted.

'Another tonic water, Petra?' Harry asked.

Antibiotics, that's what she'd told them, the sort that made you sick if you so much as looked at a glass of wine. No one had enquired what was wrong with her, but Petra didn't mind. The less her colleagues knew about her, the better. She was surprised they'd asked her to the leaving do but it was a small practice and Harry, the senior vet partner, was all for a happy ship. He had a laid-back attitude – too laid-back for Petra. 'You'll scrub that bench away,' he often said. 'It's costing me a fortune in wipes and spray.'

'Ice and a slice?'

'Please.'

Harry weaved his way through the crowd. From

behind, he didn't look much older than she did, a full head of thick platinum-blond hair, broad shoulders; it was only the deep lines on his face that gave away his age.

She stared around the bar, taking everything, everyone in.

Had she been wrong to agree to meet him here? It was a dangerous game she was playing but, the more she played it, the more she was becoming addicted to it. And, anyway, Harry had booked a table at the curry house at half past; everyone would be gone when he got here. She would usher him out as soon as he arrived, say they hadn't time for a drink. She'd booked a table at a pub in the moors; one she and Sam had been to years ago.

'All right?' Kirsty clinked her empty glass against Petra's. She nodded, noticing which side of her glass Kirsty's had touched.

Petra opened the dating site on her phone, her finger moving quickly to the profile she was looking for. David smiled back at her. Perfect, that was the only way to describe him. How could any woman resist that? His cheeky grin, the way his dark curls flopped in front of his left eye, those biceps. David Kingfisher, all man: he looked like he could impregnate a woman just by looking at her.

She scrolled through until she found the text message.
Can't wait till tonight x

'Got an admirer?' Kirsty said, the smell of rum oozing from her.

'No.' Petra stuffed her phone into her bag.

'I'll tell sexy Sam.'

Petra felt her stomach drop as if she'd just swallowed a heavy stone. Sam couldn't know. Must never find out what she was doing. It would be the end of them.

'Petra's got an admirer, Petra's got an admirer,' Kirsty sang.

'What's this?' Harry lowered a full tray of glasses onto the table.

Kirsty pointed a wobbly finger at Petra. 'Something's going on. You're not wearing a T-shirt. And you've not got your hair in that horrible plait. The quiet ones are the worst, that's what my mum says. And she should know, she's on her fourth husband.' A high-pitched giggle escaped Kirsty's mouth.

'She's drunk,' Petra said, pulling up the sleeve that kept slipping off her shoulder. She'd picked up the top in the supermarket, knowing it was important to look her best.

'We'll let her off, it is her leaving do,' said Jane.

'I'm only joking.' Kirsty let out a loud burp. 'About your admirer.'

'What admirer's this?' Harry sat down opposite Petra, handed her a glass wet with condensation.

'Nothing. No one.'

Harry winked at her, leant slightly forward. He smelt of cigar smoke, antiseptic. 'I thought you were going to give me first dibs if you ever got rid of Sam.'

Petra looked at the others but they were back to their gossip, discussing a woman who'd come in with two dead goldfish earlier. They hadn't heard what Harry had said. She let out a long breath. 'I'm not getting rid of Sam; I've told you before.'

Harry held his hands up. 'You can't blame me for trying.'

Petra rolled her eyes. He smiled and picked up his pint. She couldn't be angry with him – he was only teasing, trying to draw her out of the shell she'd holed herself up in. And Harry was lonely and she knew what that was like. Loneliness was a sickness no doctor could cure. It got inside your head, told you lies about yourself, that you deserved the emptiness that filled your mind, your body, that made you bury yourself so deep you couldn't see any way of scrambling out of it. It suffocated you, made you gasp for air. It had nearly suffocated her. Her fingers itched to get her phone out of her bag, to read the message again.

'Oh shit, I think I'm going to be sick.' Kirsty's head lolled forward.

The others moved away from her, even mother hen Jane. They all looked at Petra. *Why me*, she wanted to ask, but, of course, she knew why – she was the one who could be relied upon to clean up the mess of a haemorrhaging dog, fish up eyes that had popped out, wipe shit off fur. Petra looked at her watch; she still had another half hour before they were due to meet. Hooking Kirsty under the arm, she levered her up.

'Come on, you need some fresh air.'

'Want me to come with you?' Harry was half out of his seat.

Petra shook her head.

She guided Kirsty through the packed room, her gaze darting back and forth. Despite the lack of vodka, despite the pissed-up Kirsty rambling in her ear, she was happy. Soon he would be here.

They made it to the beer garden. Her colleague didn't seem too unsteady on her feet, even though she had quaffed at least six rum and Cokes in the last hour and was wearing four-inch stilettos. Petra looked down at her own sandals as they walked – tan strappy affairs. Bought five years ago and never worn. She wasn't used to wearing heels, preferring her trainers, but tonight was a special occasion.

'It's hot out here.' Kirsty fanned herself with her hand.

'Sit there.' Petra led her to a bench a group of men had just vacated and plonked her down on it, ignoring the stare of the one who lingered, taking the last puffs of his cigarette. 'Take some deep breaths.'

Kirsty did some theatrical heavy breathing, rocking back and to on the bench.

'Better?' Petra asked.

'Hmm.'

Petra looked around the beer garden. Red faces, necks, bare legs, short skirts, office workers with their ties off, everyone puffing away. People were making the most of the heatwave – and quenching their thirst with anything alcoholic. She could smell it on the air, hops, apples, the sweet aroma of rosé wine.

She wondered where Sam was now. A quick pint with Jacko, he'd said. She hadn't wanted him to go.

Jacko was a bad influence on him, and she didn't need that. And nor did Sam: things had been better between them recently. A lot better. It was almost as if David were a magic charm.

'Am I doing the right thing?' Kirsty said.

'Yes, fresh air is good for you. Still feel sick?'

'No, I...'

Petra looked down at her. 'There, I told you. Though why you have to drink so much, I don't know.' The words came so easily; words that, if said to her, she would have scorned.

Kirsty hiccupped. 'You sound like my mother.'

Petra's stomach lurched. Mother. She sounded like a mother. But would she ever be one?

'I meant,' Kirsty said, taking a deep breath, 'am I doing the right thing, getting married, moving away?' She grabbed at her arm and pulled Petra down onto the bench, not giving her a chance to wipe it clean first.

Petra inched away from her. She should have left this to one of the others. Mess, she could deal with, heart-to-hearts, she couldn't.

'I do love him. And he's going to make a great daddy.'

'You're pregnant?'

Kirsty laughed as if Petra had just told the funniest joke in the world. 'After the shock I had last year? No way. Not yet.' She shook her head. 'I've been very, very careful.'

Petra had been there when Kirsty had burst into tears in the middle of their morning break at work. She'd

he was looking forward to tonight, to finally being with her? Her leg jumped again but this time she caught it just in time, pushing her bitten nails down into the rough denim of her jeans before her hand moved to her stomach. He couldn't let her down. He couldn't.

CHAPTER 7

I thought I wouldn't be able to recognise them, that their photos would turn out to be lies, plucked from faded albums, their faces and bodies aged so they were shadows of their forgotten selves.

But I can still spot them from the look that lights their eyes, the slight parting of their lips, the way they're flicking their hair back. They're ready to give themselves to David Kingfisher.

How long will they wait? How long will it take for them to realise I'm not coming, they've been stood up, that I have no intention of meeting them? Not yet, anyway.

They are in love with me. They've told me. After weeks of slowly opening up like delicate flowers, their words, protestations of love, came out quickly, prematurely even.

I am the man for them. They've told me. Not only with what they said but with the things they've done. They love me and how ridiculous is that, for they don't know me at all. Yet they've convinced themselves they do, even though I've walked up to them, brushed past them, smelt the floral scent of their perfume. Not one of them has recognised me.

I feel like I'm itching all over, so great is the desire to tell them I'm David Kingfisher. But I must wait until the time is right.

They're moving, grabbing bags, upending glasses, sucking at the last drops of liquid, the anaesthetic to being stood up. Again.

I mix into the crowd around them that's pushing through the door. They are so close, close enough to touch. I clamp my hands into fists, give them one last look and set off for home.

CHAPTER 8

Denise pressed the button to call the lift. The sun was glaring through the huge swathes of glass, strip lights throwing out a harsh brightness, and the radiator next to her was pumping out heat, despite the temperature outside touching nearly thirty degrees. Why did they keep hospitals so hot? Surely heat was a breeding ground for germs? Fishing in her bag for a pear drop, she remembered she'd slipped the last one into her mouth as she came through the entrance door.

The lift beeped and she stepped in. Mirrors surrounded her on all sides. Sucking in her cheeks, she pulled in her stomach, pushed back her frizzy hair, forced herself to take in her full length, and gave a shaky smile.

Yes, her face had filled out a bit but she was still... if not quite attractive, then pretty. Hadn't David told her so? She smiled at herself. 'You are gorgeous,' she said out loud, as she said to herself every time she passed a mirror. Three weeks, the book had guaranteed, three weeks until you would believe it. She frowned at herself. Another book to return to the library.

The lift bumped and started to move. Up and up it went until a number 6 flashed over the door. Denise sighed; she hadn't pressed the button for the fourth floor. She hoped David was still here. He'd had a difficult operation to perform this morning. That's why he'd cancelled their date – he'd needed to get an early night. She couldn't be angry with him. They had all the time in the world while that poorly child most likely didn't. It was just the way it was. That was his career and his life and she had to respect that. He could be called out at any time of the day or night, like he had been two weeks ago when Mother had lost her sleeping tablets and Laurence had come to fetch her. There'd been a text waiting for her when she got home. She'd been so pleased she hadn't missed him, that she wasn't the one doing the standing up.

The lift doors opened. Denise stabbed her finger on the button marked 4; she wasn't going to get caught out again. She looked at her watch. Nearly one. The operation would surely be over by now. It had to be, she needed to see him. Three months of longing had been building inside her, three months of wanting to finally see this man she had fallen in love with.

And there was another reason why she wanted to see him: the money.

David had promised to bring it with him last night. *Just a week*, he'd said, when he asked if he could borrow it. *Just a week and I'll get it straight back to you.* It had now been three.

He probably wouldn't have it on him at the hospital though. But that was okay, she would wait until his shift ended. She wanted to see where he lived anyway. He had described it to her: a chocolate-box cottage in Dalton, a village outside of town. He had renovated it himself, was now working on the garden. The photos he'd sent added to those images in her head, the world she was building, the one she hoped to share with him.

The lift doors were sliding slowly together when another person stepped in. The doors opened again, the woman smiling a thanks at Denise, asking her something. But Denise wasn't listening, all she could do was stare straight ahead of her. David. David had just walked past, she was sure of it. Before she could get out of the lift, the doors closed. It had only been a glimpse but it had to be him: that shock of dark curls, the squareness of his jaw. But what was he doing on the sixth floor? Paediatrics was on the fourth floor. Maybe the X-ray department was on the sixth floor, or the labs, or something. Should she go back up and try to find him? No, better to wait for him in Paediatrics. He was probably on his way there at this very moment.

The lift stopped at the fourth floor. Denise stepped out into a riot of colour, cartoons on the wall, nurses dressed in colourful uniforms, worried-looking parents and doe-eyed children. The smell was different in here to the rest of the hospital – an overpowering lemony aroma, air freshener perhaps, drowning out the antiseptic fug that lingered on the other floors.

She went over to the reception desk.

'Can I help you?' A woman in oversized glasses looked up at her.

'I'm here to see David Kingfisher.'

'Can I see your letter please?' The woman – Linda, according to the badge pinned to her white blouse – held out her hand, her eyes fixed to the computer screen in front of her.

'I haven't got a letter.'

'Appointment card?'

Denise shook her head. 'It's a personal matter. I really do need to speak to him.'

The receptionist sniffed. 'Who was it you wanted to see?'

'David Kingfisher. I just saw him up on the sixth floor. I don't mind waiting. I know how busy he must be.' Denise clamped her lips shut, aware she was gabbling.

'Kingfisher?'

Denise nodded. 'That's right.'

'We don't have any Kingfishers in this department.'

'This is Paediatrics, right?'

Linda rolled her eyes.

'He definitely works in Paediatrics. He was doing a big operation on a boy this morning.'

The woman turned back to her screen. 'Not in this hospital. We don't operate on Thursdays in this department.'

'Oh.' Relief surged through Denise's veins. 'He's had to go to another hospital?'

'What? No. I don't know a David Kingfisher. He doesn't work here. Perhaps you've got the wrong place?'

Denise leant forward. 'Is that a telephone list for the

department?' She pointed at a sheaf of papers stuck to the side of a filing cabinet to the left of the desk.

Linda sighed before reaching over and retrieving the list. 'It's for the whole hospital.'

The receptionist quickly flicked through the pages. Denise waited. Someone behind her coughed. Another tutted. A baby started to cry. She turned around. There was a queue of people scowling at her.

'No, definitely no David Kingfisher.' Linda pursed her lips and nodded towards the queue. 'If you wouldn't mind.'

'Could I take a look myself? Please?'

The baby let out a high-pitched squeal. Linda thrust the list at Denise. 'I need it back.'

'Thank you.' Denise moved out of the way. The man with the squealing baby stepped into her place.

Denise longed to sit down but the only free chairs were children's ones, small brightly coloured plastic stools. She stood against a wall, next to a door marked 'Disabled toilet'. Flicking through the pages, her eyes reached the surnames starting with a K. She scanned them once, twice. And then read down the whole list, starting at the front and then, when she'd done that, beginning at the back. The receptionist was right: there was no David Kingfisher.

But Denise had seen him, she was sure of it. With a quick glance at the woman behind the desk she stuffed the telephone list into her holdall and made her way back to the lift. She'd go up to the sixth floor, start there. And then work her way through the rest of the floors, walk along every corridor. She decided she'd ask at the main information desk; perhaps Linda had an out-of-date telephone list? She would find him. As she pressed the button for the lift, images swam around her brain: his cottage, the cleft in his chin, those sea-green eyes... And the latest bank statement for the charity showing the balance was ten thousand pounds less than it should be. She had to find him.

A week, he'd said. A week. The charity wouldn't mind, not when they knew it was helping to fund lifesaving treatment for a little boy the NHS had decided they couldn't do any more for. But she'd rather not explain it to them. They might think she'd stolen the money when, of course, she would never do anything like that. She'd borrowed it. She had access to the online bank account. Laurence had said it would be easier that way, so that she could pay the invoices that came in. A couple of clicks and the money was in the bank account David had asked her to send it to.

She looked around her, at the man jigging his baby up and down, trying to make it laugh, at a couple of toddlers squabbling over some building blocks on the floor, at a young couple gripping onto each other's hands. There was nothing to worry about. This wasn't a life-or-death situation like the ones these children might be facing. This was just money. And David had promised to give it back to her. She had made a mistake. Got the wrong hospital, that was all. It was typical of her, mixing things up. There would be an explanation. There had to be. Because if there wasn't, how was she going to explain the missing ten thousand pounds to the charity?

CHAPTER 9

Petra opened the oven door, letting out a yelp as two hundred and twenty degrees of heat hit her in the face. Why hadn't she made a salad, or told Sam to do a barbecue? She must be mad, cooking a casserole in this weather. But it was Sam's favourite, which was good as it was the only thing she could cook, and it was her way of trying to make up for the last few months. Not that her husband was aware she had some making up to do, but her guilt had driven her to the supermarket on her lunchbreak, choosing four large shanks, stuffing them in the staffroom fridge, marking them with a big 'Petra – do not touch' sign so it wouldn't be mistaken for food for the 'overnighters', as they called the animals that had to stay in. She'd picked up a frozen cheesecake at the supermarket too, meaning to grab some fresh raspberries to put on top of it, but she'd forgotten.

One side of the kitchen was open to the garden, the bifold doors pushed back; heat crowded in through them, mingling with that from the oven. She spritzed antibacterial spray over the worktops, got out a new cloth from under the sink, rinsed it in nearly scalding water, and started to wipe. After circling three times around the kitchen she was satisfied. Everything was ready, the table was set, and there were still twenty minutes to go.

She made herself a chamomile tea and perched on a stool at the kitchen island. All she needed to do was slip into some clean jeans and a T-shirt and dab on a bit of lip balm. As she picked up her phone, Jude skittered into the kitchen and flopped down at her feet.

The first story on the local news site was full of 'Canal Carole', as the locals had called her, the woman found drowned by Bishopsgate Lock in the city centre three months ago. Her husband had been sentenced earlier, after confessing everything the day after she'd been dragged from the water. He'd discovered she'd had an affair but, instead of confronting her, had bided his time, watching, waiting. Until one night, on a walk down the towpath, he could, according to the local hack who'd written the piece, watch and wait no longer. He'd pushed his wife into the canal and then jumped in after her, holding her head under the water until she drowned. There was a photo of a neighbour, hair scraped back, a toddler on her hip. *I can't imagine how she felt, poor woman. It's awful to think it could happen round here.*

Petra scrolled through the other articles, tutting at the woman's lack of imagination. *She* could imagine it: the air wanting to burst out of your lungs in a scream, the water pressing against every opening. You would hear no sounds, all sights gone apart from those in your head, a metallic taste in your mouth. And then there would be nothing. Just silence. Petra had thought about it a lot. Especially last year, after what had happened. And now, too. Sometimes the images were so vivid, so persistent, she longed for that silence. A minute of panic, perhaps two, and then there would be nothing. She put her hand on her stomach, sighed, and opened up Facebook.

She brought up the local community forum. There was the usual ranting about cars parked on pavements, numerous requests for prizes for a primary school's summer fayre, someone desperate for a room to rent. Petra scrolled through the posts. And then her finger stopped.

Her knee jumped once, twice. She gripped the edge of the bench with one hand, blinked, looked back at her phone screen.

Do you know David Kingfisher? He may be a doctor somewhere in the area. He's disappeared and I need to find him urgently. Message me.

Petra tried to swallow. Her knee bounced up and down. Jude lifted his head, whimpered. An icy shiver worked its way down her back. What was this? It couldn't be her David Kingfisher, could it?

But of course it was. How could it not be? Not many people were called Kingfisher around these parts. It was him. It had to be. But disappeared? That was ridiculous. What was this woman on about? He hadn't shown up for the date the other night but he'd had a perfectly reasonable excuse, as he'd had the other times.

The clock on the cooker said twenty past. Sam had gone to pick up Jacko and Miranda: she had ten minutes at most.

She raced up the stairs and into the bedroom, not bothering to switch on the light, ignoring the fusty smell that hit her as she flung her phone onto the bed. Her Kindle was in the top drawer of her bedside cabinet. She took it out, her fingers first reaching for the bottom drawer, longing for the bottle hidden underneath. No. She needed a clear head.

After much hinting, Sam had given her the Kindle for her birthday. It was so much easier to sit in bed at night, pretending to read a book on the small screen, rather than having her laptop on her knee. It gave her the perfect cover for keeping up with the emails passing back and forth between them, the messages of love, of devotion. Sam never asked her what she was doing, never noticed the smile that would sometimes flit across her face. And when he was asleep, his snores coming soft and low, she would slip out of bed, and make a call, an eye on the living room door, the TV on low to drown out the sound of her voice.

Opening David's last email, she read it once, twice.

So sorry to let you down again, sweetheart, but my job has to come first. You're a special person, a caring person, so I know you understand that. I cannot wait to hold you, to have you in my arms. I love you. You are the world to me.

I saw Daniel's parents this morning. They were so

grateful. It brought tears to my eyes. They are flying out to America on Monday and the operation will take place on Wednesday. You have done a marvellous thing, darling. I thank you from the bottom of my heart. I pray to God, as I know you do, that Daniel will pull through and I hope that, one day, I can bring you to meet him.

Are you free next Wednesday? Shall we go to Picasso's? My treat, of course. The bank has finally released the funds. Would you prefer the money in cash or a cheque?

Darling, I have to go now. I love you xxx

Picking up her phone, she read the post on Facebook again, before clicking on the woman's profile. There was nothing to see, her details hidden from those she wasn't friends with. Even her picture gave nothing away; a swan floating on a lake. Petra looked back at David's email. This Denise woman had said David Kingfisher had disappeared. She flicked through David's messages. There was nothing to say he wasn't honest, that suggested he had other women on the go. The woman was obviously unhinged.

Petra sat down on the bed and leant back on the pillows. But what if Denise went to the police? What if they investigated and it all came out, about Sam and David and what she'd done? How would she explain the ten thousand pounds? An image of Sam's face swam into her mind: the shock, disbelief etched on it as he read the messages. He would ask her why she'd done it, say he'd thought they were doing okay, were back on track, that she should have had more faith in him. He would never believe she was doing it all for him.

Pushing her jumping leg down with her elbow, she started to tap out a message, her fingers shaking, stumbling over the buttons.

'There you are.' Sam burst into the room.

She jumped, screamed.

'Sorry, didn't mean to scare you. Were you on the phone?'

'No. Wrong number.' She pressed the *off* button on her mobile, pushed it back into her drawer, dropped the Kindle on top of it, turned around slowly, her hand on her heart to stop it hammering so loudly.

'Are you coming down?'

'Yes, sorry. I didn't hear the car?'

'Some idiot in a BMW was blocking the drive so I parked at the top of the cul-de-sac.'

'You should have told him to move.'

'By the time we'd walked down, he was gone.' He pushed his hair away from his eyes, held out his hand. 'Come on, we'd better go and offer them a drink.'

'Here she is, my favourite sister-in-law.' Jacko got off the stool he was perching on and sauntered over to her, holding her by the shoulders and smacking a kiss onto each cheek. 'Forgiven me for keeping your husband out the other night?'

Petra didn't answer.

'You're looking great – isn't she, Miranda?' he tried instead.

Petra turned up the corners of her mouth into something she hoped resembled a smile. He was so full of shit. The T-shirt was too big for her and the jeans she was wearing were faded and worn. She looked at Miranda. A silver off-the-shoulder dress made the most of her brown shoulders, while her sparkly flip-flops had probably cost more than everything Petra was wearing.

'Good holiday?' As Miranda kissed her cheek Petra tried not to breathe in the coconut sun-cream smell she reeked of. It reminded her of trips abroad with Sam, lying face down on a sunlounger, his hands rubbing, warm on her back, how he would lead her back to the apartment, make love to her with no thought as to whether there would be a baby at the end of it.

'Bliss. Absolute bliss. Though with this weather, I don't know why we bothered going abroad. I swear it's hotter here than in Italy.'

'No gorgeous Italians here though.' Sam held out the bottle of rosé to her. 'Hey?'

'I only have eyes for my husband.' Pushing her glass towards him, Miranda raised an eyebrow at Jacko, who shrugged in return. 'You're supposed to say you only have eyes for me.'

Jacko threw a nut into the air and caught it in his mouth. 'Darling, do you even have to ask?' He pinched at her waist.

'Oi, get off.'

Petra got a glass out of the cupboard and opened the fridge. Two bottles of rosé, six cans of lager and a bottle of Prosecco stared back at her. She shut the door, trying not to slam it.

'I picked this up on the way.' Sam rushed over to her, a carton of posh fruit juice in his hand. 'Sorry, forgot to put it in the fridge. Shall I put some ice in it?'

Petra ignored him, opened the oven door, reached for her oven gloves, drew out the casserole dish.

'Something smells good,' Jacko said.

Miranda giggled. 'That's me, silly.'

Petra clenched her teeth as she took the casserole to the table. Why did they have to act like a pair of love-sick teenagers all the time? They'd been married for nearly as long as she and Sam had. They were nearly forty for God's sake. She plonked the dish down onto a mat on the dining table.

'Shall I cut the bread?' Sam waved the bread knife in her direction.

She ignored him.

'This doesn't bother you?' Miranda sat down next to her, holding her wine glass in front of Petra's face.

Petra could smell the sharp tang of strawberries, the acid of the alcohol. Saliva pooled in her mouth. 'Not at all.'

'I don't know how you do it. I would literally die if I couldn't have a drink.'

There was silence. Sam stopped sawing the bread. The nut Jacko had thrown into the air missed his mouth and dropped to the floor.

'Sorry.' Miranda put her hand on top of Petra's. 'Me and my big mouth.'

'Don't worry.' Petra pulled her hand free, itching to pick up the nut.

'Jeez, you must have bad circulation or something. Your hand is freezing. In this weather, too.'

There were so many things Petra could have said: that the blood had stopped coursing through her veins, she was dead on the inside, that that's what loss did to you. And loneliness. That ache of realising that, no matter who was in the room with her, she was completely alone, as if she were shut behind a glass wall only she could see.

The messages helped, the words of love, of longing. For the first time in a long time she was connecting with someone. Ironic really when all she had were emails in her inbox, the sound of a voice at the end of a line, a text message hastily read and then deleted. But at least the past three months had given her something to get out of bed for, something to believe in. Live for. David. She needed him. He was going to help bring Sam back to her. The woman who'd posted on Facebook was obviously mad. David Kingfisher hadn't disappeared at all.

'Any luck on the baby front?'

'Miranda!' Jacko rolled his eyes.

Miranda tipped back the last of her wine. 'What? We're all friends here, aren't we? Your doctor said it was a slim chance but, if it happened once, it can happen again, right?'

'Right,' Sam said. 'We're very positive about the whole situation, aren't we, Pet?'

Petra smiled. 'Of course, it is going to happen. I'm sure of it.'

'We're keeping our fingers crossed, aren't we, Jacko?' Miranda said.

He raised his glass. 'All you need is a bit of luck.'

'We don't need luck.' Petra felt her knee bounce. Luck? Luck was for idiots. You had to plan and prepare, be determined, find a way when it felt like there was none.

'Here we go.' Sam put a bowl of chopped-up French bread in the middle of the table. 'And here's your drink, Pet.'

Petra forced herself to open her mouth, push out the word 'Thanks', pretend her mind was in the room with them as well as her body, that it wasn't turning the words of some random Facebook post this way and that.

'So, how was your holiday?' she said, trying to bring her attention back to their guests. 'Apart from the Italian men.'

'You can see it all on social media. As ever, she's plastered the photos on there for everyone to see.'

'You should have come. We said, didn't we, Jacko, you two would have loved it. The scenery is to die for and it's so relaxing. And you're only half an hour away from Verona in one direction and the Lakes in another.'

Petra ripped off a bit of bread, tossed it to Jude. 'Work, you know.'

She ignored the look that passed between them. She had known for a long time they saw her job as a little hobby, something she did to pass the time.

'I don't know why we bothered taking the kids. Fraser was holed up in his room, on his iPad, the whole time. And Izzy spent most of the time wandering around town with a girl from the villa next door.'

'Made out they were only going for the ice cream.' Jacko downed his wine, winked at Sam. 'Hey, Sam?'

Sam laughed.

'Not everyone's got your morals, boys.' Miranda shook her head, pretending to be annoyed.

Petra's knee jumped but she caught it before it hit the table.

They all jumped as a phone started to ring.

'Bloody hell, Miranda, do you ever switch that thing off?'

Miranda shrugged. 'Not my ringtone.'

Sam cocked his head to one side. 'It's coming from the living room. That's not your ringtone either, is it, Pet?'

An iciness slipped down Petra's back. Her knee jumped again, this time knocking the table, making the glasses jump. 'It's my work one.'

Sam looked at her, his fork halfway to his mouth. 'You don't have a work one.'

'Aye, aye.' Jacko winked at her. 'That's what they all say.'

'They've given it to me. For emergencies.' Petra's chair scraped on the tiles as she pushed it back. 'Sorry, won't be a min.'

She scooted through to the living room, diving on her rucksack, her fingers fumbling to find the inside pocket. Idiot. How could she have been so stupid? She always shut off the burner when Sam was at home. She eventually found it, running up to the spare bedroom, praying it wouldn't stop ringing. She pushed the bedroom door to, leant against it, took a deep breath.

'Hi, sweetheart,' she said. 'I thought it'd be you.'

She lay back on the bed, the smile on her face making her cheeks ache. Disappeared? That Denise woman was mad. David Kingfisher hadn't disappeared at all.

CHAPTER 10

'As I said, Clarissa is doing really well.' Anna stood up, hoping the couple staring at her across the desk would do the same.

'So you definitely think she'll get in to Oxford?'

'There are no guarantees, Mrs Gilbert. What I can say is she is well on her way to achieving an A star.'

Mrs Gilbert stuck her chin out. 'That's what her history and French teachers said. I can't see how she wouldn't get in with those grades. And she's got an exemplary out-of-school record. Duke of Edinburgh, hospice volunteering, the coast-to-coast walk she did for—'

'I'm sure she'll do very well.' Anna looked at her watch. 'Sorry, but I do have other parents to see.' And she wanted to be out of here. It was already gone half past eight and late-night shopping finished at ten. If she didn't get the dress tonight, she'd be ringing Benson in the morning, telling him she had excruciating period pain. Worked every time. David was taking her to the new fusion restaurant in Manchester tomorrow night and she wanted something new to wear, something to show him exactly what he'd been missing.

Mr Gilbert, at least twenty years his wife's senior, levered himself up. 'Philippa.' It was the first time Anna had heard him speak.

Philippa opened her mouth but, seeing the expression on his face, closed it again.

Anna held her hand out but they had already turned away, Mr Gilbert grasping his wife's tanned elbow firmly.

'Sorry to keep you waiting.' Anna glanced at her watch again as a woman approached the desk. Grey eyes peeped out from a grey face, a brightly coloured scarf wrapped around her head. 'Mrs James?' She was last on her list. Five minutes, ten tops, and she'd be able to escape the stifling heat of the room, the desperate scent of desperate parents.

'Call me Lorraine. No need to be so formal, is there?'

'Please, sit down.' By the time the woman had lowered herself into a chair, Anna had sat down too and was pretending to read through her notes. This was going to be difficult. She took a deep breath, clasped her hands together, plastered a smile onto her face.

'You don't have to be nice.' Mrs James pointed at her headscarf. 'Just because of this.'

'I...' Anna studied the papers in front of her. The woman had caught her out – she had been all set to give Tyler's parents a warning about his absence from school, his laziness when he did attend. But she couldn't do it. The headscarf, the lack of eyebrows, eyelashes, the pastiness of the woman's face had thrown her. 'Is

Mr James joining us?' she said instead. Maybe she could put this on him, leave his poor wife alone.

'There isn't a Mr James. Well, there is, but he's not here. He's not with us. We're not together.'

'Right. Right.'

'Gone back to South Africa. Says he can't cope. With this. With Kai. Tyler. Everything. And then his business.'

Bastard, Anna thought, but didn't say it. She didn't need to know this, didn't want to get involved in pupils' lives, she was just there to teach them. And yet perhaps it explained why Tyler had been playing up recently.

'Well, Tyler…'

'I didn't think things could get any worse, the big C, you know, and then he tells me the house is being repossessed. And what does he do? Bugger off. Excuse my French. I don't mind for me, but you know, what with Kai.'

Anna hadn't got a clue what was happening with Kai. She didn't even know who he was – a brother, she supposed. 'Well, Tyler…'

'Do you think they'll give him a scholarship for his final year? It's only lately, what with all this trouble. And he's so close to Kai. He just wants to be with him, you know. And, when he's not, then he's trying to earn the money to send him…' She coughed, a loud hawking cough that sounded like it was coming from deep within her. Picking her bag up off the floor, rooting through it, she found a handkerchief and covered her mouth with it.

'Sorry,' she said, a soft rose lighting the grey tinge of her cheeks. 'My lungs.'

'I'm sure he'll get back on track, Mrs James. Like you say, he's had a lot on—'

'He's the man of the house now.'

'I can quite imagine.' And she could. Over the last few months, when Tyler had deigned to make an appearance at school, she'd noticed how he'd broadened out, the gangly legs, the spots around his mouth, no more.

Mrs James reached forwards, placing her hand on Anna's. 'You'll put in a good word for him, won't you? Tyler says he gets on well with you. Thinks you're all right.' She smiled. 'Quite a compliment coming from a teenager.'

Anna shifted in her seat. She'd seen the way Tyler looked at her; it wasn't the first time a sixth former had had a crush on her.

'I can't promise anything. It probably has to go to the governors. But I'll have a word with Mr Benson.'

'Please.' The woman gripped her hand.

'I'll see what I can do.'

'Why should his future be messed up, just 'cos mine and Kai's is?'

'I'll see what I can do.' Anna pulled her hand from under Mrs James' and closed her notebook. The clock over the door said ten to. She'd have to put her foot down all the way there.

'Anna!'

The clack of stilettos rang in the still air. Siobhan. Anna was tempted to ignore her, had tried to ever since she found out her so-called friend had told Richard

Leek about David. There was only so much she could do to escape her though: she was often paired with her for lunchbreak cover or she would go into the staffroom, and Siobhan would wave her over, patting the seat next to her, the only free one in the room.

Anna was jabbing at the button on the car fob when she felt a tap on her shoulder.

'Going deaf or just ignoring me?'

She turned. 'Sorry, didn't hear you.'

Siobhan laughed, pushing Anna's long hair back from her ear. 'Bloody hair. Jeez, I don't know how you can stand it in this weather. You should have an up-do.' Siobhan gestured at her hair piled on her head, clips and rubber bands holding it in place. Anna didn't like having her hair up; it was one of her best features, everyone said so.

'Fancy going for a drink? A post-parents piss-up?'

Anna tried to mime a stifled yawn. 'Love to but I'm knackered. A glass of wine will finish me off.'

Siobhan narrowed her eyes. 'Got a better offer?'

'No.' The word came out too quickly.

'Is it off then? Not seeing him no more?'

Any longer. She sighed to herself. Was it any wonder they were only expecting fifty percent of year elevens to pass English?

'Are you then?'

Anna opened her car door. Part of her wanted to make Siobhan jealous, to say yes, she was still seeing him, and yes, he was the best thing that had ever happened to her. But the other part, the part that now understood what a gossip her so-called friend was, won. She shook her head.

'Phew.' Siobhan blew out an exaggerated sigh from between purple lips. 'Kingfisher. That's his name, isn't it? I thought at the time it was made up – I mean, I've never heard it round here before – but, well, I didn't like to say. And I know you won't mind me telling you 'cos we're friends, but I thought there was something iffy about him right from the start. I mean, he was so desperate to see you, said all those nice things, and, well, the photos. And then he stood you up left, right and centre. And a doctor, come on, why would a doctor need to do internet dating, with all those nurses tottering around? *Yes, doctor, no, doctor. Three bags full, doctor.* I said to...' She coughed.

'What? Who?'

'What? No one. I said to *myself*, there's something funny about him, Siobhan, something not quite right. My bullshit-ometer was spot on as usual.'

Anna put her hand up. 'Siobhan. What on earth are you on about?' She looked at her watch. Nine. If she didn't leave in the next minute, she wouldn't make it. The Joseph dress, spotted online in her lunchbreak, was perfect: low-cut, with a scalloped edge, ice blue. All she had to do was try it on and pay for it. Twenty minutes to get to Selfridges. She had to get going.

Siobhan rooted in the bag hanging from her shoulder, taking out her phone. 'Here. Hold on, let me find it.'

'Can we do this tomorrow?'

'Won't take me a minute. Right, here we are.' She

thrust her phone in front of Anna's face but, before Anna could look at the screen, Siobhan had pulled the phone away from her and stuffed it back into her bag.

'Yoo-hoo,' Siobhan shouted, peering over Anna's shoulder.

Anna turned around. Richard Leek was making his way over to them. 'How about it?' He lifted his hand to his mouth, miming a drinking motion. 'Reckon we deserve it after that.'

'Yes, let's.' Siobhan blushed.

'No.' Anna shook her head, looked at Siobhan's glowing face. She didn't fancy the slimy creep, did she?

'Come on, a little drinkie would loosen you up,' Richard said, standing so close to Anna she could smell the coffee on his breath.

Siobhan put her hand on his arm. 'Are you going to The Vaults? I'll meet you there. Won't be long.'

'What do you say, Anna?' he asked.

She shook her head. 'I'm tired.'

He winked at her again, pretended to yawn. 'I'm quite tired, too. Could do with a lie-down myself.'

Siobhan was clenching her teeth; Anna could tell by the way her cheeks were sucking in and out.

Anna rolled her eyes, crossed her arms.

'No? Another night then, ladies.' He wiggled his fingers at them as he walked backwards across the car park.

'Wanker,' Anna said, not caring if he was out of earshot or not.

'He's all right when you get to know him.'

Anna threw her bag onto the passenger seat. She needed to go. Now. 'I'll see you tomorrow.'

Siobhan fished her phone out of her bag. 'Just look at this. It won't take a min.'

Anna sighed as Siobhan scrolled up and down the screen.

'It's on Facebook, in the local community forum. Are you a member of it?'

Anna nodded. She'd joined when she'd moved to the area, thinking Robbo might be on it. But he wasn't.

'It's usually a load of bollocks, people moaning about dog muck, rats being seen around the park, that sort of stuff. Couldn't believe my eyes when I saw it.'

'Siobhan, show me tomorrow. I have to go.'

'Found it!' She shoved the phone in front of Anna's face. 'There. Look.'

Anna looked.

'That's your man, isn't it? That's David Kingfisher?'

The camera flashed, making her jump. 'Fuck,' Anna shouted, banging the steering wheel and slamming her foot on the brake. She already had six points. They'd probably make her go on one of those stupid driver-awareness courses. Sod it, she'd take the points. It was nearly school holidays – she wouldn't give up a day of her own free time to be lectured at. There was another flash. The idiot behind her had been caught too. Served him right: he'd been on her bumper for the past three miles.

The monstrosity of a shopping centre loomed up ahead

of her like a palace out of the Arabian desert. Pressing the accelerator, she shot through the traffic lights on amber and took the corner at forty, hitting the kerb with her wheel. She headed for the undercover car park nearest to the shop. The clock on the dashboard winked at her: nine twenty-five. Pulling the car to a stop, she yanked the handbrake on and pulled her keys out of the ignition.

Her hand shook as she pulled down the visor and checked her reflection. Her face was as grey as Mrs James' had been. Her make-up, perfect at seven that morning and retouched before the parents had trooped in, was nowhere to be seen, in its place a shiny nose, dark circles under her eyes. A deep furrow creased the skin above her nose. She couldn't go into the mall looking like that. She reached over into her bag, knowing a bit of Touche Éclat and lipstick would do the trick but, instead of her fingers finding her make-up bag, they found her phone.

She tapped in the password and opened up Facebook, searching for the local community forum, scrolling until she found the post.

It couldn't be, could it? Not David, not *her* David? Surely not? No, this couldn't be about him.

But, as Siobhan had said, how many Kingfishers lived in the area? She'd never heard the name before. There were none at the school. Then again, he didn't come from around here; perhaps there were plenty of them in the Peaks where he'd grown up. A whole roost of them, a whole flock, or whatever a group of kingfishers was called.

He's disappeared and I need to find him urgently.

No, this wasn't about her David, her David hadn't disappeared.

'Have you hooked up with him yet?' Siobhan had quizzed her last week. She'd lied, not wanting the nosy cow to spread another rumour about her: that she was in love with a man she'd never even met. Siobhan wouldn't understand that David gave one hundred percent to his job. He had to, he was a surgeon, always on call, the one to turn to for those life-and-death situations. And, anyway, she was the one who'd let him down last time. She hadn't wanted to but what could she do? Lisa had wanted her to go wedding dress shopping and so she'd spent the weekend in London, oohing and aahing over her sister as she'd tried on dresses. 'It'll be you, next,' Lisa had said, and although Anna had scoffed she'd been secretly pleased her sister could see how much David meant to her.

Throwing her phone back into her bag, she got out of the car and slammed the door shut. Her finger hovered over the lock button on the key fob. 'Sod it.' She got back into the car.

Why hadn't she thought of it before? She would ring him, pretend she was checking on arrangements for tomorrow, casually ask him if he knew anyone called Denise. And then he would say no, she would breathe a sigh of relief, and she could go and buy the damn dress.

She scrolled through the call log until she reached his number, pressed the screen and waited. It rang on and on as she tapped the steering wheel with the fingers of her free hand. No answer. Maybe he'd been called to the hospital? His phone was probably in his locker, or his desk drawer, silent, throbbing away.

She was about to hang up when she heard something on the line, the sigh of heavy breathing, a click followed by silence. And then his voice.

'Hello, you. Just checking what time you're picking me up tomorrow,' she said, talking over him.

'Seven thirty, I think we agreed?'

She could hear panting down the phone. 'Been for a run?'

'Just got back. You just caught me.'

'Ooh, are you all hot and sweaty then?'

'Naughty. Just hold that thought until tomorrow. Look, darling, I really need to get a glass of water.'

'Sorry, I'll let you get on. Don't want you dying of thirst. Not before tomorrow.'

He laughed. 'There's no way I'm doing that. It's been too long. Far too long.'

Anna took a deep breath. She could just put the phone down, pretend she'd never seen the Facebook post, convince herself it had nothing to do with David. But the fluttering under her ribs, the fact she cared, really cared about this man, that she'd spotted the wedding dress she knew would look perfect on her, made her take another deep breath and open her mouth.

'David,' she said, 'do you know someone called Denise?'

CHAPTER 11

Denise rummaged in her bag, found a pear drop and popped it into her mouth, her gaze sweeping the room. The bar wasn't as busy as when she'd last been here. She didn't want to think about that time, about the nerves fizzing away, her excitement, and then disappointment when Laurence had appeared. Naïve, that was one word for her. Stupid. How could she ever have thought a man like David Kingfisher would be interested in her? He could have any woman he wanted. Why would he be attracted to an overweight nobody?

She pulled in her stomach and looked around her. The place seemed brighter today – perhaps they dimmed the lights only at the weekends, trying to create an atmosphere in the cavernous room. She should be able to find them in here, no problem.

'How will we recognise each other?' one of them, the one who'd called a couple of days ago, had asked.

'I'll be carrying a book.' When the woman hadn't replied Denise had offered to send a photo of herself.

Making her way to the bar, she scanned the room. It was mostly couples, a group of men who looked like they'd decided to have a quick one after work that had turned into two, a gaggle of older women who were sitting at a small table, grouped around a couple of bottles of Prosecco in an ice bucket, talking over one another. There was a woman on her own, gorgeous, long strawberry-blonde hair like Denise's favourite singer, Adele. Just the type of woman David would go for. Denise tried to catch her eye, waved her book in the air, but the woman didn't respond, just stared at her phone. And then a man walked past, his gaze flicking towards Denise before it rested on the woman. For a second, Denise thought it was David but, no, he was shorter, and, anyway, she couldn't imagine David wearing a shirt that loud.

The oversized clock at the far end of the bar told her she was nearly twenty minutes late. Maybe they'd gone, had tired of waiting, thinking perhaps it was all a joke, that she was some mad woman with a grudge, or a fantasist. Or perhaps they hadn't even turned up? The one who had called her last night had been tetchy, wanting to know what all this was about, refusing to give her name.

'Do you know him?' Denise had asked. 'Do you know where I can find him?'

'I might do,' the woman had said and then: 'But I need to know why you want to track him down. What's he done?'

Denise had taken a deep breath, not knowing where

to start, but then Laurence had appeared at the back door and she'd had to let him in. Denise had waved him away, upstairs, avoiding his eye, waiting until she'd heard him say hello to Mother.

'Are you still there?' the woman had said. Denise apologised, asked if they could meet. The Vaults, tomorrow, seven thirty?

She had heard the woman sigh. 'Look, I really think my David Kingfisher is nothing to do with your David Kingfisher.'

'Is he a surgeon?' Denise had said.

She heard a sharp intake of breath at the end of the line and then the woman had ended the call.

Denise ordered a Coke with plenty of ice, holding the glass to her forehead for a few seconds before making her way to a table in the centre of the room. She sat down and looked around her. They had to turn up, they had to. She needed to know where David Kingfisher was. It had been three weeks. She hadn't heard from him since the night before she'd gone to the hospital to see him, despite the numerous calls and messages she'd sent. She'd even caught the bus to Dalton, found the chocolate-box cottage and knocked on the door, but no one had answered. She took a sip of her Coke. She needed to find him. She needed to get the money back.

Petra headed straight for the bar, mesmerised by the rows upon rows of bottles she could see on the shelves towering high in front of her. How did the bar staff reach them up there? It was at least twelve feet high. She considered asking for a drink from one, perhaps from the bright yellow bottle shaped like a pineapple, just to see how they managed it. But then she thought of the dust, the microbes of skin, particles of hair and dirt clinging to it and her stomach lurched. Maybe she should hide her vodka somewhere dirty; bury it in the garden, deep under the soil?

'What can I get you?'

The boy in front of her had the height of a man, the muscles slowly forming in his tanned arms, but the softness of his face, free from lines, showed he was still trying to shake off the remnants of childhood.

'Erm….' She cast her eyes over the bottles. She stood on tiptoes and peered at the ones in the glass-fronted fridges banked up in a row behind him.

'Shall I come back?'

The boy moved to speak to a man further along the bar. She tried to guess what he would be drinking. The in-your-face shirt, designer beard, the jeans made her think he would go for a gin and tonic.

He must have sensed her gaze upon him: he gave her a quick smile, a nod of recognition that they were both on their own, raised his nearly empty pint glass. She'd never been a good judge of character. Wasn't that why she was here? She turned away from him, feeling uncomfortable. He seemed familiar. Had she seen him the last time she'd been in here, at Kirsty's leaving do? She wasn't under any illusion he was flirting with her; she wasn't the sort of woman men came on to. While the boy behind the bar was slowly morphing into a man, Petra would forever be classed as a girl – her slightness, the straight up and down of her, didn't appeal to the opposite sex. Nor did men like bending down to speak to her. She couldn't even class herself as petite, a little doll they would want to care for. Catching sight of her reflection in the mirror behind the bar told her what she already knew: she was short, an imp with a permanent scowl etched onto her forehead. Especially since last year.

'Decided?'

Vodka, vodka. The words screamed inside her mouth, threatening to spill out of her lips. 'Tonic water, please.'

'Ice and a slice?'

She shook her head. Despite the heat outside, she was cold. How high did they have the air conditioning on? She longed to undo her plait, to let her hair tumble down her back and pull it around her as if it were a cardigan.

'Anything else?' The boy plonked a glass of bubbles in front of her.

'Do you do hot drinks? Tea? Chamomile?'

He shook his head. 'Not after five.'

She handed him a two-pound coin, said: 'Keep the change.'

Turning, sipping at the water, shuddering at the coldness of it, she looked around her. A woman was sitting at a table in the centre of the room, a book on the table in front of her. Was that her? She looked different than her photo, older, a bit more old-fashioned.

The woman looked up and then down at the rucksack hanging by Petra's hip, her face lighting up as she clocked the book sticking out of the back flap. Petra put her hand protectively on it. The woman stood up, a huge smile on her face. It was her.

It wasn't too late to leave. She didn't have to be here, didn't have to do this. She could just put down her glass, walk to the door and go back home to Sam. Forget the whole David thing, think of it as an idea born from madness, three months of madness, concentrate instead on Sam, on their marriage. Her eyes were drawn to the woman. If this Denise went to the police, if they started to investigate David Kingfisher, then they would want to speak to the other women who had been involved with him. Petra's leg jumped; she should never have come here. Should never have given this Denise her real name. What had she been thinking? What if the police found her, interviewed her? What would Sam say then? She put her hand to her stomach. How could she explain she'd been doing all this for him?

Her feet started moving, but not in the direction of the door.

'Thanks for coming.' Denise stood up, wrapping her arms around Petra. Petra could smell a mixture of peach and fried fat in her hair. She tried to pull away, felt as if she were suffocating. And yet, for a second, the sensation of being held sent a jolt of warmth through her.

Denise finally let go and they both sat down. There was an awkward silence until Denise opened her mouth.

'Can't believe the weather, can you? A hundred degrees, that's what they're saying. A hundred! Hotter than Spain. And the Caribbean. I've never known it to be—'

'Is it just the two of us?' Petra said.

'Someone else has been in touch. I thought it was that lady.' Denise turned her head. 'Oh, there was someone sitting over there, I thought it was her. She was gorgeous. I wouldn't be surprised that David would go for someone like her. Not that that matters, after what he's done. I just didn't believe he could do something like this. Did you?'

Petra took a sip of her drink, wishing it was vodka, before shaking her head. Would this Denise ever shut up? She was right though, wasn't she? Petra had never thought David would do something like this. Ten thousand pounds. What would Sam do if he found the bank statement? He would go mad. He would say she was mad. And she was. Her being here was testament to that. Ten thousand pounds. How could she have been so stupid?

Anna lifted her face to the sun, taking a last long drag of her cigarette before stubbing it out in the ashtray. It was the first one she'd had for ages. She allowed herself only to smoke in times of extreme stress: Robbo's phone call to her, eight months ago, had been such a time. As was tonight. Reaching into her bag, she found a pack of chewing gum, flirted one out of the silver wrapping with her thumb and stuck it in her mouth. Ridiculous, really. She was getting herself het up over nothing. She didn't have to be here. But it was time to put this Denise straight. For David's sake, as much as for her own.

David had explained everything: how he'd got chatting to Denise last year by email but decided not to take it further. She'd gone ballistic, that was the actual word he'd used, had said she would track him down, make him see what he was missing.

Anna had spotted her as soon as she'd arrived. Denise was holding a book as she'd said she would be, but her eyes were darting this way and that, looking anywhere but at the page. She could see why David had decided Denise wasn't for him. She seemed a little mumsy, a little dowdy with her flowery skirt and a satiny top that had seen better days. Anna felt sorry for her in a way. She'd obviously pinned her hopes on David and, when he'd rebuffed her, had concocted some loopy story to get her own back on him. And it *was* a loopy story, something about David taking money off her.

Anna hadn't got much sense out of Denise on the phone, had decided the best course of action was to meet up with her and put her straight. She would point out that Denise had to move on. God, she might even mention Robbo, tell Denise that being dumped happened to everyone. And if Denise refused to give up on David, if she carried on with her stupid lies, then Anna would point out that what she was doing could land her in court. Still, she didn't think it would come to that. When Denise saw that David had a girlfriend, was in a serious relationship, she might back down, move on to some other poor bloke.

Anna had gone outside to the beer garden when she'd seen the other woman go up to Denise. Denise hadn't said there was someone else. Anna took a swig of her drink. It was probably a friend, someone she'd bribed to go along with her story.

'All right?' Tyler was standing to her left, his fingers clutching four pint glasses, ready to lift them.

What was he doing here? Didn't he say he only worked Fridays and Saturdays? She thought of his mother, of Kai, the errant father, his mother's pleas to help Tyler get a scholarship for the final year. He must really need the money.

'You'll never be up for school,' she said.

'Neither will you.' He arched one eyebrow, a grin spreading across his face. 'You teachers must be getting end-of-term happy?'

'Oh?'

'Haven't you seen him? Letchy Leeky?'

Richard was here? That was all she needed.

'He was with the group by the door. I think it's a pool team thing. They always come in here before they play the match. A quick one to warm them up, you know?'

Zipping up her bag, Anna stood up. He'd be gone by now then. She hadn't seen him when she'd come in but had he seen her? If so, there'd be more gossip around the staffroom tomorrow, and he would be pumping Siobhan for details. Siobhan had promised she wouldn't say anything about the Facebook post but Anna knew her friend's promise stood for nothing.

'Meeting friends?'

She nodded, although it really wasn't any of Tyler's business.

'Not been stood up again, then?'

She pursed her lips, gave him the look she used to dish out to the unruly ones at the comprehensive in Exeter.

'Sorry.' He grinned at her and picked up the glasses.

She relaxed her face muscles, allowed a smile to creep onto her face. He was obviously going through a tough time; she didn't need to add to it.

'I meant to ask you.' He put down the glasses and started to stack them one on top of the other. 'Well, it was my mum, really, who suggested it.'

Oh, God, he was going to ask her about the scholarship. She'd not had a chance to have a word with Benson yet but, with Tyler's attitude lately, it would be hard to convince the head he was worthy of the financial support.

'Do you do private lessons?'

'Sorry?'

'Teach after school? You know I'm falling behind. Mum told you what's been going on?' He didn't wait for a reply, put his hand up to shield his eyes from the lowering sun. 'I was thinking I could do with catching up. I'm not sure I could pay much but...'

Anna glanced over his shoulder, could just about make out Denise and the other woman in the gloom of the pub. She didn't have time for this now.

'My mum, you know...'

Anna wanted to sigh but stopped herself from doing so. How could she refuse to help him when his mother was ill?

'You will?' He must have taken her silence for agreement, for his face lit up, his blue eyes regaining some of the brightness she'd seen in them when she first arrived at St Edward's.

'I can't promise anything,' she said. 'I'd have to run it past Mr Benson.'

'Sure.' He picked up the pint pots, a large tower of them. 'That would be mint.'

'I thought it was you.' Denise stood up as the woman she'd spotted earlier, the gorgeous one who'd been sitting on her own, stopped in front of their table. 'I'm Denise. We spoke last night.' She held out her hand, smiled, although disappointment tugged at her; the woman was everything she wasn't. 'Sit down, sit down,' Denise said, sucking in her stomach.

The woman pulled out a stool and sat, crossing her long legs, smoothing her skirt towards suntanned knees.

Denise wiped at her own skirt, wishing she'd dressed up a bit. Then again, she had nothing to dress up in. 'This is Petra.'

The woman gave Petra the briefest of smiles before taking a sip of her wine.

Petra didn't return the smile; she fiddled with the straggly end of her plait as she stared at the woman.

Denise tried to smooth down her own frizzy hair. 'Sorry, I didn't catch your name.'

'Anna,' she said, looking towards the entrance and then back at them. 'I'm Anna.'

'Nice to meet you, Anna. Before you called I thought there was just going to be the two of us,' she said, smiling at Petra, 'but then I thought, if he's done this to you, Denise, then there'll be others, there's got to be. Men like this, they can't stop themselves, can they? And then you rang last night and I thought, yes, I'm right. I was just saying that to you, wasn't I, Petra? Men like David…'

'Has he had money off you?' Petra leant towards Anna, her elbows resting on the table, her chin cupped in her hands.

Denise held her breath. If there were three of them, three of them he'd conned, then surely there was power in numbers, surely, between them, they'd be able to find him, get the money back? She had just under four weeks until the charity's AGM when the accounts would be picked through with a fine-tooth comb.

Anna put down her wine glass, smiled at them. She had perfect teeth. Denise wondered if they were naturally that colour or whether she'd paid to have them whitened. 'Ladies, you've really got to stop this.'

Denise sank back into her chair. 'Stop what? He's taken money from both of us. Ten thousand pounds each.'

'Why are you doing this?' Anna reached into her bag and got out her phone, scrolling the screen before holding it up. 'You need to delete this post. And stop spreading these rumours. Don't you know you could be done for slander?'

'It's only slander if I'm lying and I'm not.' Denise felt her cheeks flame and picked up a menu from the table, fanning herself with it. 'I'm not.'

'Look.' Anna took a deep breath. 'David told me all about you. I know it's not pleasant when someone dumps you but you need to move on.'

Something inside Denise shrivelled. It was bad enough he'd stolen the money. But the fact he'd let her down, dumped her, stung even more.

'I'm not lying.' Her voice came out like a whisper. She looked over to Petra. 'We're not lying, are we?'

Anna turned to Petra. 'You need to tell your friend to let this go.'

'I'm not her friend,' Petra said, emphasising the word 'her'. 'I saw the message on Facebook and came to find out what she knows about all this, about David.'

Denise swallowed. She'd been hoping the three of them would be friends, would together track down the man who had conned them.

Anna looked at the entrance again. 'Why would David want money off you? He's a top surgeon, for God's sake. He has a place in Dorset, and a lovely cottage on the other side of town. What would he want with your money?'

'Are you still with him?' The words flew out of Denise's mouth as Anna glanced at her watch. 'Is David Kingfisher your boyfriend?'

'Yes,' she said.

Denise clapped her hands together and smiled at Petra. Petra raised an eyebrow back at her.

'So you know where he is?' Excitement fluttered in Denise's chest: this woman was going to lead her to David Kingfisher. She was going to get the money back. She nodded at Anna, willing her to say more, but Anna crossed one leg over the other and sipped at her glass of wine.

'He's a surgeon at the hospital?' Petra asked.

Anna sighed. 'That's right.'

Denise looked at Anna's perfect cupid's bow lips. She didn't want to think of David kissing them. 'But I went to the hospital and they said no one called David Kingfisher works there.'

Anna smiled. 'They don't just give out information to anyone, do they, these days? Data protection and all that.'

Denise blushed. Was she right? Did David work there, after all, even though his name wasn't on the telephone list? Had the man she'd seen been him? That shock of dark curls, that square jaw – he was either David Kingfisher or his twin brother. Or had she been imagining it?

'I know someone who works at the hospital and they checked for me. There's definitely no one called David Kingfisher who works there.' Petra folded her arms. Denise let out the breath she'd been holding. She had been imagining it, the man who had walked past the lift wasn't David. But if not, then where was he? Tears clogged the back of her throat. She took a sip of her Coke, swallowing them down.

Anna shook her head. 'You obviously don't believe

a word I'm saying. Why should I believe what *you* say? David Kingfisher is my boyfriend. He's a top surgeon, he works at the hospital. Perhaps you're confusing him with someone else?'

Denise looked at Petra. Perhaps they'd both got it wrong?

Petra gave Anna a tight smile. 'Have you met him?'

'What?' Anna shifted in her chair, put her wine glass to her lips.

Denise bounced in her chair. 'Have you met him? He kept promising to meet me but then never showed up.'

'Me too,' Petra said. 'He always had some excuse or another.'

'They're not excuses, he's a busy man. His career is very important to him. If you knew him, you'd know that.'

'You haven't, have you?' Petra said.

'It's none of your business.'

'I thought so.' Petra took a sip of her drink. 'You've never met him and yet you've been in a relationship with him for how long? Let me guess. Just over three months? Don't you think that's strange?'

Anna pushed her hair back over her shoulder, smiled tightly. 'As I said before, none of your business.' She turned to Denise. 'I know as much as anyone what it's like to be dumped. You've really got to move on. Forget this. It's been what, a year since you chatted to him? There are plenty of other men out there.'

'A year?' Denise shook her head. 'I only signed up three months ago, the night David messaged me.' She

131

reached down into her bag for her phone, thrust it towards Anna. 'You can check. He stopped messaging me three weeks ago. I asked him to give me back the money I'd lent him and then he just went silent.' She looked at Petra. 'Is that what happened to you?'

Petra nodded, started fiddling with her necklace.

'Oh, you've got the same necklace.' Denise leant towards Anna. 'It is, isn't it?'

Petra shot forwards. 'Did he buy you that?'

Anna put her hand protectively over the locket, shook her head. 'No.'

'Liar.' Petra spat out the word.

Denise looked back and forth between the women. David hadn't bought her a necklace. She'd obviously never meant anything to him. Nothing at all. Anna and Petra were both sitting with scowls on their faces. This wasn't going the way she'd planned. But, then again, how had she expected it to go? All three of them had been in love with him, probably still were. They weren't going to be the best of friends. She couldn't ever see herself being friends with Anna. The woman was convinced David Kingfisher could do no wrong. Perhaps he just hadn't asked her for money yet. But he would. Denise knew he would. That was his game. She stared out of the window. At least Petra was on her side; between them they'd given him twenty thousand pounds.

A car flashed past outside, a car that looked suspiciously like Laurence's. He hadn't followed her, had he? After the initial awkwardness between them, in the past

132

month or so he'd started to laugh and joke with her again, despite her monosyllabic responses. And he'd wanted to know where she was going tonight. She'd made up a story about meeting up with some women she used to work with. She could never tell Laurence about all of this. He could never find out about the money. He was on the board of the charity, had helped set it up. She glanced at Anna. The woman sitting in front of her knew where David Kingfisher was. She was the key to finding him and getting the money back.

Anna stared at her watch. He was late. He'd promised he'd be here by quarter past. He'd promised to clear everything up. Between them they were going to put this Denise woman straight. Where was he? Her earlier excitement, the bubbling inside her stomach, was starting to flatten, to disappear. He'd promised.

She couldn't believe David had cheated on her, even if it was virtually, not with anyone, and certainly not these two. She was being mean, she knew it, but one looked like her idea of a night out was a game of bingo at the local village hall and the other had a boyish look to her, a spitefulness in the pinch of her face. The denim jacket she was wearing swamped her. And her hair. A long plait, like a schoolgirl might have. No, David wouldn't go for these women. He wouldn't.

And yet a tiny sliver of doubt had been itching away at her. They were right: she hadn't met him yet and although she'd let him down a couple of times, lately it was always he who cancelled their dates. She thought of the Joseph dress, still hanging in cellophane in her wardrobe, the dinner at the fancy restaurant in Manchester they'd never enjoyed. He'd had an excuse, he always did. But he'd wanted to confront this Denise woman too, had said he was looking forward to finally getting her off his back. He would make short shrift of her, he'd said, and then he would whisk Anna off to Picasso's. He'd even texted to say the table was booked.

'I checked the electoral register. He's not listed.' Denise pulled a folder out of the large canvas bag hanging on the corner of her chair.

'What's that?'

'My notes.' Denise opened the plastic wallet, spreading papers in front of her. 'Here. The telephone list for the hospital. He's not on it.' She held it out to Anna, but Anna crossed her arms.

'Are there *any* Kingfishers on the electoral roll?' Petra picked up her glass.

Denise shook her head, rifling through the papers on her knee. 'I've checked this town and all the outlying districts.'

'Doesn't surprise me,' Petra said. 'I did a search on the internet and could only find a David Kingfisher in Ireland and one in Australia.'

Anna leant forward, picked up the telephone list off the table. He would be here in a minute to put an end to all this nonsense, but it didn't hurt to look. Denise didn't seem the brightest; she'd probably missed his name. Her eyes searched through the Ks – Karim, King, Kennedy but no Kingfisher. Anna thought back. She'd assumed David worked at the local hospital but perhaps he worked at another Manchester hospital?

'I told you.' Denise sighed. 'He's taken our money, and now he's done a runner. I don't know how I could have been so stupid.'

Anna turned to Petra. For someone who had supposedly been diddled out of ten thousand pounds, she didn't look on edge; in fact, she had a blank expression on her face, as if she were elsewhere. 'How did you give him the money?'

'I sent it to an account number he gave me.'

Denise clapped her hands. 'Me too. See, this is what he's like.'

'Not with me.' Anna thought back to the emails, messages, the texts, phone calls. Not once had David mentioned money, never mind asked her for some. She glanced at her watch. He was now forty minutes late.

Denise grabbed her arm. 'I went to his cottage, where he said he lived. If he was there, he didn't answer the door. If you know where he is, please tell us. I have to get the money back.'

Anna shrugged her off. She couldn't blame David for not answering the door to this mad woman. She checked her phone wasn't on silent. Perhaps he'd texted her? There was nothing.

'Please.' Denise sniffed and rubbed the back of her hand across her nose.

'I'll ring him,' Anna said. She dialled the number. Listened to the ringtone. Waited. There was a click and then an automated woman's voice: the answerphone.

'Not answering? Probably doing a lifesaving operation on a poorly child.' Petra slammed her glass down onto the table.

Anna scrolled through her phone, rang another number. 'Could you tell me if my boyfriend has arrived? We have a dinner reservation for eight thirty. Kingfisher.'

She listened to what the man on the end of the phone was saying.

'Are you sure? Maybe you have the wrong time? Or the wrong night?'

Anna bit her lip. Waited. 'Okay, thank you.'

Denise grabbed her hand, refusing to let it go this time. 'He's stood you up, hasn't he? Hasn't he?'

The strangest feeling came over Anna. She couldn't tell if it was anger or humiliation. It shot through her, warming her veins, making her right eye hurt, the beginnings of a headache coming on. It was a feeling similar to the one she'd had when Robbo had accused her of moving here to be with him.

'There'll be a perfectly reasonable excuse,' she said, as she waited for the man on the end of the line to check his appointments book.

'There always is,' Petra said.

Anna had met women like her before: sarcastic, spiteful even, a huge chip on their shoulder because they were short, plain. From the look on her face, the caustic words coming out of her mouth, it seemed Petra, like Denise, had been pinning her hopes on David.

'And the most reasonable one, the most sensible one, is that he doesn't exist.'

Petra nodded at Denise's words.

'No, sorry, madam.' The man's voice came back on the line. 'We have nothing for this week or next in the name of Kingfisher.'

It was as if someone had stepped on her stomach. Anna gripped the arms of the chair, feeling like she was falling. David was her soulmate. David loved her. David was taking her to his cottage in Dorset in the school holidays. She'd spent a fortune on new clothes, especially underwear. She looked at the women in front of her. They were mad, the pair of them. David was probably stuck at work. Or she'd got the restaurant wrong. Yes, that would be it. He was more than likely sitting in the curry house up the road right now, waiting for her. But why hadn't he turned up here? He'd said he would.

Denise and Petra were staring at her.

'Now do you believe us?' Denise asked.

Petra smirked. 'He's a con man. Admit it.'

Anna stood up. 'I don't know what game you're playing, but you have to stop. Leave me and my boyfriend alone or we'll go to the police.'

The colour drained out of Denise's face so that it was nearly as white as Petra's. 'Not the police.'

So, she had been right. The only con going on here was the fast one these two women were pulling. They were probably lonely, had nothing better to do. God, there were some weird people about.

'We're not lying, please.' Denise tried to grab at her arm but Anna was too quick for her, hitching her bag over her shoulder and striding towards the door.

They were lying.

David Kingfisher was her soulmate. She believed that and she had to, for she couldn't face what would come if he wasn't: the soul-destroying loneliness that would envelop her like it had done before, when Robbo had walked out of her life.

CHAPTER 12

They really are stupid. Have they got no idea I'm here, watching them? Breathing in every last bit of them, going over the messages, the conversations we've had.

I watch them and they have no idea I can hear every word they say.

Maybe I should reveal myself, give them the answers they want. And yet I can't. Like them, I want the game to continue until we reach the final outcome. Until she is no more.

CHAPTER 13

Anna had driven past David's house before, of course she had. It had been easy to find. He'd told her about the cottage many times. How it had been a wreck when he'd found it, how he'd been doing it up bit by bit, whenever he got a spare hour or two. She'd said she'd love to see it and he'd sounded a bit embarrassed on the phone, telling her it still needed a lot of work, he couldn't show it to her yet, for whatever would she think of him if she saw it in its current state? 'You'd run a mile,' he'd said. And she'd laughed, wanting to tell him she would never run from him, but not letting the words out of her mouth. She could see now she'd been too needy with Robbo; she wouldn't make the same mistake with David.

It was a small cottage, black and white beams criss-crossing the outside, making way for tiny windows. She wondered if David hit his head on the doorframes, for he was tall, six foot two, he'd said.

He'd told her the garden was a mess but it wasn't,

there was box hedging and pink roses, lavender too, framing a gravel path to the front door. Maybe he'd concentrated on getting the outside done first before moving on to the interior. She looked up at the roof and saw the weather vane David's parents had bought him when he'd moved in: a black wrought-iron kingfisher sitting proud atop a black arrow.

So she knew this was his house, knew he lived in the village of Dalton, had driven past many times, wanting to stop her car and go up the gravel path and knock on the door. But his car had never been there and the cottage always seemed empty, no sign of life, so she hadn't stopped, telling herself she would wait to be invited, reminding herself about not coming across as too needy.

It had been less than twenty-four hours since she'd met those mad women in the pub. She'd kept checking the Facebook group but there had been no messages since. And she'd hidden her number the time she'd rung Denise so she couldn't ring her back. They'd probably moved on to someone else by now, someone they could con.

David had texted her at three in the morning. She had been awake, waiting to hear why he hadn't turned up. A boy had been knocked off his bike on the high street. A hit-and-run. He'd been operating on him for eight hours, trying to put him back together. He couldn't leave him, he hoped she understood. She did, of course, she did.

This morning she'd scoured the local news online for the story of the poor boy. There was nothing but perhaps it wasn't big news. A hit-and-run though, a critically ill boy? She'd expect it to be the top item. She'd watched the regional news on TV. Nothing. She rang the hospital, asking to be put through to David Kingfisher's office. The operator told her to wait. She suddenly felt silly as she listened to the piped music. What would she say when he came onto the line? But he didn't, there was just the operator's bored voice, asking her to repeat David's name, telling her there was no one with the name Kingfisher who worked there. Anna had hung up. Had she got it wrong? She'd scoured through his emails, texts, gone over their conversations. He'd never actually said he worked at the local hospital, she'd just assumed it.

She slowed her car, her heart leaping as she saw a Porsche parked on the gravel area at the side of the cottage. He was home! Finally, finally, she would get to meet him.

'Graceland' by Paul Simon came on the radio as she stopped the car. She smiled. It was surely a sign, yet her hand shook as she angled the rear-view mirror so she could check her make-up. She took a deep breath, telling herself there was nothing to be nervous about. David was in love with her, so why shouldn't she just turn up on his doorstep? She looked good; she knew she did. She'd had more highlights put in her hair that morning and treated herself to a facial yesterday after work. Her skin was glowing.

She was getting out of the car when her phone buzzed. Was this him?

She opened the message on her phone. It wasn't him. Lisa. Did you ask David about Dorset?

Lisa and Joe were off to the south-west for a camping trip. When Anna had told her sister they were going to David's place in Dorset for a fortnight, Lisa had suggested that she and Joe could call in on their way to Cornwall. 'Just for a day,' Lisa had said. 'I need to make sure he's good enough for my big sis. Give him the once-over.' Me and you both, Anna had thought but, of course, she hadn't said anything; she hadn't got around to telling Lisa she hadn't actually met David yet.

Anna switched off her phone and threw it back into her bag.

Her mouth was dry – she should have brought a bottle of water with her. She walked along the road to David's cottage, her legs feeling as if they were going to give way under her. She hoped he wouldn't be angry at her turning up like this, but why would he? She was his girlfriend, after all.

The garden was better close up, the grass neatly cut as if he'd taken a pair of nail clippers to it, the roses perfect buds, their delicious smell mingling with that of the lavender. She smoothed down her hair before lifting the lion's head knocker, letting it fall limply.

No one came and yet she could hear music in the house, something classical, something familiar, but a tune she couldn't name.

She lifted the knocker again and banged it against the door.

From behind the door came noises: a chain being pulled back, a key turning in a lock.

She pushed back her shoulders, tried to soften the grin that was making her cheeks ache.

'Can I help you?' An old woman with small pink curlers in her hair stood at the door.

'You must be David's mother?' David had said his mother lived in Spain. Anna had imagined someone much more glamorous than the slightly scruffy woman in front of her. She held out her hand.

The woman squinted at her through thick glasses. 'Can I help you, love?' she said again.

Anna dropped her hand. 'I'm Anna. David's girlfriend. Is he in?'

The woman shook her head, her curlers bobbing. 'You've got the wrong house, love. There's no David lives here.'

Perhaps David's mother was suffering from dementia. 'But his car's here.' Anna nodded towards David's car. She knew he had a Porsche, a silver one, he'd promised to take her out in it.

'That's my daughter's.'

A woman, fifty-something with a short buzz cut, suddenly appeared. 'Can I help you?'

'I'm looking for David Kingfisher.' Anna tried to see past the two women into the gloom of the cottage.

'Got the wrong house.' The daughter sniffed.

Before Anna could say anything else, she'd closed the door.

Anna felt the heat rise in her cheeks. A sob caught in her throat. Had she got it wrong? Had she got the wrong house? She strode along the gravel path, the heel of her sandal catching on a loose stone, propelling her forwards, making her gasp as she struggled to catch her balance, her new Stella McCartney skirt catching on a branch of a rose bush. She didn't fall. She picked up her bag, which had dropped to the ground, flicked back her hair, refusing to turn around to see if she was being watched, and headed back to her car, slamming the door as she got into the hot interior. There was a pull in her skirt. She rubbed at it, leaving a grimy mark on the white material. Tears welled in her eyes.

She looked up. The weather vane stood tall and proud on top of the cottage, the kingfisher peering down as if it were mocking her. She put her hands onto the steering wheel, let her head rest on them, Petra's words coming back to her: *He's a con man.* She got out her phone and found the photo David had sent her. She hadn't got the wrong house, the image showed the same one she'd just knocked at, so did that mean she'd got the wrong man? Anna banged her head against the steering wheel as tears spilt down her cheeks.

Her phone buzzed again. She lifted her head and rummaged in her bag for it. Lisa. We can't wait to meet him. Never known you this happy. So thrilled for you. Glad you've put dickhead Robbo behind you.

Robbo *was* a dickhead. He'd promised her everything and then taken it away from her. Anna let out a sob. She'd allowed it to happen again, hadn't she? She had to face up to it: David Kingfisher was leading her on. Three months and she'd never met him. Three months of lies. What was it with men? Why did they think they could do that to her? She stared into the rear-view mirror. Her face was flushed, her lip gloss gone. Tears were streaming down her cheeks, leaving a silvery track through her Chanel foundation. She might have let Robbo get away with treating her like shit, but she wouldn't let David. She wouldn't let another man do that to her.

She rang his number. There was no answer. She rang again, twice, three, four times. On the fifth, she spoke to his answerphone. 'I'm outside your house. Only it isn't your house, is it? You've never lived there. And you don't work at the local hospital. In fact, I doubt you work at any hospital. You're a fraud. Delete the photos and never call me again.' She hung up and scrolled through the numbers on her phone until she found the one she wanted. She waited, her pink-polished nails tapping the steering wheel.

She was about to hang up when she heard a click and an excited 'Hello?'

'Has he given you the money back yet?' Anna held her breath, wanting the woman on the end of the line to admit it had been a joke, or even some terrible mistake. That would do.

'No, he hasn't,' Denise whispered. 'Do you know where he is?'

'No, but we're going to find him, Denise. We're going to find him and we're going to make him pay.'

'I believed him.' Denise's voice was quiet. 'He said he loved me. He said I was the only one.'

Anna let out a long sigh. 'He's just another liar, Denise. Just another liar.'

CHAPTER 14

Three days later

'Shall I put the sat nav on?' Anna reached forward to get her phone out of her bag.

'It's okay. I know the way.'

Anna turned to look at the woman in the driver's seat. They were in the depths of the Peak District, driving along a single-track lane, the grey concrete cutting a path through the green hills. 'How come?'

Petra's gaze slid to the left quickly before moving back to the road ahead. 'My dad was big into walking. Had us tramping over these hills every Saturday for the whole of my childhood.'

'At least it wasn't Sunday too,' Anna said. She couldn't think of anything worse than expending energy just to get a view of some fields. She looked down at her gold sparkly flip-flops; perhaps she should have worn trainers. There might be dirt, or cow muck.

Petra let out a *huh*. 'Sundays were for him.' She flicked her head upwards. 'God.'

'Oh, your dad's religious?'

'Was then.'

'Not now?'

Petra indicated past a parked tractor, even though the car behind them was further down the hill. It was the only one they'd seen since they left town.

'He was a vicar.'

Anna thought of her own father, a Methodist lay pastor, and shuddered. Thank God her only brushes with religion these days were the odd wedding and funeral she found herself at. Lisa and Joe were getting married at some fancy hotel in London – no bell-ringing, no hymns, no eternal vows to get through, and with any luck her father and stepmother wouldn't be going.

Turning her head, she glanced at Petra. That she was a vicar's daughter came as no surprise. There was something of the Bible-basher about her that reminded Anna of her stepmother: a plainness, a streak of penance in the furrow of her brow. And now, with her bright white crop, even more so. She looked like she'd been tarred and feathered and dipped in bleach. What had possessed her? Anna almost hadn't recognised her when she'd picked her up this morning. That long dark plait had been the only feminine thing about her.

As they hit a bump in the road and flew down the other side, Anna's stomach lurched, her head throbbed: the after-effects of the glasses of wine and countless mojitos she'd polished off last night. 'Does the air conditioning go any higher?'

Petra pressed a button.

Ice-cold air rushed at Anna, soothing the tight band across her forehead. She hoped she wasn't going to be sick. Images of last night flipped through her head like a slide show, jumbled-up snippets of conversations coming back to her, faces laughing. One glass of wine with the other teachers, the last day of term, just to be sociable, that's all it was supposed to be. After all, she had nothing else to do. But then someone got another round in. And after that Siobhan bought a bottle and kept topping up her glass. Taxis arrived and she was bundled into one. They'd headed straight for The Vaults. Richard had convinced her to have a mojito, Tyler had given her a free one, bringing it out to her in the beer garden. What had she said to him? Her memories were hazy, clouded by alcohol, but an image of her showing him her phone kept flashing into her mind.

A hot sweat broke out on the back of her neck, flooding her face, her body. She hadn't shown him the photos she'd taken of herself, had she? And then it came back to her: Tyler staring at the photo of David, telling her to leave it with him. And then, just when she was about to head home, the room already starting to spin in front of her, Robbo had appeared. She'd thought she was hallucinating, conjuring him up, but the spicy scent of his aftershave, his warm hand on her arm, convinced her he was real. He steered her back into the beer garden, made her sit down. And, in a slur of words, she told him about David. Boasting at first, calling him the love of her life, saying he would never let her down, emphasising the *he*, scowling at Robbo one second, grabbing for his hand the next. And then the truth came tumbling out of her mouth: how David had led her on, the unanswered calls, the dates that had never happened, the house that wasn't his.

Robbo had pulled her towards him, kissed the top of her head, told her to be careful. Clinging to him, never wanting to let him go, she put her lips to his but he had pulled away. 'There are blokes out there who play women, who get a kick out of it. He's probably done it before, will do it again.' She started laughing then, because wasn't that what Robbo had done to her? And then she was crying. 'Why, Robbo, why?' But there had been no answer, he'd just pushed his fingers through his hair and helped her back inside. Why wouldn't he tell her why he didn't love her anymore?

Another image came into her head: Richard to one side of her, Tyler leaning over the bar, Robbo holding her up. And while they argued about who should take her home, she helped herself to another glass of wine someone had left. The next thing she remembered was the taxi, tongues and hands everywhere, clothes pushed up, touching, squeezing. And then they were in her bed and she was sitting astride him, the room spinning, and she knew she was doing a very bad thing indeed.

'Hangover? You reek of booze.' Petra swung the car to the left, following the sign for Ashbourne. 'Help yourself to the water.' She reached down to the side and passed an unopened bottle to Anna.

Anna broke the seal, flicked back the cap and took a long drink. 'Had one of those nights,' she said. 'Ended up in The Vaults. On the mojitos.' The water was luke-warm, but it was better than nothing. 'Want some?' She held it out to Petra.

Petra grimaced and shook her head.

Anna shrugged and screwed the top back onto the bottle. What a cold fish Petra was. She'd hardly said anything on the forty-minute journey, apart from that mention of her father. It didn't sound like she was still in touch with him. Was her mother still around? Sisters, brothers? Anna didn't think so. Petra seemed so insular; she couldn't imagine her being part of a big family. She was definitely a loner. For a second, she wondered how David could have been interested in someone like her, until she remembered David hadn't been interested in Petra at all, just her money. Anna sighed. Since she'd left him the voicemail message, telling him she knew he was a fake, she'd texted him again to demand he delete the photos of her. There had been no reply.

Anna uncapped the bottle, took another swig. 'Denise should be here.'

Denise had rushed out when they'd pulled up outside her house this morning. 'I can't come, Mother's not well.'

Petra had shrugged. 'Probably a waste of time anyway.'

'No!' Denise's head had pushed through the car

153

window, bringing with it a smell of pear drops. 'No. You two go. Please.' She had glanced back at the house, lowered her voice. 'Please, Petra. We need to find him, don't we? We need that money back.'

Anna turned the air vents towards her so that icy air blasted her face. She was never drinking again. 'I hope this isn't a wild goose chase.'

Petra slowed the car. 'Shall I turn around?'

'We're nearly there now, aren't we?'

The car picked up speed again. Anna closed her eyes, felt herself nodding off until she heard Petra's voice.

'Denise and I want our money back... but what do you want from him?'

Anna kept her eyes closed. She had to find David. Not for Petra's sake, although she would love to see the exchange between them, nor for Denise's, because she couldn't help thinking the foolish woman had brought it on herself. No, she wanted to find him for herself. She wanted to scream and shout at him and tell him what a bastard he was, that he couldn't go around promising women the earth and then deliver nothing. And, of course, she needed him to delete those photos. An image of Benson calling her into his office, asking her to 'go quietly', flashed through her mind. She couldn't lose her career; it was the only thing she had left.

She opened her eyes, saw Petra looking at her. 'Answers, I suppose, like you do. I want to know why he lied to me.' She turned her head to the window. 'I want to hurt him. A woman scorned and all that.'

'A woman like you could have any man she wanted. So he let you down, so what? At least he didn't get your money. Move on. He doesn't deserve you.'

'I just want answers.' And she did. She hadn't been able to get them from Robbo, so she was damn sure she was going to get them from David.

They passed a pub, its hanging baskets dry and dusty, no end in sight to the hosepipe ban.

'Ever been married?'

The question startled Anna.

'No.'

'Why not?' Petra followed the sign for Bickley. 'Never found Mr Right?'

'I did.'

'And?'

She shrugged. 'I suppose I wasn't his Mrs Right.'

'Were you in love with him?'

'Er, I just said he was my Mr Right?' Anna was aware she'd raised her voice at the end of the sentence in that annoying way her students did, a habit picked up off some awful American TV show.

'But he didn't love you?'

'Said he did. But perhaps not enough.'

'There was another woman?'

'Shit.' Anna flung her arms out in front of her as the car lurched to a sudden stop.

'Sorry. I couldn't kill it.' A pheasant skittered back and forth across the road in front of them, before making its mind up about which way to go and diving under a hedge.

Anna picked up the bottle from the footwell where it had landed. Her hands were shaking. It wasn't because of the emergency stop though, it was because of what Petra had said. Another woman? She thought of the girl with the blue hair. Millie. He hadn't ditched her for a bloody student, had he? A horrible thought suddenly struck her. A wife? No, not Robbo. Her mind was running away with her. She had asked him if he was married that first night they spent together at the conference. She remembered the conversation word for word, the way she had clenched every muscle in her body, holding the air inside her lungs until he said, 'No, who'd have me?' He'd reached over, cupped her face in his hands, touched his lips to hers. And she'd tried to smile as a sob built in the back of her throat. Because he knew she would have him in an instant.

Men lied, of course. It came as naturally to some of them as breathing. But she'd driven past his house, parked at the end of his street every Saturday, and she'd never seen evidence of someone else living there. There was no wife kissing him goodbye, no second car on the drive. She thought of his hands, those strong fingers, no sign of a wedding ring hastily removed.

Petra pulled up at a give way sign. 'Maybe you're right, maybe he just didn't love you enough.'

Anna's stomach flipped. She was all for plain talking, she had to be growing up with Lisa, but really this woman could run rings around her sister. What gave the imp the right to speak to her like that? But was Petra right? She thought back to last night, to Robbo's arms around her in the beer garden. He cared for her, that was plain to see, but had he ever really loved her? Had any man?

She pushed the thoughts away. 'What about you? Ever come close to getting hitched?'

Petra made a snorting noise she hoped sounded non-committal. How could she confide in the woman next to her that she was married, that Sam was at home now, probably in bed where she'd left him? No, she couldn't tell Anna about Sam; she didn't want her to think she was the sort of woman who cheated. And, anyway, she wasn't. Not technically. And yet... if Sam read David's messages he would think she'd been cheating on him. But he must know she would never do that? David was just someone she'd been using to get what she wanted. She mentally checked she had her laptop and Kindle safely in the boot. She shivered, switched the air con back to heat. Sam couldn't find out. He wouldn't believe she'd been doing all this for him, for them.

'Did he say he'd take you to his cottage?' For a moment, Petra thought Anna was talking about Sam. 'In Dorset?'

'What? Yes.'

'I wonder if he ever asked Denise? I doubt it.'

Petra bit her top lip and concentrated on the road ahead, trying not to look as Anna crossed one bronzed leg over the other. Anna really thought she was something.

'I suppose you're wondering what he sees in me?'

157

Petra ran her head over her shorn crop, still not believing she'd had the courage to chop it all off and dye it. 'You think he couldn't possibly love someone like me. You think I'm deluded, don't you? You think he prefers you to me?' She closed her mouth before any more words could tumble out of it.

'I wasn't thinking that at all.' Anna sniffed. 'And what does it matter, anyway? He's conned us all, hasn't he? He doesn't love any of us.'

Petra stopped the car on the far side of the village green.

'I recognise that from the photo.' Anna pointed at the pond before scrabbling for her phone in her bag. 'Yes, here he is.' It had been Denise who'd spotted the village sign in one of David's photos. Bickley. It was as good a place to start as any. Someone had to know who he was. And, more importantly, where he was.

'Shall we ask in the pub?' Anna stretched like a cat as she got out of the car.

'No. Let's start over there.' Petra pointed at the village shop.

'Spoilsport. I could do with something to refresh the spirits. Hair of the dog.'

'You go in,' Petra said as they reached the single-storey red-brick building.

'Sure.' Anna pushed open the door, the tinkling of a bell announcing her arrival as she entered the shop.

Anna swung a pink-striped plastic bag as she came out of the shop. 'I treated us to lunch. They didn't have much choice though. Cheese and pickle okay? I got crisps too.'

Petra shook her head. 'I'm fine.'

'Well, I'm starving.' Sitting down next to her on the bench, Anna ripped open the cellophane and took a huge bite from the corner of the sandwich. 'You sure?' she said, through a mouthful of cheese. Petra didn't answer her, just stared at the ducks that were waddling towards them. Anna took another mouthful. Was Petra anorexic? Was that why she was straight up and down, wore that horrible denim jacket that swamped her? There was certainly something wrong with her. Her cheekbones were too close to the skin, the skin itself a bluish tone.

'Did you ask?'

Anna swallowed her mouthful of bread. 'Never heard of him.'

'I knew this was a waste of time.' Petra stood up.

Anna grabbed her thin wrist. Her skin was icy cold despite the fact it was, what, over thirty degrees? 'They said to knock at the cottage over there, the one at the end of the row. Some old bloke. Lived here all his life apparently.'

Petra snatched away her hand. 'He's probably got dementia.'

Anna stood up, dropping the sandwich wrapper into a wastebin. 'We can't give up that easily.' She nodded in the direction of the cottage. 'Come on. It's worth a try.'

Anna lifted her fist to knock but the door flew open before her knuckles touched the wood.

'What?'

A man in his late twenties stood before them, a baseball cap pulled down low over his forehead. His T-shirt, grey with oil stains on it, was stretched at the neck. Tracksuit bottoms flapped two inches above bare feet.

Anna took a step back; the smell coming from him made her want to gag.

'Police?'

Anna put her hand to her nose. Did they look like the police?

'Who is it, Mickey?' An old man, a walking stick in his right hand, appeared in the hallway. 'Come away.' He steadied himself by leaning on the wall while he swiped his stick at the back of the younger man's legs. 'And what can I do for you two ladies?'

'We're wondering if you could help us. We're trying to find a David Kingfisher.'

The man shook his head, turned to Mickey hovering behind him. 'Go and make some tea.'

'Don't want tea.'

'Just do as I say.'

'But—'

'Mickey.'

The old man waited until they were alone. They heard a door bang.

'Sorry,' he said. 'He can't help it. Did you say David Kingfisher?' He touched his hand to his ear. 'My hearing's not what it was. Have I got it wrong?'

'No,' Anna said at the same time as Petra said, 'Yes.' 'We're looking for David Kingfisher.'

The man's eyes clouded over and he leant heavily on his stick.

'Please. Do you know where we can find him?'

'Granddad.' Mickey appeared in the hallway. 'Yer want sugar?'

'Two, please.' He waited until his grandson had disappeared again. 'He's asked me the same question for over thirty years.'

Anna put her hand on the door jamb. The man obviously knew something. 'Do you know where we can find him?'

The man closed his eyes, rubbed his liver-spotted hand over his face.

'Please.'

He opened his eyes. 'You'd better come in.'

CHAPTER 15

'Here.' Mickey thrust a mug at Petra with such force that milky tea slopped over the side of it. There was a chip in the rim, brown cracks cobwebbing out from it. She itched to put it down, to get the bottle of hand sanitiser out of her rucksack, but there was no table and, although the moss-green carpet looked like it could stand another tea-stained ring on it, the warmth of it made her keep it in her hand.

'Too much milk?' the old man, who had introduced himself as Bert, asked. 'Always telling him, I am. Goes in one ear and out the other.' He lifted an arthritis-swollen finger to his ear. 'Doesn't it, Mickey?'

Mickey shrugged, plonked himself down next to Anna, curling one leg under him. There was a rip in his jogging bottoms; Petra could see a bruised bony knee poking through it. She was glad she'd chosen the chair now. Anna shifted away from Mickey, put her hand to her face, covering her nose. It smelt like he hadn't had a bath for a year.

'So, David Kingfisher?' Anna took her hand away from her mouth for long enough to let the words out.

'Mickey, go up to your room.'

Mickey slurped at his tea, picked up the TV remote and pointed it at the screen. Music, old-time, blared out of the small box in the corner. Petra turned: a black and white film – Ginger Rogers and Fred Astaire were dancing across the screen.

'Turn that off now.'

Mickey pressed the *off* button and threw the remote. Petra ducked as it flew overhead.

'Stop acting like a child. Now go up to your room. And say sorry to the lady.'

Petra wondered how Mickey could stop acting like a child when Bert treated him like one. The man-child caught her eye, staring at her as if he could see right inside her, see the thoughts swirling around inside her head. Petra looked down.

There was a rush of the bitter smell as Mickey left the room. She lifted her head as the door shut with a bang.

No one spoke as they listened to the thump of feet on the stairs. Another door banged and then the bass of heavy rock music kicked in, so loud the thud of it reverberated through her.

'Don't mind him. A bit—' The old man tapped the side of his forehead. 'Not very good around strangers.'

'He thought we were the police,' Anna said.

Bert's eyes widened. 'You're not, are you?'

Anna shook her head.

'No wonder he didn't want to let you in. Had a bit of trouble, you see. A while back. Something and nothing, but the police came. I've told him, it's not good being on that blinking computer all the time.'

'Oh?'

'Like I said, something and nothing. A misunderstanding. And he gave the money back. No harm done.'

'Money?' The word was out of Petra's mouth before she could stop it. She put her cup down on the carpet, fearful of spilling the hot liquid over her legs.

'Thought you said you weren't the police?'

'We're not.' Anna scowled at Petra, gave Bert a reassuring smile. 'We just want to find David Kingfisher.' Her voice was a hushed whisper. 'Do you know where he is?'

'Aye, I do.' Bert sucked at his tea.

'Where?' Anna smiled again, leant forwards.

Bert downed the last of his tea before wiping his mouth with the back of his hand. 'In the cemetery, isn't he?'

'What?' Anna and Petra said at the same time.

'Aye, such a shame.'

'He's dead?'

Dead. Petra stared at Bert. Dead. Her leg started to jerk. Dead. She wanted to clamp her hands over her ears but they moved to her stomach instead. Dead. She didn't want to hear the word, she couldn't.

Petra watched as Anna's face crumpled, her arms wrapping themselves around the thin body rocking back and forth. Was this what grief looked like? But how could you grieve for someone you hadn't met? Petra knew what loss felt like and it wasn't like this. This felt like panic. She pushed down on her leg to stop it from jumping.

'Was it a car accident?' Anna's eyes were wide.

'A car? No.' Bert shook his head. 'Drowned, the poor lad.'

Anna gasped. Petra's breath came in short gasps. There was no air. She longed to push open the tightly shut windows. Her leg jumped again.

Anna started to cry. 'Oh my God, I can't believe it.' She rummaged in her bag, pulled a handkerchief out of a packet, dabbed carefully under her eyes so as not to smudge her mascara before her head whipped back up. 'This explains everything. Everything.' She narrowed her eyes at Petra as if this were all her fault. 'Where did it happen?'

Bert looked at them, confusion furrowing his brow. 'In his back garden, wasn't it? They had a pond, you see, only two foot deep but—'

'He drowned in a pond? David? But he was over six foot. Grown men don't drown in two feet of water. Unless he was drunk,' Anna said.

'Six foot? You did say David Kingfisher, didn't you?' He turned to Petra, obviously seeing her as the less emotional one, the one he could count on to give him a straight answer.

'That's right,' said Petra, her voice cracking. She coughed, pressed as hard as she could onto her jumping knee.

'He was four.'

'Four? No.' Anna shook her head.

'Four or five. Died a good twenty years ago, it must be. Broke his mother. The whole family, come to that. After what had happened to their Susie. No one could believe it. To have one child drown is bad enough, but two. And in such a short space of time.'

'Hang on.' Anna wiped her nose. 'Are you saying David Kingfisher died when he was *four*?'

'Four, five, something like that. He was just a young 'un.'

Anna let out a long breath and blew her nose. 'Well, it's not the same David Kingfisher then. We're looking for a thirty-seven-year-old man.'

Petra stood up, brushing at the back of her jeans. 'Sorry, we've wasted your time.'

'So you know another David Kingfisher? Well, I never.' Bert scratched his head. 'One hell of a coincidence. Not a common name, is it? Kingfisher, I mean.'

Petra shook her head.

'Are you thinking what I'm thinking?' Anna looked at Petra.

Petra opened her mouth but no words came out.

'His name's not David Kingfisher at all. He's used a dead child's name.' Anna shook her head slowly. 'What a bastard.'

'What's that you say?' Bert cupped his hand behind his ear.

Anna turned to him. 'Do you know when his birthday was?'

'Haven't a clue. Our Mickey was friends with him but better not to ask. He was never the same afterwards. He was there, you see. Thought it was all a game. It'll be on the poor lad's gravestone though. The church is just past the green on the right, down the lane at the end. He's buried there. Bit of a mess. No one bothers with it. His mother and father both had cancer. Went within a year of each other. People said it was the shock. His sister's still here, of course.'

'I thought you said she'd drowned?'

'Aye, that was Susie. Fourteen she was. No, I'm on about Davy's twin sister. Lives in the farmhouse on the Ashbourne road. And his brother, now what was his name? A lot older than the others, he was.' He narrowed his rheumy eyes. 'Jonathan, aye, that was it.' He clicked his fingers. 'Some top surgeon up in Manchester, last I heard of him.'

'A surgeon?' Petra didn't believe in coincidences, but surely this was a big one? Anna was staring at her, her eyebrows raised.

'Well, if there's nothing else,' Bert said, trying to lever himself out of the chair. 'I don't like to leave him alone for too long. Gets himself into mischief on that computer.'

Petra and Anna stood. 'Don't get up.' Petra followed Anna to the front door. 'We'll see ourselves out.' She felt disgusting, the smell in her hair, in the pores of her skin, what Bert had told them contaminating her thoughts.

'Did he say the cemetery was to the left or right of the green?' Anna strode down the path.

'The right.' As Petra pulled the gate to behind her, a movement at an upstairs window caught her eye. Mickey's face was against the glass, staring at her. He disappeared behind the curtain when he saw her looking, but not before pointing his finger at her as if it were a gun.

'Here it is.' Anna pushed back the grass covering the front of the gravestone. 'Eighth of November, that's…'

'David's birthday.'

He really was a bastard. Anna pulled at the grass, tugging up small handfuls. How could he do that? To pretend to be someone else was bad enough, but a dead child? It was obscene, horrific, an insult to the little boy who lay here. Who was this person? What sick game was he playing? And if he could do this, what else could he do? Bastard was too good a word for him. Reaching into her bag, she found a packet of tissues, took one out and wiped away the dust cloaking the headstone.

'Didn't Bert say he had a sister? Fancy letting it get in this sort of state. Poor little mite.'

She glanced at Petra. 'You okay? You look like you've seen a ghost.' Deathly pale, even more so than usual, the blackness of her eyes stood out against her milky skin. And her hair didn't help. Whatever had possessed her? Her skin couldn't take the harshness of the bleached colour.

'Petra, what is it?' Anna straightened up. Was she going to faint? Maybe seeing the gravestone, realising what David, or whatever his real name was, had done

169

had finally hit her: she was never going to see her money again. Anna swallowed. The photos. Some bastard had the photos of her. What was he intending to do with them? She had to find him, had to get him to delete them.

'Can I have that water?' She pointed to the bottle sticking out of Petra's rucksack. 'We can buy more at the shop.' There was no answer. Anna picked her way carefully through the grass. 'Hey.' She touched Petra's arm. God, she was freezing. And yet the sun was burning. How could anyone be that cold? Maybe she was sickening for something? She didn't seem like the sort who could handle germs, not robust enough by far, and Bert's place had certainly been full of them. 'Petra.'

Petra blinked.

'Are you okay?'

'It just brings it all back.'

'What?' What was she on about? 'David?'

Petra blinked again. Colour flooded her face, not a lot, just the merest hint to show blood was still pumping through her veins. She stared at the gravestone, her eyes wide, unblinking.

Suddenly, Anna understood. 'Oh no,' she said. 'Has this happened to you? Have you lost a child?'

Petra seemed to come around. Her eyes focused, bored into Anna. 'What?'

'You've lost a child, haven't you? Oh my God, was it a baby?' Anna's hand flew to her mouth. 'Oh, how awful. I'm so sorry. Was it recently?'

'I don't want to talk about it. Especially not to you.'

Petra pulled her denim jacket around her and strode through the overgrown grass, back to the path.

Anna let her go. It was grief. Grief and shock. There was no need to be rude though, she was only being kind. Petra obviously thought they were still love rivals. Didn't she understand there was no David? That they'd all been as stupid as each other? Didn't she get that he'd duped them both, Denise too? They weren't rivals any longer. The only rival they had was the sick bastard who had stolen a child's name. And their money, her photos. Who was he? Where was he?

She turned back to the grave. Would this poor child's sister know who was doing this to them?

A tune played out across the air, something classical. She looked over to see Petra scrabbling in her pocket before lifting her mobile phone to her ear.

As Anna wandered over to her, she heard the ping of a message on her mobile. Tyler.

She clicked the screen, read the words, turned to Petra, saw the same shock she herself felt etched in the whiteness of Petra's skin, the blood sucked away from it.

'What is it?'

Petra looked like she was going to faint again. 'Petra, what is it?' She snatched the phone from her hand. It was a message, from Denise. She'd seen a photo of David in the local paper. He worked at the hospital. His name was Alex Michaels. The same name Tyler had just texted to her.

CHAPTER 16

'You've missed the turning. The car park's back there.'
Anna reached down into her bag.

'I'll drop you off at the entrance.'

'We're more likely to find a parking space if we're
both looking.' Anna unzipped her Mulberry purse.
'What's the betting we've got no change between us?'

'I'm not coming in.'

'Sorry?' Anna shifted in her seat so she could get a
better view of Petra. 'Denise has found him and you're
not coming in?'

Anna dropped her purse back into her bag. It had
to be something to do with earlier. Petra had definitely
been in shock in the graveyard and she'd hardly spoken
on the way back, except to ask how Anna had known
Alex Michaels' name. It had started to come back to
her: she'd been telling Tyler she thought her new
boyfriend was conning her. Had she googled his photo,
he'd wanted to know, telling her you could check where
an image had been used before. She must have texted

the photo to Tyler. She was sure it was just that one. It had to be. If he'd seen those photos of her... Petra had wanted to know the details but Anna really couldn't explain how Tyler had done it. Did Petra think she was lying? Did she somehow think she was involved in all of this?

Then she'd gone silent. And, after numerous attempts at starting a conversation and being met with a shrug of the shoulders or silence, Anna had sat back in her seat and closed her eyes, trying to think of exactly what she would say when she finally saw David, Alex, whatever his name was. She felt the anger like a hard ball in her stomach.

The car slowed to a stop. 'Are you sure?' Anna unclipped her seatbelt. 'Don't you want your money back?'

'I don't feel great.'

'You look like shit.'

'Thanks.'

'Get some food inside you. And sleep.' Anna opened the car door and got out. 'Leave it to me and Denise. We'll get the money back, don't you worry.'

Petra smiled weakly.

Anna slammed the door shut and watched as Petra's car headed along the road away from the hospital.

Anna strode down the corridor. Denise had texted half an hour ago, saying she was still waiting to see him. Apparently, the receptionist wasn't happy but Denise had told her it was important, life or death, and she only wanted a minute with him.

A sign for a disabled toilet loomed up ahead. Anna went in, locked the door, careful to pull the cord for the light switch and not the one that would scream emergency. After using the loo, she peered at her reflection in the mirror. What a mess. Her hair, normally so shiny and bouncy, had frizzed up in the heat. Spidery red veins cobwebbed across the whites of her eyes. She opened her make-up bag and set to work. Within ten minutes she was resembling her normal self. A touch of powder, slick of lip gloss, quick flick of eyeliner, squirt of eye drops and a spritz of perfume and she was done. She wanted him to see exactly what he had let slip through his fingers. Anger fizzed inside her. How dare he do this to her? She wanted an explanation, a reason as to why he'd led her on, why he'd let her down. And she wanted him to delete the photos. Then she wanted nothing more from him.

Denise looked around her. Only the man with the plaster cast up to his knee to go. She had been timing the other patients: they were with David for an average of twenty minutes each. So that meant she had another twenty to wait, maybe half an hour at most. And then she would finally get to ask David, or Alex Michaels, as she now knew his name really was, why he had done this.

The receptionist glanced at her and tutted. Denise, pretending not to have noticed, picked up a magazine from the chair next to her and flapped it in front of her face, trying to get rid of the blush spreading upwards from her chest. The receptionist could tut at her all she liked – she wasn't going anywhere. Not until she'd seen him. Not until she'd got some answers. Not until she'd got the ten grand back. She shifted in her chair. She had to get it back. The AGM was only just over three weeks away. She bit down on the pear drop in her mouth. The money was only a part of it though. She also wanted to find out why he'd strung her along. And she wanted to know if he'd ever loved her. Had he felt the way she had, that sense of being complete, of being wanted? Or had it all been a lie?

The slap of flip-flops came along the corridor. Denise didn't have to turn around to know Anna had arrived: the scent of Chanel No. 5 filled the reception area. A memory of Ian kissing her neck came back to her.

'Is that him?' Anna took the chair next to Denise and nodded at the door to the right of the reception desk. 'Alex Michaels? Is that him?'

Denise took the newspaper out of her bag and opened it to the page where a grinning Alex Michaels stood, clad in running gear and kissing a medal that hung around his neck. He had raised nearly fifty thousand pounds for the hospital by running the equivalent of seven marathons around the grounds. Was her ten thousand part of the total? Was there no Daniel, no eight-year-old boy who needed lifesaving treatment in America?

'A consultant,' Anna said after a minute of studying the picture and reading the article underneath it. 'One thing he didn't lie about then.'

Denise looked at Anna. It seemed like she'd calmed

down a bit. She'd been livid on the phone earlier, had sworn and cussed, saying it was disgusting, stealing a dead child's identity.

Denise sucked her stomach in and tried not to think about what Alex or David, or whoever he was, would say when he saw her. She imagined the look of horror on his face, the disgust. Would he hand over the money straightaway, sign a cheque perhaps, anything just to be rid of her? Denise closed her eyes. She had imagined a future with him, had even stuck images of their perfect life together on a visualisation board and studied it every night. How could she have been so stupid? He'd got the only thing he wanted from her: money.

She felt tears clog the back of her throat. Without David in her life, what was left? Laurence? She shuddered. No, no way. She couldn't think of anything worse. If only she didn't have to rely on him so much. She'd hated ringing him, asking him if he'd mind Mother while she popped out. But she couldn't not come to the hospital when she'd seen the photo of Alex Michaels in the paper. 'No problemo, Denise,' he'd said. 'I'm glad you've called. There was something I wanted to ask you.' And then he'd invited her out to dinner, an official date. He was aware they were doing things the wrong way around, he'd said, but he really did like her and would like to treat her. Picasso's in town was very good. 'What about Mother?' Denise had shot back. Laurence had chuckled: 'You know she doesn't like anything foreign.'

She looked at the clock on the wall. Laurence had

said he could only stay with Mother until seven. It was nearly four o'clock – there was plenty of time.

'We mustn't let him talk us round.' Anna nudged her in the ribs. 'What he's done... stealing a dead child's identity, it's disgusting. He's disgusting. We mustn't let him charm us.'

'No.' Denise shook her head. 'Is Petra in the loo?'

'She went home. Doesn't feel great. She—'

'What? Is she okay? What is it?'

Anna leant forward. 'She lost a baby.' She put a finger to her lips. 'Don't say anything though, will you? It's not really my secret to tell.'

'What? When?'

Anna shrugged. 'Don't know. She just clammed up.'

Denise nibbled at her thumbnail. How awful for Petra. And then hearing David Kingfisher was dead and finding out he was a child, a child who'd died. It must have been a shock for her. Must have brought it all back.

Denise stuffed another pear drop into her mouth, licked her thumb and finger, sucking the stickiness off them. A baby. She munched on the sweet so hard her right incisor caught on the inside of her bottom lip. Her eyes watered as she held in a yelp. She would never be a parent, never hold her baby in her arms, she had to accept that now. David had talked about children, whether she wanted them, how he longed for a son or daughter. And so she'd built up this fantasy. Their baby. A part of her. A part of David. She noticed Anna's suntanned legs as she crossed one over the other. Had

178

he said the same thing to her? She couldn't imagine the woman sitting next to her being the motherly type; she'd be too worried about breaking a nail or getting baby sick on her designer top.

Denise looked up as the door to the consultant's room opened. The man with the plaster cast hobbled out.

'That's us, come on,' Anna said, grabbing at her arm.

'You can't just—' Denise heard the receptionist say, as she followed Anna through the door and into Alex Michaels' office.

CHAPTER 17

Heavy footsteps pounded up the stairs. There was no time to read over the message she'd been composing for the past twenty minutes. Petra pressed *send*, pushed the Kindle under the duvet and laid her head on the pillow. Keeping her eyes firmly shut, she slowed her breathing until a wave of panic washed through her: had she put the vodka bottle back in its hiding place? As she pulled the duvet up around her, emitting a sigh as if simply stirring in her sleep, she half-opened one eye and glanced down at the carpet. It was okay, it wasn't there. Before he'd made it to her side of the bed, she'd shut her eyes.

'How are you feeling, Pet?'

She opened her eyes. He wasn't going to go away. But how could she explain, how could she tell Sam what she had seen today, the memories it had stirred inside her, memories she had been trying to lock away in a place where no one could get at them? Her hand moved to her stomach, rubbed back and forwards.

181

Sam looked down to where the duvet was moving. 'Eaten something dicky?'

A *yes* formed in her head, moved into her mouth but refused to come out. It did feel like that, like there was something rotten inside her, something she wanted to get out, to flush from her system.

He sat down on the bed, put his hand on her forehead, her cheek. It was comforting, warm, familiar. 'You're freezing. Must be coming down with something. There's summer flu going around at work.'

'I'm fine.'

'Or maybe it's cutting your hair.' He smiled at her. 'You're like Samson. Lost all your strength.'

'I knew you didn't like it.'

'I love it.' He moved his fingers gently through it. 'I'm not saying it wasn't a shock; you've had long hair all the time I've known you. A change is as good as a rest though, eh?'

She didn't answer, just snuggled further under the duvet.

'At least we can rule out morning sickness.'

She felt as if he'd punched her in the stomach.

'I'm sorry.' He ran his hand across his face. 'I shouldn't have said that.'

'No.'

He kissed her cheek. 'How about some tea and toast, honey?'

Honey? Was he asking her if she wanted honey, or was he calling her honey?

He got off the bed, went to the window, looking down at the garden. 'I've piled up all the rocks behind the greenhouse. Just the hedge to do now.'

Honey? He never called her honey. Where had that come from? She felt the words building inside her, tried to swallow them down. 'How's the hangover?'

His shoulders tensed; her own rose too. Taking a deep breath, she willed herself to shut up, to pull the duvet over her head until he'd gone away. She wanted him to go away.

He turned towards her, his outline dark against the bright sun streaming through the window. She couldn't read his face.

'I had one too many. You know how Jacko is. You were asleep when I came in.'

She nodded, although she hadn't been asleep.

'Tea and toast then? I have to pop up to the hospital for an hour, there's a meeting about the clinical placements for next year. I'll pick us up something nice for dinner on the way home. What do you fancy?'

In the past, she might have said 'you'. They would have laughed, he would have tickled her, smothered her neck with kisses, stripped his clothes off and made love to her, thinking about her, and not about the baby he so wanted to make. But that was then. The silence was thick in the room, thicker than the stagnant air, that musty smell that shrouded everything.

'Go,' she said. His hand came towards her again, the words *I love you*. She pushed him away, praying he would leave. She couldn't handle that now. And, anyway, she wanted him gone, she had something to do.

She stood at the window, watching as his car backed out of the drive, hearing its familiar roar as he pulled out of their street. She padded back to the bed, knelt by the bedside cabinet, slid out the bottom drawer. An inch left in the bottle. That's all there was.

As the warmth of the vodka hit the back of her throat, she allowed her mind to go where it had wanted to all afternoon: the hospital. Were they with him now? Was Denise crying, Anna shouting? Was he hotly denying it, telling them to leave him alone, threatening to call security perhaps? What if he said yes, though, that he knew what this was all about?

Putting the bottle to her lips again, she shook it, trying to get every last bit of liquid into her mouth, her tongue licking greedily at the rim.

The Kindle was poking out from under the duvet. She picked it up, sank down onto the floor, leaning back against the side of the bed, and switched it on, clicking on her inbox. Would there be a reply? A glimmer of hope in all this darkness?

A creak as the door opened slightly. She held her breath, her leg jumped. Jude came around the corner of the bed. He flopped down beside her, put his head on her lap. As she fondled the soft fur of his ears, rubbed her nose on the top of his head, breathing him in, she read her email.

Darling, what can I say? My mother hasn't been well again and then I got called abroad for a conference. It was all very last minute but I had to go. The South of France. Sounds glamorous but wasn't at all. A nondescript hotel on the outskirts of Nice. Now it would have been glamorous if you'd been there though. Can you forgive me? I know it's unforgiveable to go incommunicado but I've thought about you every second of the day. Say you'll forgive me, darling, and say you'll meet me. I want you. I need you. I love you xxx

Her leg jumped again. Exhilaration shot through her. It was going to be okay. All of it. She was worrying for nothing. She put her hand to her stomach, remembering Sam's howl when she'd told him she'd lost the baby. David Kingfisher hadn't disappeared. He wanted her. Needed her. It was going to be okay. David was going to make everything okay.

CHAPTER 18

'David Kingfisher? Nope. Never heard of him.'

Denise pulled out the plastic wallet from her holdall and opened it, flicking through the pieces of paper until she found what she was searching for.

'Here,' she said. 'That's you.'

As he took the printout of the photos from her, their fingers touched for a moment and, despite herself, Denise acknowledged the tingle of excitement that shot up her arm. His head bent over the images, she studied him, the way his dark curls flopped forward into his eyes, the smattering of stubble on his chin, this man she'd thought she knew so well. He was ridiculously good-looking, his photos not doing justice to him in the flesh. She bit her bottom lip. She wanted to hate him so much, for the misery, the fear he'd caused her, and yet, at this precise moment, all she could think of was planting a kiss on those perfect lips. He was everything she'd expected him to be. The man she had wanted to spend the rest of her life with. A sob worked its way to the back of her throat. Why had he done it? Why?

'That is you, isn't it?' Anna stabbed a pink-polished nail at the photos Denise had printed out.

The smirk playing on his face disappeared. 'What? I don't understand. Yes, that's me. Val d'Isère, I think, or was it Courchevel?'

'So, you're not denying it?' Denise interrupted.

'Look, that is me. But I haven't been on any dating sites.' He shoved the printouts across the desk towards her before turning around a silver photo frame to the left of his computer. 'I'm married.'

Denise stared at the photo. He had his arms around a slim woman, two teenagers standing in front of them. She noted he hadn't said happily married. He wouldn't be the first man with a wedding ring to try his luck on a dating site.

'Are you sure you're not David Kingfisher?' Anna said.

He smiled at her, laughed. 'Would it be wrong to say I wish I had been?'

Denise closed her eyes, breathing in deeply, trying to push away the tug of jealousy in her stomach. She'd been such a fool. To think a man like this, a man who could have any woman he wanted, would be in love with her. She dug her bitten nails into her knee, trying to dissolve the pain she felt, the shame threatening to overwhelm her, the despondency that darkened her future.

She opened her eyes. 'I want my money back. I've

188

got all the messages you've sent me, the texts, the emails. I want it back.'

'Yes, give her the ten thousand back.' Anna pointed her finger at him. 'And tell me why you've done this to me. Or I'll tell your wife everything.'

Alex stood up, placed his two hands flat on the desk in front of him. 'You won't tell my wife anything.' He turned the photo away from them. 'Because there's nothing to tell. Do you think I need your money? What was it? A poxy ten grand? I can earn that for a couple of private operations.'

'It's not a poxy ten grand to me.' The sob at the back of Denise's throat threatened to escape. She rummaged in the pocket of her skirt but found nothing but a scrunched-up piece of toilet roll.

'Here.' Anna picked up a box of tissues from Alex's desk and held it out to her.

Denise grabbed a handful and wiped at her eyes.

'Are you saying someone's stolen your identity?' Anna said to Alex, putting the box back down.

'It looks that way.'

Denise swallowed, blew her nose. It couldn't be true, it couldn't. Why was he saying this? The man in front of her had to be David Kingfisher. She needed that money back.

'How do we know you're not lying? And how did they get hold of your photos?' Anna said.

Alex went to the window, gazed out. 'Facebook? My wife is always posting things on there.' He turned back towards them. 'Someone's obviously having a laugh at both our expense. I was going to say I could see one of my mates doing it; we're known for our pranks. But not when money's involved. How much did he have off you?'

Denise looked at Anna. Now came the moment of truth. Anna had told her and Petra she hadn't given David Kingfisher anything, but neither of them were sure they believed her.

'Nothing.' She parted her lips. 'This is not about the money for me. He promised me things, he…' Her words petered out.

'How about you give me your number? Just in case I think of anything.' Denise saw a split second of hesitation before Anna read out her number.

'I hope you manage to find him,' Alex said as he scribbled in his notepad.

'Come on, Denise.'

'Just one last question.' Denise levered herself up out of the chair, stuffing the plastic wallet back into her holdall. 'Have you ever been to Bickley?'

'Bickley? Rings a bell.' Alex put his finger to his lips, tapping away. 'But, no, I don't think I've ever been there. Why?'

'No matter.' Denise swung open the door, swept through it. She'd almost believed him, almost believed he wasn't David Kingfisher. But he'd lied about going to Bickley: they had the photograph to prove it.

Striding along the corridor, leaving Anna in her wake, she reached in her holdall for her phone. She would call Petra. Petra would know what to do. As she scrolled through her contacts, she realised in her anger, her desire to get her money back, she'd completely forgotten to tell this Alex another woman had been conned.

There was no answer. A voice came on the line, telling her to leave a message. 'Hi, Petra. It's me, Denise. It's not him. Or at least he says it isn't.' A beep sounded in her ear. Was that Petra now, trying to ring her back? She ended the call. No, it was a text. Her legs stopped moving. Someone behind her swore, banged her shoulder as they walked past. She tapped the screen.

Leave me alone, you stupid bitch. You'll never find me and you'll never get the money back. And you wouldn't want me to come looking for you, would you?

She spun around, her eyes searching this way and that, only to see Anna and Alex Michaels, moving along the corridor away from her, his hand on the small of her back.

CHAPTER 19

For fuck's sake, that was close.

To be honest, I thought they were stupid, especially her, dozy Denise. Funny what the need for something can do to you. And I don't think it's the money that's gnawing away inside her, making her veins throb with longing. It's me. The lies she keeps telling herself: that, after everything that's gone on, I still want her.

I feel sorry for her, in a way. Look how far loneliness can push you, chasing after something that isn't there, following the images you've made in your head, the words you've told yourself. Pushing, pushing you. Until you fall in love with an illusion.

But they want to make that illusion real. And it seems like they won't stop until they find me, until they find David Kingfisher and get what they want.

I must stop thinking of them, must concentrate on me. On the plan. If I let myself get distracted, who knows what will happen?

Rule number one: I can't let them find me. I can't.

If they find me, the whole thing will come crashing down. I've got to keep one step ahead.

They've drawn a blank this time but what if someone talks? What if Fate conspires against me? What if someone puts two and two together?

The time has come. The time has come to put an end to all this.

CHAPTER 20

The scalpel dragged across the shorn skin, leaving a red line of blood in its wake, a metallic tang in the air that reached her nose despite the mask. Petra opened her mouth, sucking the thin plastic in with each breath as she stroked the dog's head; the anaesthetised animal couldn't feel the love she was pouring into him but it comforted her, gave her a sliver of hope the dog would make it.

'Petra, clamp, please.'

'Sorry.' She reached for the clamp and handed it to Harry who fixed it firmly into place. 'How did you go on?' she asked. 'At the hospital?'

'Oh, just routine.' His eyes swivelled away from her, back to Maisie on the operating table. 'Forceps, please. The consultant said there was nothing to worry about. Name me any man over sixty who hasn't got a dodgy prostate.'

Petra hoped he wasn't lying. According to Jane on reception, his bitch of a wife seemed determined to take him for everything he'd got. An illness to worry about, on top of that, would be too much.

Petra leant forward. 'Are they?'

He grimaced. 'Seems like the scan was right. They're all dead.'

She busied herself, getting a needle ready to stitch Maisie back up. She should have said no when they'd called her earlier. It was her day off. Damn the new vet nurse. She hadn't shown up. 'At least I can always rely on you,' Harry had said, as she'd swept in through the door, sucking vigorously on a mint. It had been a risk, driving after the vodka, but it had only been a couple of inches – she wouldn't be over the limit for that much, surely?

She put a hand to her stomach. Sam would ask her how she'd gone on, would curse Harry for asking her to come in when she was sick. Should she tell him about this? How could she explain, put it into words? It'd only hurt him, bring it all back. No, she'd keep quiet, hold tightly to the pain, let the guilt fester inside her. Her mouth was dry, the plastic of the mask sticking to her lips with each in-breath. The supermarket should still be open; she'd call on her way home, buy a bottle, maybe two. She imagined the cool liquid rushing over her tongue, down her throat, mixing with the guilt, dissolving it.

Harry was already sewing the dog up. 'Do you mind?' He handed her the foetuses in a bag.

She grabbed it and hurried from the room, her jerking leg propelling her forwards.

'Someone to see you.' Jane peered over the reception

desk and nodded at a woman in the far corner of the room.

'Denise?'

'Petra? I didn't recognise you. I'd forgotten you'd had your hair done. I wondered who it was when you pulled up at the house this morning.'

Denise stood up, apologising as she skirted around a Great Dane, gently pushing a small boy with a brown box in his hands out of the way. 'This is the third vet's I've been to. I've been ringing you. Wow, you look so different. It suits you. It really does.'

Petra ran her hand over her short hair. She didn't need to see Jane's face to know she was smirking. 'My phone was off. What is it?' Petra's leg jumped. The small boy stared at it, fascinated.

'I wanted to discuss... you know.' Denise's eyes swivelled to the right, away from the prying Jane to the left.

'I'm working.'

'Are you okay? Anna said you weren't well?'

'I'm fine.'

'Are you sure? You shouldn't be working if you don't feel up to it. You've had a shock today and—'

'I'm fine.' Petra crossed her arms. 'What is it?'

Denise's eyes turned towards Jane, who was flicking through some files. 'We can't talk here. What time do you finish? It says six on the door. I can wait. Laurence is with Mother, although he has to leave at seven and it'll take me half an hour to get back on the bus.'

'I have to clean up. I have things to do. I don't know how long I'll be.'

Denise looked at her, a line furrowing her brow. 'Don't you want to know what we found out?'

'You left me a message.'

'Oh, so you got that. You didn't reply.'

'You said it wasn't him.' The words hissed out of Petra's mouth. She glanced at Jane to check if she was earwigging. Whatever was going on in Petra's private life, she never brought it into work – she kept those two parts of her life completely separate. Sam had once asked her what they'd said about the baby, whether her colleagues were as excited as they were, but, of course, she hadn't told them. It had made it difficult when she'd needed time off after it had happened but she'd booked a week's annual leave and then said nothing when she'd gone back in, had pretended they'd been to the Lake District in a chalet with a hot tub.

'I said *he* said it wasn't him,' Denise replied, her eyes widening. 'But there's something else.'

Petra was aware Harry had come into the waiting room. He was leaning on the reception desk, talking to Jane, his eyes flicking between her and Denise. Heat was rising up Denise's neck, making her face shiny, pink. Did she and Harry know each other?

'I'll wait outside,' Denise said.

Petra sighed. 'Okay.'

'This is so good of you.' Denise nodded at the clock on the dashboard. 'Is that right? My watch says half past.'

'It's ten minutes fast.' Petra gritted her teeth. 'So, you said there was more?'

Denise shifted in her seat. 'Was that your boss, the bloke with the grey hair?'

'Harry?'

'He looked familiar. He's very attractive.'

So, that was it, Denise fancied him.

'I'd say he's got a bit of a thing about you.' Denise rummaged in her bag, pulled out a pear drop.

'Don't be stupid. He's my boss.'

'You should have seen the way he was staring at you. You should go for it. It's never too late to seize a bit of happiness.'

'You've been reading too many self-help books.' Out of the corner of her eye, she saw Denise blush, angle her face towards the window. 'Anyway, he's over sixty.'

'Is he?' Her head turned back towards Petra so quickly she thought she might have whiplash. 'Ugh, no,' she said, grimacing, 'he'll be all wrinkly. Down there.'

'You sound like you have experience of that.'

Denise blushed. 'I'll tell you about it someday.'

'So, was it him?'

'What? Who?' Denise held out a bag of pear drops in front of Petra.

Petra waved her hand away. 'David? The hospital?'

'He said it wasn't. Said someone had stolen his photos.'

'Do you believe him?'

She shrugged. 'I asked him if he'd ever been to Bickley. He said he hadn't. We know that's a lie, don't we?

We've seen the picture of him with the sign in the background.'

'What did he say about the money? Did you mention me?'

Denise slipped another pear drop into her mouth. 'I… oh, look, I forgot. I was so het up and he was just sitting there smirking and… I'm sorry.' She reached over, squeezed Petra's arm quickly.

'What did Anna do?'

Denise sucked on her sweet. 'She was pretty mad. Had a right go at him. She still gave him her number though. And they walked off together, I saw them.'

Petra's leg jumped. She flicked a glance into the rear-view mirror. A car, something flashy, had been following them for the last ten minutes. She tried to make out the driver but the sun visor was down, obscuring the person's face from view. Now she was just being paranoid. She looked into the rear-view mirror again, caught sight of her narrowed eyes, the line like an exclamation mark between her brows. Was she jealous that this man in the photos, the perfect man, they'd all agreed, was attracted to Anna? But of course he would be. Anna with her endless legs, her long strawberry-blonde locks, those curves; she had everything men found appealing. Petra took a deep breath. What did it matter anyway? Alex Michaels wasn't David. Her hand went to her stomach. She thought of what he had said: he loved her.

Denise rustled through her bag. 'He seemed, as Mother might say, a bit of a ladies' man.'

'Anna doesn't strike me as a lady.'

Denise laughed and popped another pear drop into her mouth.

The crunching of boiled sweets filled the car. Petra had the strong desire to turn the radio on, to tune into Classic FM, something to soothe her. Her eyelids were heavy. All she wanted to do was have a shower and sink into bed.

'Have you heard anything from him, from David?' Denise said, in between crunching the sweets.

Petra's leg jerked so hard it hit the steering wheel. 'No.' She could sense Denise looking at her bobbing leg. 'No. Have you?'

'No. Not a thing.'

The woman was a poor liar. It showed in the way she was twisting the paper bag between her fingers, the way her foot was tapping in time to the music. Petra hoped she herself wasn't so easy to read.

'Next road on the left and then it's the third house along on the right.'

Petra pulled the car to a stop opposite a drab 1930s semi. Grey lace curtains hung in both windows, a dog's head poking under the upstairs ones, watching, waiting. So, Denise was a dog lover, like her. She didn't know what she'd have done without Jude this past year. He could always be relied on to be there, to listen without judging, to let her hold him when she needed to feel the warmth of another body against hers. She waited as Denise unplugged her seatbelt, stuffed the sweets back into her bag and opened the door.

'What did you want to talk to me about?' Petra

wasn't going to let her leave without finding out what had been bothering her.

'I was thinking. We ought to try and find the real David Kingfisher's brother.'

Petra's head was starting to pound. 'Who?'

'The surgeon. Anna told me on the phone. Just seems a coincidence that he has the same job as our David Kingfisher.'

Petra rubbed her hand across her face.

'Are you okay? Still feeling bad? You're ever so pale.' Denise gave her a warm smile. 'If you ever need someone to talk to—'

'It's just a bug.'

Denise's eyes widened. 'Hope it isn't the same thing Mother has. She was throwing up half the night.'

'How is she now?'

'She was okay when I left earlier. I think it was just a twenty-four-hour thing. I hope I haven't passed it to you.' Denise leant over and patted the back of Petra's hand. 'I meant what I said – anytime you need to talk.' She opened her mouth and then closed it again.

'What?'

Denise took a deep breath. 'Anna said you'd lost a baby.'

Petra gripped the steering wheel tighter. Bloody bitch. Couldn't she keep anything to herself?

'You'd pinned your hopes on David, hadn't you? Like I had.' Denise tried a smile. 'I wanted a family too. Thought he'd be the one, like you did.' She suddenly laughed. 'I mean, for God's sake, I'd even chosen names for our kids. How stupid am I?'

Petra shook her head. 'You're not stupid.'

Denise got out of the car. 'You'll find someone, Petra. I can't imagine what it's like to lose a baby, but you'll find someone and you'll have another baby, I'm sure of it.'

Tears welled at the back of Petra's throat. She swallowed them down.

Denise slammed the car door shut and crouched down, signalling to her to open the window, leaning through it. 'And we'll get the money back too. He's sure to be in touch with one of us again. He just can't seem to help himself, can he? This seems to be all a game to him.' She smiled. 'We'll find him, Petra. We will. We've got to, haven't we?

Petra nodded, although she'd forgotten about the money. Sam and the baby that never was, they were all that had been occupying her mind, making her lie awake at night, staring into the blackness. Despite her throbbing headache, she smiled. Denise was right: David had to be the answer to it all.

CHAPTER 21

Why hadn't she told Petra about the text she'd received at the hospital? She would understand, would know what to do. Denise put down her holdall and slipped her feet out of her sandals. She hadn't told her because she was embarrassed, pure and simple. David hadn't turned on the others, hadn't called them a bitch, had he? Just her. Petra had said she hadn't heard from him and Denise believed her and, well, even if Anna had heard from him, she doubted he'd call her a bitch. How could he hate her so much when a few weeks ago he was telling her he loved her? And, anyway, it was she who should hate him. Not just because he'd stolen ten thousand pounds off her, no, she hated him for much more than that: he'd stolen the hope she had nurtured, that she had finally found someone who would love her.

She switched on the hall light. Had Alex Michaels lied to them? Was he really David? He'd been so adamant it wasn't him, that someone had stolen his identity. And why would a surgeon need the money

205

anyway? She'd been so stupid. Heat rose from her chest, hitting her face. She was hungry, her blood sugar low. There was some chocolate in the fridge. She started to walk towards the kitchen and then stopped. It was quiet. Too quiet. Something wasn't right. There wasn't a moment, not a second, a minute of the day when the chatter of BBC News couldn't be heard throughout the house. Mother was deaf, usually had the volume so loud Denise could hear word for word what was being said even when she was in the kitchen. What if she'd got worse? What if it hadn't been a twenty-four-hour bug? What if the ambulance had taken her away?

She hurried as fast as she could up the stairs, threw open Mother's bedroom door and bustled into the room. 'What are you doing?'

Mother and Netty, who was sitting on the edge of the bed, stared at her, their mouths hanging open, their lips trying to form words. Barney, Netty's Irish terrier, jumped off the ottoman under the window and bounded up to her.

'Is that my laptop?' Ignoring the dog, Denise went over to the bed and snatched the laptop off the overbed table.

Mother tutted. Netty was so red she was virtually crimson.

'That's mine.'

Mother tutted again and leant back on her pillows, while Netty slipped off the bed. 'Really, Denise, you sound like a petulant child, doesn't she, Netty?'

Netty looked from Mother to Denise, clearly unsure

what to do or say, before bending down to stroke Barney.

'I was just giving Netty some lessons on how to use a computer. She wants to find a little holiday for her and Barney, and I was just showing her how to search for one. Isn't that right, Netty? Netty?'

'Yes,' Netty said, her gaze firmly fixed on the dog.

Denise clutched the laptop to her. It was hot, the heat pushing through her thin top. They must have been using it for a while. How had they got in? They'd need a password. But, of course, Mother would know what it was: she had embroiled Denise in a big debate on computer passwords when a story had hit the news about hackers. And she'd happily told Mother what hers was, knowing her disability meant she'd never be able to get to her laptop. Or so she'd thought.

'What about your iPad?'

Mother sniffed. 'It's broken. I dropped it.'

Netty straightened up and picked the iPad up off the bedside cabinet, holding it aloft so Denise could see the shattered screen.

Denise started to shake; she wasn't sure if it was from low blood sugar or fear. Please God don't let them have checked the history or have opened her emails. She'd kept every single message from David. There were details about the money. Everything. She bit her lip, looked up at the ceiling. They couldn't have. No. And yet there was something about the way Mother was watching her, her mouth struggling to keep straight, to not morph into a smirk.

'Where's Laurence?' Denise asked.

'He couldn't wait any longer for you. Thank heavens for Netty. Without her, I'd be all on my own. Anything could happen to me while you're off gallivanting.'

'I wasn't gallivanting.'

Mother sniffed. 'Anyone would think you'd had enough of me.'

Denise's legs wouldn't hold her any longer. The blood was heavy in her veins, droplets of sweat pooling on her forehead. She sat on the edge of the bed.

'Don't sit there, Denise. You'll ruin the mattress.'

Denise ignored her, turned to Netty. 'So, did you find a holiday? There's not many places that will take dogs.'

Netty opened her mouth but no words came out. Her eyes slipped back down to Barney.

'There was nothing suitable, was there, Netty? Nothing you liked.'

'No,' Netty said, suddenly becoming more animated, her grey perm bobbing up and down. 'Nothing I liked.'

'Where was it you were wanting to go?'

'Scotland,' Mother said as the word 'Wales' flew from Netty's lips.

'That's a long way to go with a dog. I thought he got car sick.'

'They'll go on a coach, Denise.' Mother tutted. 'Anyway, enough of this chit-chat. Netty, you can go now. And don't forget,' she said as the dismissed woman shuffled to the door, 'you've got the number.'

Netty held her hand up to show a telephone number

scrawled in black ink across her palm, before grabbing Barney's collar.

'I thought she didn't find anywhere,' Denise said as Netty and the dog left the room.

Her mother flicked her good hand in the air. 'Oh, that's something else she's helping me with.'

'You don't have to bother Netty.' Denise stood up slowly. 'I can help you with whatever you need.'

'Not with this, Denise.' Mother picked up the remote control and pointed it at the television. 'Now a cup of tea would be lovely if you can be bothered to move your fat arse. I'm parched.'

Denise was just putting the plastic cup down onto the overbed table when Laurence burst into the room. She jumped, lost her grip on the cup for a second and watched as it tipped over. Luckily, the lid was on fast.

'Denise,' Mother said. 'Be bloody careful.'

Denise righted the cup and looked at Laurence.

'My, how handsome you are.' Mother directed at him.

'Thank you, Veronica.' Laurence tugged on his bow tie and did a twirl. 'Not bad, eh?'

Denise attempted a smile but her lip and cheek muscles refused to budge. Laurence was the furthest thing from handsome she could think of. Thoughts of what she'd done with him, the weight of his stomach crushing hers, came rushing into her mind. She tried to push them away, to think of other things. Of Alex Michaels, of the way his dark curls flopped over one eye. Of Netty's red cheeks, the phone number on her hand. But it was no use: heat rose up her body, her eyes watered. She relived every moment of that night in ten seconds. How could she have done it? She looked at Laurence, trying to find something nice in his face, some feature she found attractive, anything to make her feel better about what she'd done. But she couldn't. All she could see was his yellow skin, a round belly hanging down over his waistband, the hairy mole on his chin. She swallowed. She would never drink again.

'I have a favour to ask.'

'Anything, Laurence,' Mother said. 'You've helped me so much. Your wish is my command.'

'Not of you, Veronica. Of Denise.'

'Oh?' Mother and Denise both said at the same time.

Laurence rubbed his hands together. 'Well, I know it's short notice and everything, and I'm really running late, but Polly – you know my niece, Polly, don't you, Veronica?'

'Lovely girl. So slim.'

'Well, not at the moment. She's just gone into labour a month early and, well, I can't expect our Eileen to come with me now. I mean she's gutted. She hasn't been to a black-tie event since she was at uni but well, you know, it's her first grandchild and all that. Children come first.'

'Of course they do, Laurence,' Mother said.

Denise tried to keep the look of surprise off her face, but her muscles worked involuntarily, shooting her eyebrows up. She had never come first in Mother's eyes. Never.

210

'I wondered if you'd like to come? To the golf club dinner dance?'

Denise turned around to see if he was talking to someone behind her. 'Me?'

'Her?' Mother snorted. 'No, Laurence. No.'

'Why not?' Laurence pulled on his jacket cuff. 'It would do her good to get out.'

Mother closed her eyes, sank back into her pillows. 'But what about me?'

'Netty will come round. I've already asked her.'

'I don't want that woman here again. I've only just got rid of her.'

'You like Netty.'

'I put up with her. She could bore for England.'

'Now, Veronica.'

'What?'

Denise put her hands in the air. 'There's no need for Netty to come.' She looked at Laurence. 'I have nothing to wear.'

'Could you lend her something, Veronica? I remember you had some wonderful ballgowns.'

Mother laughed, a shrill bark. 'Laurence, don't be silly. I'm a size eight. Always have been, always will be.'

'You could squeeze into something?'

'I'm not squeezing into anything. Sorry, Laurence. I'm not coming.' Denise walked as quickly as she could out of the room.

She made her way down the stairs. It would have been nice to go to a ball; the last one she'd been to was with Ian, what, eight, nine years ago? She'd worn an emerald-green, off-the-shoulder dress. Ian hadn't left her side all evening. But a ball with Laurence? No, thank you. She bit her lip. What was she going to do? He just didn't get it, did he? She wasn't interested in him. Not one jot.

The bedroom door creaked. She turned around to see Laurence thudding down the stairs after her. He caught up with her in the hallway, putting his hand on her arm.

'Please, Denise, it promises to be a lovely evening. Dancing. A five-course meal, although we've probably missed the starter by now. You love dancing, you told me. I'm quite a mover myself.' He wiggled his hips. 'Come on. It'll be fun.'

Denise did love dancing, but not with Laurence. Couldn't think of anything worse.

'I'm not coming.' She tried to wrench her arm free from his grip but it was too firm.

'What's wrong, darling? I thought you liked me?'

It was dark in the hallway. All she could see was the flashing of his false teeth. She took a deep breath. Now was the time to say it.

'No, Laurence—'

'No, Laurence, what? You weren't so reticent before, were you?'

'What do you mean?' She tried to contain the wobble in her voice.

'You know.' He nodded towards the kitchen. 'Don't tell me you've forgotten?'

212

Denise peered up into the darkness of the stairwell. 'Mother will hear you.'

'And we wouldn't want that now, would we?'

Denise yanked her arm away from his hand with such force she staggered backwards. She caught hold of the corner of the console table to steady herself. 'No, we wouldn't. I don't think Mother would be very enamoured with you, if she'd found out what you'd done.'

'Hey, I was only joking,' he said. 'Of course we don't want her finding out, do we?'

She stepped back, but Laurence moved closer.

'Such a lot of secrets, Denise.'

Her bottom was wedged up against the table, the knob on the drawer digging into her flesh. 'What do you mean?'

'Oh, I think you know what I mean.' The smell of stale alcohol filled her nose as he leant forwards. 'I've been having a gander at the charity's online accounts. Let's just say they make for very good reading.'

Denise clung to the table. 'You don't... you don't have the password. I changed it. Just to make sure it was secure.'

He raised a bushy eyebrow. 'But you use the same password for everything, don't you, darling? At least, that's what Veronica told me. You know she tells me everything.'

'I don't know what you mean,' Denise said again, so quietly she wasn't sure if the words had come out of her mouth.

He moved closer, pushing his knee between her legs

and kissing the tip of her ear. 'I'm sure you don't need me to tell you the missing money needs to be back in the account before the AGM. Ten thousand pounds, Denise. My, that's a lot of money. What have you done with it?' His eyes widened. 'You haven't given it to some con man, have you?'

Before she could stop it, a sob escaped her lips.

'Oh, Denise, what were you thinking?'

'Of course I haven't.' She pushed him away from her and hurried into the kitchen.

He followed her, standing behind her as she filled the kettle.

'Then what have you done with it?'

'I – I – borrowed it. I want to buy a car.'

'A car? But you can't drive.'

'I'm going to learn.'

She reached for a mug off the mug tree but he caught hold of her hand. 'I can teach you.'

'I've changed my mind.' She snatched her hand away from his. 'I was just borrowing the money. I'll put it back.'

'So you still have it?'

'Yes.'

'Oh, Denise.' He helped himself to a mug and dropped a teabag into it. 'You're a terrible liar, you know. How about we come to a little arrangement? I pay the money back for you and you… well, let's just say, you entertain me like you did the other week.' He grabbed her hand and placed it on the front of his trousers.

The hardness of him disgusted her. She tried to pull

her hand away but he had his firmly clamped over the top of it.

'So, do we have a deal?'

His mouth loomed in front of hers. She twisted her head to the side and shoved her whole weight into his left shoulder. He stumbled backwards, catching the back of a chair to save himself from falling.

'Feisty. I like that, Denise.' He straightened his bow tie, walked towards the kitchen door. 'Just think about it, darling, that's all I'm asking.'

She stood holding onto the table, waited for the bang of the back door before she let out a breath. Mother couldn't find out about her and Laurence. The charity couldn't find out about the money. It wasn't going to happen. She wouldn't let it.

Denise put her shaking hands to her face, tears welling up, spilling through her fingers. Everything was such a mess, such a bloody mess. It was only three weeks to the AGM. She had to get the money back by then. The trustees would go to the police. Without a doubt. The orphanage in Kenya needed that money; it was going to pay for a new roof on the schoolhouse. It was on the last meeting's agenda. They would want to go through the accounts in detail. She ripped off a piece of kitchen roll, wiped her nose on it. Why had she done it? Why? She wasn't a thief, she gave money back to shop assistants when they gave her the wrong change, she'd returned a pack of batteries she hadn't seen in her trolley before she left the shop.

Laurence. The money. She sniffed, shuddered. She

215

would never take it from him. She would rather go to prison than do that with him again. A thought flashed across her mind, one so horrific she couldn't bear to think it. Laurence hadn't done this to her, had he? Laurence wasn't David Kingfisher? He hadn't taken the money from her so he could blackmail her? She shook the thought away. Of course he wasn't. Laurence couldn't have written those words of love, it just wasn't in him. And, anyway, she'd spoken to David – the husky tone of his voice was nothing like Laurence's horrible whining tone.

David Kingfisher. This was all his fault. The man she'd hoped to spend the rest of her life with. He had taken her in, exploited her. But she had let him. Tears spilt from her eyes. God, she was angry with him, but she was angrier with herself. Why did she keep making the wrong decisions? She dabbed at her eyes. She knew why: she was lonely, hollowed out, her soul crying out for someone to love her, to take away the gaping hole that filled her. But a man wasn't going to fill that emptiness, not David Kingfisher, and especially not Laurence.

She stopped sniffing and wiped her eyes on the back of her hand. There was still time to put things right, to find David Kingfisher – no matter what he threatened.

CHAPTER 22

'Shush.'

Anna sat down, her eyes swivelling towards a sour-faced woman who was scowling at them over the top of half-moon glasses.

Tyler snorted out a laugh.

Anna mouthed a 'Sorry' at the woman and gave Tyler a look. Couldn't she nip to the loo without him causing trouble?

'What? Told you we should have gone to yours,' he said.

Yours? Anna picked up her bag and started gathering up the books in front of them. Tyler was talking as if they were out on a date. 'Come on, we'll go to O'Hare's.' There was no way she was having him in her flat. She was already giving him extra tutoring under duress: his mother had been to see Benson and the headmaster had accepted on Anna's behalf. 'Now we've given him a scholarship, thanks to you, Miss Farrow, we must ensure that his A level grades are good, mustn't we?' He'd left the question hanging in the fetid air of his study. There was no argument to offer. If she could get Tyler through his A levels then she was sure to have a one hundred percent pass rate, something none of the other teachers would achieve. And knowing she was good at one thing, at least, was keeping her going. It had to stand her in good stead if – and she didn't even want to think about it – those photos ever came out.

'Great. Their toasties are mint.' Tyler pushed his chair in, making the loudest screeching sound he could, and followed her out of the library. Mrs Sour-Face tutted as they passed.

The café was busy but she managed to find an empty spot by the window and, after ordering a black coffee for herself and a Red Bull and a toastie for Tyler, she upended her bag, spilling textbooks onto the table.

She found her leather notebook in amongst the pile and opened it, smoothing down the pages. 'Right. Here's the next question. Discuss and—'

Tyler leant forward, his eyes sparkling over his sun-darkened freckles. 'You've got an admirer.'

For a second, she thought he meant himself, thought he was flirting with her. A blush spread across her cheeks.

'Don't turn around but there's someone staring at you.'

'Where?' Anna tucked her hair behind her ear while glancing over her shoulder. The café was full. A group of mothers, fussing toddlers bouncing on their knees, a gaggle of young girls, a middle-aged married couple sitting staring at each other with nothing to say.

'Over there. Behind the newspaper. He put it up as soon as you turned around.'

She peered in the direction Tyler had indicated. All she could see was a pair of hands, a broadsheet in them, a cuff of a shirt. 'Don't be silly.' She picked up her notebook again. 'Stop trying to distract me.' This question and the next to get through and then she was calling it a day.

Tyler's eyes widened. 'Hang on, wasn't he in the bar with you? You know that night when—'

'Enough,' Anna said. She'd already apologised to Tyler, said she'd had one too many, asked him not to say anything to his friends. She hoped to God he hadn't taken a photo of her, that it wasn't doing the rounds on social media.

Tyler leant back on his chair, a slow, lazy grin spreading across his face as his gaze flicked over her shoulder. 'You were very drunk. Have you forgotten what happened?' He laughed as she reddened. 'He's still looking.'

Pretending to rummage in her bag, she moved her head slightly, got a good look at the guy. For a second, she thought it was David and then reminded herself that David didn't exist, his face belonged to someone else. Alex Michaels. She'd spent all of the previous evening going over what he'd said when she and Denise had confronted him. He'd been adamant he wasn't David. But what if he'd been lying?

'He was in the bar, wasn't he?' Tyler said.

Anna realised it was the guy she'd seen in The Vaults, the cute one with the beard who'd offered her a cigarette the first time David had stood her up. As she straightened up, he put the paper down, smiled at her and mouthed 'Hello', then reached for his phone.

'See, told you it was that guy. Do you know him? Do you fancy him?'

'Stop trying to distract me.' She picked up her notebook. 'Write down five points you'll need to answer the question. I'll give you ten minutes.'

Tyler tipped back on his chair, balancing on the rear two legs. 'Did you find that bloke? The one in the photo? Alex Michaels, wasn't it? What did he say? I can do some more digging, if you like.'

Shit. Anna was grateful Tyler had helped her, that he'd found Alex Michaels online, but she never should have involved him in her private life. She only hoped he hadn't seen the photos of her when she'd been flicking through, trying to find the one of David. The photos. Still no reply to her message to David, asking him to delete them.

'It's all sorted.' She gave him her best smile and got her phone out of her bag. 'Come on, ten minutes.'

He started tapping away on his phone. She'd long since given up getting him to write his answers in a notebook. She checked he was engrossed in what he was doing before opening her inbox and typing out a message. Texts hadn't elicited a response from David. Had he blocked her number? Perhaps an email would work. Delete the photos I sent you or else I'm going to the police. She wouldn't, of course, she couldn't risk it. She only hoped her threat would be enough.

The bell over the café door tinkled. Picking up her cup, she gulped greedily at the hot liquid, grateful for

220

the shot of adrenaline from the caffeine. And then she saw him: Robbo, standing by the door, trying to spot a free table. His eyes moved around the room. Relief and disappointment washed over her as she realised he hadn't seen her. And then he walked towards the back of the café, heading for the table where her admirer was sitting. Did they know each other? It didn't look that way. No words passed between them as Robbo pulled out a chair.

Had Robbo seen her and deliberately ignored her? Anna couldn't blame him. After what had happened the other night, it was no surprise. Why had she drunk so much? The night was a blur. Bits of it had come back to her slowly but she was still none the wiser as to who she'd taken to bed.

She glanced at Tyler. It couldn't have been him. She wouldn't have done that, no matter how much she'd drunk. He was a schoolkid, in her care. She had to get out of here. A migraine, that's what she'd say; not a lie, her right cheekbone was starting to pulse, a threat of pain to come. But she didn't want him going back to Benson, saying she hadn't done the time. She needed to keep him on side. Could she do that for another year until he left the school?

Another year. It stretched before her. Would her life be any different then, better? Or would she still be sitting in this café, still bumping into Robbo, half of her hating him for letting her down, the other half still fizzing with longing whenever she saw him? Would she still be worrying about the photos that David, whoever he was, had of her?

She took a sip of coffee, this time grimacing at its bitterness. Should she go over to Robbo? Apologise for last week? She twisted her silver heart pendant between her fingers.

Pretending to scratch her shoulder, she shot a glance in Robbo's direction. He was tapping away on his phone. A shot of jealousy coursed through her. Who was he texting? A friend, a work colleague? It wouldn't be a woman. It couldn't be. Not after what she'd said to him the other night. Her face started to burn as she recalled the words that had spilt from her lips, the demands to know why he didn't love her any more, her assurances she still loved him. Her stomach clenched. Did she have no shame?

Her watch said five to; another twenty minutes and she could escape.

'I left my cap in the library.'

'What?'

'My cap. My mum got it me for my birthday. I won't be long.'

'Go on then.' The less time she had to spend with Tyler, the better.

Making sure he'd gone, she flipped back to her email account on her phone, opened her inbox. Nothing. She scrolled down to her spam box. Just in case. And there it was. A message from a week ago telling her how sorry he was, churning out yet another excuse, something about a conference in the South of France.

And, suddenly, it was all too much. Tyler and his smirks, Robbo sitting so close but just out of reach, the photos, blue shirt man shooting her looks, this town with its cloying heat. Her fingers stabbed at the screen.

I mean it, you sick bastard. I'll go to the police.

She put down her phone, got her lip gloss and compact mirror out of her make-up bag and angled the mirror so she could see behind her as she rolled the gloss over her lips. Robbo and blue shirt man were chatting, laughing.

'Got it.' Tyler flopped onto the chair and picked up his can of Red Bull, swigging from it. 'He's always going on about you, you know?' He put down the drink and looked at her.

What? Who was he on about? Robbo? Did he often go into The Vaults? Had he and Tyler struck up a friendship? Perhaps Robbo had recognised him from the school visit?

'Leeky. Definitely got it bad for you. I can't see you going for someone like him though.'

Disappointment washed over Anna. 'Don't be ridiculous, and it's Mr Leek to you,' she said, using a sharp tone to hide her embarrassment. Tyler was right though: the geography teacher had got it seriously bad. He had called her last night, wanting to know if she was okay, telling her not to worry about what had happened on the last day of term. Her answers had been short, clipped, as she'd sidestepped his questions about meeting up in the school holidays, and told him she would see him in September. Why had she drunk so much last week? She'd let herself down. Again. And Robbo, Tyler and Richard had been witnesses to her stupidity. She looked over her shoulder. Probably blue shirt man too.

'You're not going to go out with the tosser, are you?' Tyler took another slurp of his drink. 'You can do much better than him.'

'You shouldn't call him a tosser.'

'Why not?' He grinned at her and she had to bite her lip to stop herself from smiling.

'So, what've you got?' She reached for his phone at the same time as he did, their fingers touching.

He grinned at her again. 'You shouldn't look at a person's phone. There's private things on there, you should know that.'

She swallowed. This had been a mistake. She should have put a stop to things the first time she'd seen Tyler behind the bar of The Vaults. Should have told the headmaster. Then none of this would have happened. She wouldn't be here now, feeling this sense of unease, as if he'd got something on her. It was ridiculous, he was more than half her age. Her pupil. She should never have shown him the photo of David. She turned to see if Robbo was watching them. He wasn't. He'd gone.

'I think we'll call it a day for now.' Picking up the textbooks, she started piling them back into her bag.

'But don't you want to go through what I've done?'

'It'll wait till next week.'

'How about I call round later so we can go through it? You're up by the hospital, right?'

'What? No.' How did he know where she lived? She looked at his rosebud lips, the freckles sprinkled across

224

his nose. He seemed so innocent, so boyish, and yet there was an insistence, something dark in him that was unnerving. 'Same time next week in the library.'

Ushering Tyler out of the door, her phone buzzed. She waited until he'd headed off along the high street before opening the message. Please say you'll meet me tonight xxx

CHAPTER 23

'You look gorgeous.' He slipped off the stool, placed his hands on her bare shoulders and kissed her on both cheeks. 'G&T?'

As he gave his order to the barman, Anna stared straight ahead of her, not daring to turn around to face him, not wanting to see what she knew: that, although it was wrong and she didn't want it, she didn't want it at all, there was an attraction between them she couldn't deny.

'Shall we go through?' He didn't wait for an answer so she followed him, taking in the crispness of his shirt, the way he'd rolled his shirtsleeves halfway up his arms to reveal tanned skin covered with dark brown hair, the roundness of his bottom in his well-cut trousers – this was the man she'd fallen in love with. As he pulled back her chair, she hesitated. She shouldn't be here, it was wrong, and Petra and Denise wouldn't approve at all. And yet she was doing this for them, wasn't she? Doing it for all of them. She was here to find out the truth.

* * *

'Cheers.' He raised his glass towards her.

She smiled back – it wouldn't be a crime to enjoy herself. After everything that had happened recently, she deserved it. And she'd finally had a chance to put on the Joseph dress. It fitted her perfectly, and the ice-blue fabric brought out the blue of her own eyes.

'So, have you found him yet? The elusive David Kingfisher?' Alex Michaels asked.

Was he toying with her? Was all this some elaborate game? Had he been caught out and decided to run with it, to see how far he could push them? Or push her, at least – he hadn't asked the others out, Anna was sure of that. And was it merely a coincidence that she'd replied to David's email, telling him she would go to the police, and Alex had texted – what, five minutes later? – whereas David still hadn't replied?

She flicked her hair back over her shoulder. 'Are you sure you're not him?'

'Would you like it if I were?' The lines around his eyes crinkled as he laughed. 'Sounds like you and he were quite close?'

'You could say that.' He was obviously after details, and not of the love note variety. The expression on his face told her he wanted the more salacious ones, the heavy breathing that had gone on, the words of what she would do to him. There was a throb between her legs – she wondered if the lust had passed over her face and looked up to see if he'd noticed. 'It was all fantasy though, wasn't it?' she said.

'And you prefer reality.' He put his hand over hers, stroking the skin on her palm slowly. 'Me too.'

She took a sip of her G&T. Alex was a player perhaps, one who made a habit of cheating on his wife. But going through the rigmarole of chatting women up online, cheating them out of money he didn't need? No, she didn't think that was his style. This man could have any woman he wanted, pick them up in bars, at the hospital. He was the sort that needed instant gratification, he wouldn't want to spend months chatting up a woman via text and emails. And yet she wished it had been him, the man she'd fallen for, who'd called her in the middle of the night, made her heart leap when he'd sent her a message, instead of the faceless creep who had played her.

'You're not him, are you?' Despite her conviction he wasn't David, she needed to hear the words come out of his mouth. 'This isn't all some kind of sick joke, is it?'

He smiled. 'I may be many things, Anna, but doing that to a woman?' He shook his head. 'That's not my thing.'

'Doing what? Breaking her heart?'

'Poor Anna.' His thumb moved across her palm again before he laughed. 'No, that's just life.'

She pulled her hand away. 'Seems to be the story of mine.' Her laugh was half-hearted. What was she doing, sitting here with a married man? She'd told herself she'd come to meet Alex to find out if he was David but, deep down, she'd always known he wasn't. And yet still there was a part of her that wanted him to want her, as David had done. Needed someone to want her. Especially if that someone reminded her of Robbo, as Alex did.

Alex closed his menu. 'Shall we just skip to dessert?'

'Thanks for the coffee.'

'Thanks for dropping me home. I'm sorry...' Anna looked down, embarrassed at how she had acted earlier. He had kissed her and her mouth had responded but, as his hand moved up her leg, under her skirt, she had pulled away. It was wrong. However much she was attracted to him, he was married.

'Hey, nothing to be sorry for. Though there aren't many women who can resist my charms.'

She smiled at him. He really was gorgeous. A jumble of 'if only's, flitted through her mind. If only he had been David. If only he had been real. If only he didn't have a wife.

He slapped his forehead. 'I meant to tell you earlier. I did some digging around. There is a surgeon called Jonathan Kingfisher, practises the other side of Manchester. Completely different area to me. I checked out his bio online. He's originally from Bickley. Didn't you mention that village when you came to see me?'

Anna nodded. Jonathan. The old man in Bickley had told them that little David Kingfisher's brother was called Jonathan.

'I got you his address.' Alex reached into his back pocket, fished out a scrap of paper.

'How?'

'I know a nurse up there.' He shrugged, gave her a smile.

Anna rolled her eyes but smiled too.

'Just a friend.' He kissed her again on the cheek before making his way along the path to his car.

'Thanks for this,' she shouted, watching him lower himself into the sports car, waiting while he revved the engine and sped off. It was a full moon. David Kingfisher was somewhere out there, the same moon shining over them both. Alex was as much a victim of this as she was. He'd told her earlier he'd emailed the dating site, telling them someone was using his photos, requesting they remove the profile. They hadn't responded. Denise had been in touch with them too, asking them if they could help her to find who was behind all this. Again, there had been no reply.

Anna studied the address Alex had given her. Hale. An extremely wealthy suburb of Manchester. Was this Jonathan behind all this? But why? Someone who owned a house in that area wouldn't need the money.

There was a rustle to the side of her, along the path leading between the apartment blocks. A cat perhaps, or some teenagers necking in the alleyway. She glanced up at the spotlight over the doorway. Hadn't the landlord said he'd replace the bulb? What a cheapskate, couldn't even be bothered to do that. She headed inside, locked the door behind her and went into the living room. For some reason, she didn't switch the light on, moving to stand by the patio doors, peering out towards the road. There was something there. And it wasn't a cat, wasn't teenagers messing around. It was someone in a hoodie, someone who was staring at her window. She shivered, despite the fetid air, and pulled the curtains to, telling herself not to be silly. They were probably just waiting for a lift or something. Nothing to do with her.

Her phone pinged. She smiled and went over to where her bag lay on the floor. Alex? Perhaps he wasn't going to give up?

She swiped her phone and opened the message.

At first, her brain couldn't take in the words staring back at her.

Slag. Bitch. Whore. Think I don't know what you're up to? You'd better make it up to me otherwise the photos go viral.

Her hands started to shake. Who was doing this? She ran to the window, pulling the curtains back an inch, peeping through them, her heart hammering. There was no one there. The moon had disappeared behind a cloud, leaving just the inky night staring back at her.

The photos. Her career would be over if they got out. She looked at the piece of paper Alex had given her and then back at the message on her phone. The bastard. How dare he threaten her, how *dare* he? Two could play that game. She would find who was doing this to her, who the real David Kingfisher was, if it was the last thing she did. And when she did, she would make him pay.

CHAPTER 24

'Is this it? Do surgeons really earn this much?'

Petra glanced at Denise, who was staring goggle-eyed out of the window. The white stuccoed mansion behind the imposing gates was certainly impressive – if you were into that sort of thing. From the gasp that escaped Anna's lips it seemed she, like Denise, certainly was.

'Imagine living here,' Denise said.

Only one thing was going through Petra's head, her go-to thought when she was nervous: the cleaning – the endless rooms, skirting boards to wipe every day, toilets to bleach, walls to wipe down. It was a two-hour job for her in her own house and that was small compared to this monstrosity.

'This is my dream home.' Denise levered herself out of the car.

'Yes. I can just see myself living here,' Anna said.

Was Petra imagining it or had Anna emphasised the word *myself* as if she fitted into this world but the likes of Denise never would? Petra slammed her door shut and locked the car. Such grand aspirations for a schoolteacher.

A CCTV camera whirred into action above them. Petra hung back, letting Anna sashay her way to the intercom to the right of the gates. Before she could part her perfectly lined lips, the gates swung open.

'Shall we get back in the car?' Denise peered along the driveway.

'Come on, think of the exercise. And Petra, you could do with a bit of sun on your face – you look like death warmed up.'

'Cheeky bitch,' Petra said.

Anna held her hands up. 'Hey, I didn't mean anything by it.'

'But she's right.' Colour flooded Denise's face. 'Not about you, Petra, I didn't mean that, I just meant me and—'

'It's fine, Denise. Come on.' For a second Petra almost hooked her arm through Denise's but the thought of her clammy flesh touching her own skin stopped her.

Anna was already lifting the huge wrought-iron knocker on the door when they caught up with her.

'Yees?' A young woman with huge almond-shaped eyes and a worried expression pulled back the heavy oak door.

'We're here to see Jonathan Kingfisher.'

'You have appointment?'

'No,' Denise said, at the same time as Anna said, 'Yes.'

'Names?'

Denise opened her mouth again but Anna cut her off. 'Is he here? It's important we speak to him. Very important.'

The woman hesitated before pulling back the door and beckoning them in.

'This can't be him.' Denise turned to Petra, a frown tugging at the corners of her mouth. 'Anyone who lives here doesn't need our money.'

'People move in mysterious ways, Denise,' Anna said. 'You never know what's going on in someone's head.'

Petra's leg jumped as Anna stared at her. You certainly didn't: Anna looked as if she'd come dressed for a party – a long white gypsy dress with silver high heels, her hair was part up, part down in a style Petra would never have been able to imitate, even when she'd had long hair. As she brushed her hand through her own short crop, the blast of air conditioning hit her neck, making her shiver.

'This way, please,' the young woman said.

They followed her into a huge living room. Like the hallway, it was decked out in white. White sofas faced each other across a large white coffee table and white lilies filled the air with an overpowering scent.

'Sit, please. I tell him you here.'

As the woman backed out of the room, Anna chose the sofa facing the door. She relaxed into it, crossing one bronzed leg over the other, fiddling with the top of her dress so it showed the right amount of cleavage. Petra glanced down at her own non-existent chest. Was that what men went for? Were they all obsessed with the perfect body? Denise hesitated before plumping for the sofa opposite Anna. Petra perched on the edge of the sofa next to Denise, not sure whether her jeans were clean; she'd been halfway through the morning shift when Denise had burst in, saying they'd found David's brother, Jonathan Kingfisher. 'Go without me,' Petra had said but, even as the words had left her mouth – and even though her faith in David and what she was doing was absolute – the need to be with them, to find out what he knew, made her tell Harry it was an emergency and head for the door.

Denise took a bag of pear drops out of her holdall. 'Sugar, it's good for the nerves.'

'No, thanks,' Anna said, raising her eyebrows at Denise.

Denise sealed up the bag and left it on her knee.

Why was Anna such a bitch? Petra tried to catch Denise's eye, willing her to stand up for herself, to answer Anna back. 'I'll have one.'

Denise beamed at her as she took a large yellow pear drop out of the bag.

'Do you think it'll be him?' Denise said.

'Well, he's hardly going to just admit it, is he?' Anna rolled her eyes.

Petra looked at her. Despite her relaxed pose, she was fiddling with a loose thread on her dress, winding it back and forth between her fingers. She was worried. Definitely.

Light footsteps came from the hall, followed by a creak as the door opened.

Anna stood up, extended a brown arm in the direction of the man who was now standing next to the coffee table.

Of all the things Petra had been expecting, this wasn't it. The man in front of them had curly grey hair, navy shorts topping stubby legs, deck shoes, a linen shirt straining over a bulging stomach. He wore leather thongs around his neck and wrists.

'Ladies, how lovely. What can I do for you?' He bowed and kissed the back of Anna's hand before settling himself next to her on the sofa. He crossed one leg over the other, mimicking how she was sitting.

'This weather's a bitch, isn't it? It's no better in Villeneuve. Do you know it? Next door to Nice.'

'Nice?' Anna said.

Petra's leg jumped. David had been in Nice; he'd mentioned it in his last email.

'Yes, dear, we have a little place over there. Only got back a few weeks ago. Six months with the French is long enough for anyone. You've just caught us actually. We're off on a little jaunt around Australia tomorrow. Five months away. It's going to be wonderful.' A laugh like the tinkle of a bell burst from his lips.

'I thought you were a surgeon,' Denise said.

'Oh dear, is that why you're here?' He grabbed hold of the glasses poking out of his top pocket and stuck them on his bulbous nose while he looked her up and down.

Petra didn't need to turn to her to see that Denise had gone bright red; the heat was radiating from her.

'I... I...'

237

'That's not why we're here.' Petra sat forward. 'We're trying to find David Kingfisher.'

'David, you said? Little Davy? I don't understand. He drowned. Twenty-odd years ago.'

Petra leant forward. 'So, you *are* his brother.'

He nodded. 'Such a shock. Even for me, and I was long gone by then. I was twenty years older than him, you see. Terrible, what happened. You know my sister drowned as well? Susie. Fourteen. On the cusp of every-thing. And two days later there was Davy, face down in the pond. He was only four. Ma and Pa never got over it. Lightning can strike once, but twice? So cruel. And yet, well, it was Susie's own bloody fault. Even a width in the local baths was beyond her, that's what Ma said when I went back for the funerals. Whatever she was doing in the quarry lake, I'll never know. Showing off to her friend, Ma thought. They were always trying to outdo each other, her and Nell. School, boys. I mean, they were great friends but, well, you know what teenage girls are like.'

'It must have been hard for you,' Denise said.

Jonathan rubbed at his eyes. 'It was. Is. You never really get over losing someone you love, do you?'

Petra experienced the familiar jab of pain in her stomach, her hand moving to rub it. She noticed Anna watching her, felt Denise's hand on hers, squeezing her fingers. She snatched her hand away.

'I'm sorry for your loss.' Denise's voice wobbled. 'But someone who's calling himself David Kingfisher has stolen things from us.'

Anna stuck her chin in the air. 'Denise is talking about money. The thief is someone who has links to Bickley. That's where your family home was?'

'Oh, lordy, I think this calls for a G&T. Ah, Jean-Claude,' he said, as a tall Adonis of a man came into the room. 'Fix us some drinks, gorgeous.'

As Anna's eyes followed Jean-Claude over to a globe-shaped cabinet, Petra sniffed. Surely she didn't think she'd got a chance with him? Or with Jonathan for that matter? But, of course she did, Anna probably thought she could charm any man.

'G&Ts?' Jean-Claude asked.

Saliva pooled on Petra's tongue, the word *vodka* sat at the back of her throat. 'Just a tonic water for me.'

'Coke if you have it, please,' Denise said.

'I'll have a double then,' Anna said, smiling. 'To make up for these two lightweights.'

Petra pushed her hand down on her knee to stop it jumping. Why was the stupid cow smiling? Had she already made her mind up that this man wasn't David Kingfisher?

Jean-Claude poured the drinks and handed them around before sitting on the arm of the sofa, next to Jonathan.

'Cheers.' Jonathan clinked his glass with Jean-Claude's first and then with Anna's. 'So, back to the story, dear. If he's stolen money from you then you surely know who he is?'

Anna shook her head. 'We met him online. Internet dating.'

239

'What?' Jonathan put his hand over his mouth, coughed, made a play of being unable to swallow his drink. 'A beauty like you needs to do internet dating?'

Petra's stomach clenched and it was nothing to do with the fact she hadn't eaten a thing all day. Denise turned to look at her, the redness still on her cheeks, her mouth set in a firm line.

'Well, Jonathan, it's hard to find a good man,' Anna said.

'Tell me about it, dear.' Jonathan patted Jean-Claude's knee. 'Anyway, carry on. I've got to say this is all very exciting. We don't get this in France, do we, JC?'

'We've never actually seen him. Just photos of him. And they weren't his photos anyway. They were of someone called Alex Michaels.'

Jonathan chuckled. 'Lordy, I'm going to need a top-up in a minute.'

Petra's leg jumped. She couldn't stand much more of this. The coldness of the room, the way Jonathan was looking down his nose at her, Anna sitting there, totally relaxed, like she belonged in this house.

'Someone has used your brother's name and Alex Michaels' photos and stolen money from us,' Denise said.

'Hang on.' Jonathan put his glass down. 'You didn't think it was me, did you? How exciting.'

'We thought you might have an idea who is behind all this.' Denise banged down her glass on the marble coffee table in front of her. 'I need the money back. It's a lot to lose. Ten thousand pounds.'

'Oh, dearie.' Jonathan looked her up and down again. 'I'm sure it is.'

A strangled sound escaped Denise's lips. 'May I use your bathroom?'

'Of course. Jean-Claude, be a darling.'

Jonathan's boyfriend stomped from the room like a sulky teenager, Denise following him.

Petra glanced at Anna. She was tipping back her glass, smiling at something Jonathan was saying. Couldn't she see how uncomfortable Denise felt? Petra's leg jumped. Bitch. Bloody bitch.

'So how do you know the man who's doing this has links to Bickley?' Jonathan said.

'He sent us all photos.' Anna fished her phone out of her bag. She tapped the screen a few times and then held it out to Jonathan.

'Right.' He peered at the phone. 'Cute, isn't he? I can see why you fell for him.' He winked at Petra. 'One should never punch above one's weight though, dear. It'll never end well.'

Petra's leg jumped again. The nerve of him! What did he think he was doing with toy boy Jean-Claude, who couldn't be any older than nineteen? He had the body of a male model, compared to the bloated body of the middle-aged man sitting opposite her. She looked at the crystal ashtray on the table and felt a strong urge to throw it at Jonathan. With any luck, it would smash into his face and then bounce off it and give Anna a black eye.

'Just swipe to the right,' Anna said.

241

'Yes, that's certainly Bickley. And that's the view from the top of Colm Hill... Hang on,' Jonathan said, just as Denise and Jean-Claude came back into the room.

'What is it?' Anna moved closer to him.

'Look, look at that there.'

Petra's leg jolted, bouncing her hands up and down. She put her tonic water on the table. Denise came and sat next to her. This time she didn't move her hand when Denise grabbed it.

'What is it?' Denise said. 'What?'

'What?' Petra tried to keep the word inside her but it escaped before she could stop it.

Anna was peering over Jonathan's shoulder, studying what he was pointing to on the screen of her mobile. 'The view from the top of the hill, the one David said he took, where you can see the corner of a car in the photo,' she said.

'Yes?' Denise dropped Petra's hand and scrabbled in her bag for her phone.

Petra didn't need to look; the photo Anna was referring to was imprinted on her memory.

'You can see part of a wing mirror and, if I'm not mistaken, there's a reflection of the person who took the picture in it.' Jonathan clapped his hands together.

'Who is it?' Denise said. 'Who?'

'You want drinks?' The woman who had let them in appeared at the door.

'Not now, Elena. Not now,' Jonathan said with a wave of his hand.

242

'Who is it?' Petra didn't recognise her own voice; it sounded faint, ethereal, as if it didn't belong to her.

Denise stood up. 'Who is it?'

'It's a woman.' Jonathan dropped the phone and clapped his hands together again, his eyes twinkling. 'It's a woman. I'm sure of it.'

Denise flopped back down onto the sofa. 'So?'

'He said he'd taken it. I asked him.' Anna took a huge gulp of her drink. 'He said he does that walk on his own. A great place to clear his head, that's what he said.'

Petra tried not to flinch as Denise grabbed her hand again. 'A woman?'

Jonathan reached for his glasses and placed them onto the end of his nose.

It was as if time were standing still. Petra looked over at Anna. Her face, despite its thick layer of make-up, seemed to have lost all its colour. Denise, next to her, was breathing heavily; Petra hoped she wasn't going to have a panic attack. And, if it weren't for her own leg jerking, Petra would have believed she wasn't really in the room, that it was all a dream and she would wake up shortly.

Jonathan shook his head. 'No, it's no good. You can tell it's a woman from the long hair but it's only a faint reflection from the neck up, and most of the hair's covering her face. It could be anyone.'

'Let me see.' Jean-Claude held out a brown hand, squeezing Jonathan's shoulder as his lover handed him the phone.

243

'He won't know who it is.' Jonathan rolled his eyes. 'He doesn't know anyone in this country.'

'A woman,' said Denise, on a long exhale of breath. 'A woman?'

Petra turned to her. This was the time to put a comforting hand on her arm, or around her shoulders – a pat of the hand would do. But she couldn't manage it, even though she was starting to warm to Denise. And even though she could see what was flitting through her mind, and knew it was what Anna was thinking too – that they had shared intimacies with a woman, told a woman things they only wanted a man to hear.

'Elaine?'

They all stared at Jean-Claude.

'The girl who showed us in?' Denise gasped. 'That girl?'

Jonathan laughed. 'No, no, that's Elena. No, it's not her.'

'Then who is Elaine?' Anna said.

Jonathan was squinting through his glasses again, moving the phone back and forth, swiping the screen to make the image larger. 'You think?' He turned to Jean-Claude. 'Really, gorgeous? Elaine?'

'For God's sake, who's Elaine?' The loudness of Denise's voice startled Petra.

'She's my sister.'

'You said your sister drowned.'

'That was Susie.' Jonathan took off his glasses and rubbed his hand across his face. 'Elaine is Davy's twin.'

'And where is she now?' Denise shifted forward on the sofa.

'She's in Bickley,' Petra said.

'What? How?' Denise said.

Anna nodded. 'She lives at the farm where you grew up, doesn't she, Jonathan, up on the Ashbourne road? That old man we spoke to told us.'

'That's right,' Jonathan said. He sighed. 'It wouldn't surprise me if Elaine is mixed up in all this. She's never been right since little Davy died.'

'Do let us know what happens, ladies,' Jonathan said, giving them a cheery wave before closing the front door behind them.

'I feel sick. The things I told him. Honestly when I find whoever's behind this, I'll—'

'Stop being an overdramatic cow.'

Anna stopped. Had Petra just called her a cow? Reaching down, she tugged off her sandals. She should never have worn heels, but she'd been hoping they were finally going to meet David Kingfisher and she'd wanted to look her best, wanted him to see what he couldn't have. She thought of the text message, the vile words he'd written.

She hobbled down the long drive, gritting her teeth as bits of gravel lodged themselves in the soles of her feet. If only she were more like dowdy Denise and pinch-faced Petra. They always wore sensible shoes – Denise had on hideous walking sandals and Petra was in trainers. She smiled to herself. She would never be

245

like them, would never want to be like them. Not while she had breath in her body.

And Anna would never have been as stupid as they'd been. Fancy giving someone they'd never met money. What had they been thinking? Thank God she hadn't been that dumb.

Or had she? Money you could get back... your dignity, your reputation, your career for God's sake, they were irreplaceable. Five photos. That's all it would take. She'd been stupid enough to show her face in every one of them. She thought of the text he'd sent her. He must have been following her. He must have seen her out with Alex Michaels. He wanted her to *make it up to him*. He could go to hell. But she couldn't risk those photos going public.

She couldn't believe it was a woman. It couldn't be. Okay, a woman had probably taken the photo but it might have been a friend? It didn't mean David was a woman. They were missing one vital clue, though.

'Hey, wait up,' Anna said.

Denise started to turn but Petra tugged on her elbow, moving her forwards.

'Stop! I've thought of something,' Anna shouted, breaking into a run, not catching up with them until they reached the car. 'It can't be a woman,' she said, reaching down to brush the gravel off her feet.

'It could be an alien for all we know.' Denise opened the car door.

'But we've spoken to David, haven't we? All three of us?'

Denise nodded. Anna looked at Petra who shrugged as if to say, *And?*

'Well, I don't know who you spoke to, but I definitely spoke to a man. Without a doubt. A deep voice—'

'Husky,' Denise said.

'Exactly,' Anna said. 'Petra?'

Petra went around to the driver's side of the car. 'What?'

'Did you think you were speaking to a woman?' Anna let out a laugh. 'Even a butch woman? Well?'

Petra shrugged her shoulders. 'No. Definitely a man.'

Denise's face changed from that of a ghost to that of an excited child. 'You're right.' She turned to Petra as she climbed into the driver's seat. 'Whoever David Kingfisher is, it isn't a woman.'

Petra nodded slowly. 'It might be a reflection of a woman in that photo but it was probably just a friend, someone he'd been walking with. David Kingfisher is a man.'

Anna jumped onto the back seat. 'Exactly. A woman wouldn't do this. This is a man. And when I find him—'

'I think we should go to Bickley anyway. Talk to this Elaine and find out if she knows anything.' Denise's voice was so quiet Anna had to lean forward to hear what she was saying.

'But we're all agreed, it isn't a woman,' Petra said, reversing the car out of the drive. 'For God's sake, what is that car doing?'

Anna looked over her shoulder. There was a BMW right behind them by the gate. 'Why's he stopped there?

247

Idiot.' She peered at the driver. He seemed familiar somehow. Before she could get a better view of him, the car had indicated and sped off with a screech of tyre on gravel.

'We should at least go and find out what this Elaine knows,' Denise insisted, plugging her seatbelt in and turning to look at Anna for reassurance.

'It isn't a woman. We've all spoken to him.' Petra said.

Denise put her hand on Petra's arm. 'Please, Petra. Please? What else are we going to do next? I need to get that money back. Please.'

Petra took a deep breath. 'Okay.'

Anna leant back against the seat. It had to be a man. She could work her magic on a man, but a woman? If David was a woman, then she had no chance of getting the photos back at all.

CHAPTER 25

That was close. Too close. It's not good for my body, my mind. And yet it gets the adrenaline pumping through my veins. Reminds me I'm alive. That I'm fighting. That I can do this.

I take a deep breath and concentrate on the road ahead of me. In, one, two, three. Out, one, two, three.

They think they're oh so bloody clever. They think it's all a game, trying to track me down. But it isn't a game. When will they realise that? Haring here and there, not knowing I'm one step ahead of them every time.

A horn blares me out of my thoughts. I must concentrate. I must keep calm. I'm so close. So close to the finish line. All will be revealed. Soon.

They think they're following me, hunting me. How wrong can they be?

CHAPTER 26

Of all the things Denise had been expecting, the woman in front of her wasn't it. And yet she'd known that one day she would have to, as every self-help book she'd ever read told her, *face her fears*.

The woman sprawled on the bed was a stranger and yet Denise *knew* this woman, could recognise herself in her. The way her hands plucked the chocolate from the silver foil. The thin, dark hair plastered to her forehead with sweat, the red-veined eyes. Her arms. Denise didn't want to look at them and yet she couldn't drag her gaze away. The woman's filthy T-shirt cut into the place where her biceps should be, mottled skin hanging below. Would this be her in what, two years', three years' time, if she didn't stop gorging herself?

'Who are yer?' The woman huffed and puffed, tried to lean down, but couldn't shift her bulk more than two inches to the side. 'Got a gun, I have. I'll use it.'

As Anna stepped backwards, trying to hide her tall

frame behind Petra's diminutive one, Denise realised it was Anna's disgust that was causing her to hide. Not that Denise could blame her. The urge to escape the stench of the room, the image of this woman, to get outside, breathe, pulsed away at her. And yet she didn't run, her feet propelled her closer to the bed.

'Are you Elaine?'

'Who are yer? How'd yer get in?'

The front door had been open. Stepping over and around things in a cluttered hallway, bits of old farm machinery making it almost impossible to make a passage through, they had called out, announcing their arrival. The lack of an answer wasn't surprising; music was blasting out from a stereo Denise could now see half-hidden under a pile of clothes. Meatloaf. They hadn't followed the source of the racket at first, had gone into the kitchen, shocked at the state of it, crockery strewn everywhere, a bin overflowing, empty takeaway containers piled high. That's when Denise had had the first inkling. The hairs on the back of her neck had stood on end – there was something about the chaos, the dirt that reminded her of her own house. She'd perhaps known then what was coming, maybe that's why she'd led them into the other bedrooms first, avoiding the one with the deafening music. One bedroom had bunk beds in, looked like it hadn't been touched since the 80s, a Spider-Man poster on the wall, brown, curling, a Barbie doll, minus a leg, lying on a chest of drawers. A double bed filled the other room, net curtains yellow with age, an eiderdown with flowers on. Dust over everything. And now they were here. And here was Elaine.

'What d'yer want?' The woman lying on the bed puffed on an inhaler, her chest rattling as she removed it from her mouth. 'Are yer police? Was nothing to do with me, that Mickey business. Told the last lot. He been at it again?'

Out of the corner of her eye, Denise saw Anna and Petra exchange a glance. And then it came to her – Mickey was the slow boy, the one Anna had told her about, the grandson of the old man they'd talked to during their last visit to Bickley.

Denise looked over at Anna and Petra. Was one of them going to take the lead? They were the strong ones after all, used to dealing with people. Wouldn't let anything faze them. But they were staring at the walls of the room, at the pictures plastered over the faded wallpaper. Anna had her hand over her mouth; Petra was jigging from foot to foot.

'Mickey, Mickey.'

Denise turned back to the bed. Elaine had a phone to her ear, was wheezing down it. 'There's folks here. You need to get rid of 'em.' There was a pause and then she continued: 'No, Mickey. Now. Come now.' She slung the phone down onto the bed. 'There, Mickey'll sort you out. Get rid of yer, he will.'

'We're here about David Kingfisher.'

Elaine crossed herself. 'Davy. My Davy. What do yer know? Have yer found something out?' She rolled to the side, suddenly agile, took a laptop from under her pillow, lifting the lid covered with pink butterflies, sparkles, hearts, and jabbing with her sausage fingers at the keys. 'Asked God every day, I have, to help me.'

Denise took a deep breath. 'Someone's been using your brother's name to con women online. To cheat them, us,' she said, 'out of money.'

'No.' The jowls of fat under Elaine's chin wobbled as she spoke. 'David Kingfisher is my brother. Davy. You know something, don't yer? That's why you're here.'

'No.' Denise shook her head. 'He drowned, didn't he? Twenty-odd years ago, wasn't it? What would we know about that?'

Elaine squinted. 'Didn't drown, did he? He was murdered. God rest his soul.'

'Mur—'

'Who are these girls?' Petra had turned to Elaine, was pointing at the wall. 'Who are they?'

For the first time since she'd entered the room, Denise focused on what Petra and Anna were staring at. The wall was covered with pictures of girls, young, late teens maybe. Pretty. Barbie blonde. Were they the same girl? Different? She couldn't tell from where she was standing.

'Those are me girls,' Elaine said, her bingo wing flapping as she waved her left arm in the air.

'Your daughters?' Denise could hardly believe it; how could someone so grotesque give birth to such lovely things, and so many of them? And yet, despite her incredulity, a glimmer of hope flickered in her chest. If this woman in front of her could do it, then there was hope for her too. There had to be.

'Me girls. Yer know, girlfriends.' She tapped the laptop. 'Met them all on here.' She swung the laptop around to face Denise. 'Look.'

Denise looked. A teenage girl with a high ponytail, freckles and a pink checked shirt sitting on a fence was grinning back at her. Long legs. Tanned. An all-American girl. 'Nice.' It was all she could think to say.

'That's me.' Elaine pulled the laptop to her.

'I don't understand?' Denise said.

Anna moved her hand from in front of her nose. 'You're pretending to be someone you're not?'

Elaine picked up a bottle of Coke from her bedside cabinet, took the top off and lifted it to her lips. 'No one's going to want this, are they?' she said when she'd finished guzzling, nodding her head down to the body sprawled all over the bed.

'But that's wrong. Dishonest. You're deceiving them.'

'Bollocks. D'yer think them girls really look like that?' Elaine nodded towards the wall. 'Anyway, what harm's in it? A bit of fun, that's what it is. People pretend to be something they're not all the time. Look at yer.' She pointed at Anna. 'All prissy. Bet you're a dirty cow really.'

Anna opened her mouth to say something, but no words came out.

A strange noise came from Petra; it sounded like a laugh. Was this some sort of alternative reality? Petra couldn't be laughing, there was nothing funny in this situation. Nothing at all. Denise swallowed. Had they found David? Was this monstrosity in front of them the man they'd fallen in love with?

She stepped closer to the bed. 'Have you been pretending to be your brother? To take money from us?'

A giggle escaped Elaine's lips, so high-pitched Denise couldn't believe it was coming out of someone so huge. The laugh got deeper, morphing into a wheeze, a splutter, then a cough. It sounded like she was choking. Denise's involuntary reflex was to thump her back but she couldn't touch the woman, she couldn't. And yet she needed to know. She needed the answer.

Elaine took a huge gasp of her inhaler. Sweat beaded on her forehead.

'So?' Denise said. 'Is it you? Have you been posing as your brother online?'

Elaine moved her eyes slowly, taking in all three of them.

'Just bloody tell us,' Anna shouted.

'You ain't bad, Prissy Knickers, but yer ain't my type. I like 'em young, don't I?'

Saliva pooled in Denise's mouth. She was going to be sick. For the second time in the past five minutes she realised this woman could be her, for hadn't she been doing the very same thing as Elaine had these last seven years: pretending to be something she wasn't? A loving carer for Mother, a person who wasn't devastated when Ian left her, someone who was fine on her own, didn't need someone to hold her, love her. And then in

256

the virtual world she had reinvented herself, becoming someone exciting, fun, someone who David could fall for. And now look where all the pretence had got her. Nowhere. She was none of those things. Never would be.

'Who is he then, this man? You say he's been using our Davy's name?' Elaine spluttered, after sucking at her inhaler.

'Yes. We don't know.'

'What?'

'We don't know.' Denise could hardly get the words out. 'That's why we're here. We think he has some links to Bickley. We've seen photos of him here by the village sign, and, yes, he's been using your David's name.'

'Bastard.' She looked up at the ceiling and then back at them. 'Making me blaspheme, you are.'

'We went to see your brother.'

'Davy?'

'Jonathan.'

'Him? Don't call him me brother. Wants nowt to do with us, he doesn't. Wasn't even bothered when our Davy was murdered. Came here last year with that boyfriend of his. I sent 'em packing.'

'Why do you say murdered?' Denise asked. 'He drowned, didn't he? An accident?'

'I was there.'

Denise told herself to take deep breaths. 'Must have been awful for you.'

'I'll wait in the car.' Anna moved towards the door.

'Aye, go on, Miss Prissy Knickers,' Elaine shouted after Anna as she left the room.

Anna's leaving seemed to stir Petra into action. 'You were there?'

'I was in the house, wasn't I? And I saw someone going out of the back garden. They drowned him.'

'Why?' said Denise. She had only signed up to internet dating to meet someone. Didn't everyone deserve to find a soulmate? And now, look what had happened: she was talking to a mad woman. 'Why would someone do such a thing to a four-year-old boy?'

''Cos he'd seen what had happened to our Susie, hadn't he? Was there at the quarry the day she drowned. There was a strange man there, he said. And Nell saw him too.'

'Nell?'

'Our Susie's best friend. Thick as thieves they were. Nell had been sunbathing while Susie had gone in the water. Had offered to watch our Davy. And then she heard a scream and saw this man running off. They found Susie's body at the bottom of the quarry pit. Sank like a stone, they said. And our Davy had seen it all. And this man knew. That's why he murdered him.'

Petra coughed. 'Did you tell your parents? The police?'

'Thought I was imagining it, didn't they? Or making it all up. I was only four. An accident. That's what they all thought. I'll never give up though. Been searching all my life. It's all on here.' Elaine tapped the laptop. 'God willing, I'll find out who killed him. And our Susie.'

'But what about Nell? She must have told them about the man? She was Susie's age, wasn't she? Fourteen? They'd have to believe her.'

'Aye, they followed it up but they never found the man so they gave up. Not me though. I'll never give up on Davy. Or our Susie. I loved her too but Davy... he was my twin, you see. Got a private investigator sort coming around tomorrow, I have. Always wanted to get one but never had the money up till now.'

'You.'

The word wafted in on a smell of BO.

'Mickey. Knew yer'd come.'

'What you doing here?' Mickey pointed at Petra.

'We're just going.' Petra was already moving from the room.

'Do you swear you're not behind all this?' The question couldn't stay locked in Denise's head.

Elaine's red eyes stared at her. And then she laughed, that high-pitched giggle again.

A spasm in Denise's chest caused her feet to move, to step over the detritus in the hallway and follow Petra out of the front door. She heaved what was left of her cooked breakfast onto the weed-strewn path, trying to get rid of the thoughts tearing at her: that Elaine could be David Kingfisher and, even worse than that, that she, Denise, could be Elaine.

CHAPTER 27

'I'm just on the right up here,' Anna said. 'The next block of flats.'

Petra pulled over and stopped the car.

'We need to get hold of the laptop,' Anna said, as she shut the door behind her and motioned for Denise to open the car window. 'Elaine's laptop. We need to see what's on it. Maybe she got that Mickey to make the calls for her.'

As disgusted and embarrassed as she was at the thought of whoever was doing this being a woman, Anna would rather it was Elaine than someone else. Elaine, she could cope with. Someone who couldn't get out of bed, couldn't threaten her, no matter what spiteful insults she typed. She thought of the nasty message she'd received after her night out with Alex, the vile words hammering away in her mind, insistent, relentless.

'How can we get the laptop?' she said. If Elaine were pretending to be David then all she had to do was get hold of her laptop and delete the photos.

'Break in? Steal it?' Denise's eyes widened.

'We're not bloody Charlie's Angels, you know.' Anna rolled her eyes.

'I wish.' Denise sighed. 'What about that Mickey? We could ask him to help us.'

'Haven't I just said they might be in it together?' Anna's words came out sharper than she'd intended. 'Remember his face when he saw us that first time, Petra?'

Petra turned to her. 'What do you mean?'

'He looked like he'd seen a ghost, tried to shut the door on us.'

'He thought we were the police.'

'Did he? Or was it because he was terrified we'd found him?'

'Maybe you're right.' Denise nodded her head. 'They do seem very close. Do you think they're an item? You hear about couples like that, don't you? They get some weird kick out of doing strange things, terrorising other people.'

'I hardly think they're an item.' This time Anna did laugh.

'What do you mean?'

Anna twirled her house keys around her index finger. 'Come on, look at the bloody size of her. She'd squash him.'

'What, you think love is just for skinny bitches, like you?' Denise said.

Anna's body jolted back in response to the words. Where had that come from?

'I just meant…' Anna's words petered out. She didn't know what she was trying to say.

'I know exactly what you meant.' The car window started to rise.

Anna moved her hand just in time to stop her fingers being trapped. 'I only meant—' But it was too late, Petra had accelerated away from the kerb. Anna raised her arm, hoping to catch her eye in the rear-view mirror, but the car was gone, careering around the corner. She sighed. Did Denise think she'd been talking about her? But Denise was nothing like Elaine; it was only her clothes that made her seem frumpy and dumpy.

She waited another minute, expecting the car to come back. When it didn't, she turned and walked down the path. It was starting to get dark. Despite the continuing heatwave, the nights were drawing in – less sun to burn during the day but more heat to keep you lying awake at night, searching for a cool spot on the bed, kicking sheets to the floor. The bulb in the lamp post across the road flashed on and off intermittently. As she lifted her hand to the entry system, she glanced behind her. Was there someone there, or had she imagined the soft shuffle of footsteps? Her fingers stumbled over the buttons but eventually the door buzzed open. As she walked along the corridor, she peered up into the pitch-black stairwell before sticking the keys into the Yale lock and pushing open the door to her flat.

What a day. And one of two extremes: Jonathan's palatial house and the hovel Elaine called home. A man filled with bonhomie and a woman filled with lies, fantasies, an obsession. Anna shuddered. Those pictures on the wall. Imagine if hers had been amongst them? The woman was clearly mad.

Kicking off her sandals, she flicked on the radio as she headed for the fridge. There was a cold Sauvignon in there. Half a bottle. That would have to do for tonight. In the past, she would have walked to the corner shop to buy more but, ever since she'd seen the figure the other night, loitering on the other side of the road, she felt nervous about going out.

What had all that been about with Denise? She'd thought Denise liked her, maybe looked up to her a little bit. *Bitch*. That's what she'd said. And Petra had called her a cow earlier. The wine was ice cold in her mouth. Sod them. Why let them bother her? After all this was over, she would never see them again. Wouldn't want to see them again. And yet, in the two weeks they'd been searching for David, she'd felt like she was getting to know these two women. After all, they were in it together, weren't they? A part of her had thought they might become friends. The only friend she'd made since she'd moved here was Siobhan and she could hardly call her a proper mate.

Anna took another swig of wine. She wasn't a person who gelled easily with other women. They seemed to think she was up herself, just because she took care of her body, how she looked, the clothes she wore. She'd always been the same. Her father and stepmother had scrubbed at her and Lisa, their faces, their bodies, their hair, pushing them under the bathwater like they were trying to wash away their sin.

Her phone beeped. David? She put her wine glass down onto the kitchen counter and padded over to the hall, humming along to 'You Can Call Me Al' as it blasted from the radio. She squatted down, rummaging in her bag. Might as well get it over and done with; there was no way she could relax without knowing what he or she, whoever was doing this to her, had said. As her fingers hit the cool metal of the phone, her eyes flicked to the doorstop propping open her bedroom door, a stuffed tartan terrier. There was something that wasn't quite right about it. And then she realised what it was: the dog was facing the wrong way – its head usually pointed into the bedroom, not out into the living room as it was doing now.

Anna straightened up. Had she moved it earlier? She walked towards her bedroom, breath catching in her chest as she switched the light on and peeped around the door. Everything appeared as it should and yet there was something not quite right, a strange scent perhaps? Or was it just in her head? Had David's text the other day freaked her out more than she wanted to admit? She stepped into the room, dropped to her knees and peered under the bed, then stood up again and touched the jewellery box, the candle, the photo of Lisa and Joe on top of her chest of drawers. No, everything was in its place.

And then she noticed it. The top drawer, the one where she kept her best underwear, was open. Not by much, only a few millimetres maybe, but it was still open. And she hadn't left it like that – she always shut drawers, always. She opened the drawer wider. It had been so long since she'd been in there, so long since she'd needed to, she couldn't be sure if everything was in the right place or not.

She closed the drawer. Was she just being silly? The bedroom window was shut, the front door had been locked when she got in. Going back into the living room, she checked the patio doors – locked – and put her head around the bathroom door. The window was closed. It was impossible. No one could have got in. There was only one spare key and she kept that in a mug in the cupboard. She opened the cupboard door, lifted the mug out and looked inside it. Yes, the key was still there.

Taking a huge glug of wine, she retrieved her phone from the floor and hit the screen, just as another text arrived. She finally released the breath she'd been holding. They weren't from him.

Hey, guess who I hooked up with last night? Siobhan. And: Oh God, we went all the way. Anna didn't have to guess. She knew exactly who it would be. Letchy Leeky, as Tyler called him. She slung the phone onto the sofa. Shit, her life was a mess but Siobhan's was a whole lot worse. Sleeping with Richard was really scraping the barrel. Good luck to them.

She took another slug of wine. They were well suited. Had Richard finally given up on her then? She examined her nails, pushed a cuticle back; she would have to go to the nail bar at the weekend. Siobhan and Richard. She should feel relieved, after all she didn't fancy Richard one bit, hated how he fawned all over her. And the fact that he could transfer his affections so easily, and to a gossip like Siobhan to boot, showed exactly what sort of man he was. Her nail file was in the fruit bowl. She grabbed it and started sawing at her thumbnail. She couldn't believe he didn't like her any more though. Maybe he was just using Siobhan? Not many men went off her, it was usually her who did the dumping. The nail file pirouetted across the countertop as she flung it away from her. Apart from Robbo, of course. And David. Bloody David. But that was different. David, whoever he, or she was, was a con – he hadn't gone off her because he'd never been into her in the first place.

A knock at the door broke her thoughts. Who would be calling this late? Surely not Siobhan? Anna groaned. The last thing she wanted was to hear about her exploits.

Her phone beeped again. She took it out of her bag. Are you jealous? Of that creep? Siobhan must be unhinged.

Anna flopped onto the sofa, tucking her legs under her. She would pretend she was out. She'd done it before when Siobhan had called. When would the woman get the message?

Okay, so the light was on, she told herself, but plenty of people left a light on when they went out. Straining her ears, she listened. Footsteps receding down the path. Good. She picked up her wine glass and put it to her lips.

And then nearly dropped it as there was a loud banging on the patio doors. Her heart thundered in her chest. A yelp shot from her mouth as she clutched at a nearby cushion. She would kill Siobhan. She really would. What was she playing at?

She got up slowly. Made her way to the window. She wanted to open the curtains, to scream, shout, to tell her she was a poor excuse for a friend, that she could fuck off right now. Her fingers touched the silky material but her arm wouldn't move to inch them back.

Keeping very still, holding her breath, she listened. And, although she couldn't hear anything, she could tell there was someone out there. She could sense it.

'Who is it?' Her voice, normally so strong, came out as a croak.

This time her arm did move, the curtains parting just enough for her to peek through.

The garden was empty.

She stuck her chin out. Was it him? David?

Her mind told her there was nothing to be afraid of, while the prickle of fear on the back of her neck warned her otherwise. Anger at being made to feel like this made her unlock the door, open it and step out into the garden.

The earth was dusty under her feet, the air still, black. She stepped forwards, her breath clamped inside her mouth. She looked. Watched. Waited.

But nothing moved, apart from the flashing of the light from the lamp post. On, off, on, off, until its bulb eventually died and then Anna could see no more.

CHAPTER 28

'I am so sorry.' Denise bustled into the kitchen.

Netty was up to her elbows in soap suds. 'It's no problem. None at all. You deserve a day off, Denise. I know how difficult things can get with...' She nodded her head in the direction of the ceiling and then smiled to show she meant no offence.

'You didn't have to wash up, I can do that.'

'I've finished now. I'll leave them to drain though, if you don't mind. Barney will be wanting a walk.'

Denise looked over to where the dog was spread out under the kitchen table.

Netty dried her hands on a tea towel and picked up the lead from the back of a kitchen chair.

Barney bounded up, gave Denise a reproachful look and plodded to the back door.

'How's she been?' Denise said, as Netty clipped the lead to his collar.

Netty kept her head down.

'Same as usual?' Denise tried.

'She spent all day wondering where you were, who you were with, what you were up to.' Netty finally straightened up, staring at a point five inches to the left of Denise's face. 'Do you want my advice, lovey? Get out of here, get a life for yourself. It's not right. A woman of your age. You should be enjoying yourself. Get a chap. You need a family of your own.'

It was the most Denise had ever heard Netty speak. And she'd never talked to her about Mother before. Tears pricked the back of her throat.

'She's my mother,' she said. 'She's all I've got.'

Netty shook her head, opened her mouth as if about to say something else and then closed it again. 'Come on, Barney.'

'Thank you so much, Netty,' Denise called after her. As she watched them go along the side of the garden, down to a gate in the back hedge, Denise wasn't sure if she was thanking her for looking after Mother or for what she'd said. Netty was right: being here, living with Mother, was sucking the soul out of her. She had to get her own life.

And she was going to start now. She had something to do, something she should have done weeks ago, that would shut a firm door on the past and let her move forward.

As she waited for the kettle to boil, she glanced around the room. Apart from the three years she'd been at university and the two years she'd lived with Ian, this was all she'd known. This room in particular. Mother had never been a great cook and so the kitchen had become her and her father's domain, the place they went to when Mother was being 'difficult'. They always termed Mother's behaviour in that way. 'She's just a difficult person,' her father would say. 'Nothing to do with you though, sweetheart, that's just how she is.' He was just being kind, of course; Mother's moods *were* to do with her. She'd seen photos of her parents when they were on their own, out with friends, at a party – they seemed perfectly happy then. There had been flares and halterneck dresses, suede bags and platform heels, parties and glasses of Babycham and cigarettes. Their arms had been around each other, Mother smiling, laughing, enjoying herself. Denise had often thought the person in the photos was someone else, a secret twin sister of her mother's, someone they'd never told her about. 'She'll be fine tomorrow,' Dad would say. And she would be, Denise hoping that the mother who ruffled her hair would, this time, be here to stay.

But Mother's difficult periods grew longer and longer and came with more frequency. And then, when Denise returned home from school one day, there had been a change in the house, the way the air hung. She'd run up to the room where her father slept, pulled open the door of the old mahogany wardrobe. All that remained was a single shirt Mother had bought him for his birthday, one Denise couldn't remember him ever wearing.

She hadn't dared to ask Mother where he was. She'd gone into her room, shut the door, put the chair from her desk up against it and lain down on her bed, letting the anger come, feeling it tighten her muscles, her whole body, until she curled up like a baby. How could he? How could he? It had always been the two of them, tiptoeing around Mother, going for a walk to the park or the shops when she was in one of her tempers, cooking for each other, trying to find the light in the darkness that shrouded them. He had left her. Left her with Mother, knowing what she would have to face, what it would do to her.

The kettle whistled to its climax and for once, she didn't care that the noise might wake Mother. That moment, over twenty years ago when her father had left, never to hear from him since, had shaped her entire life. She picked up a mug off the draining board, barely noticing the soap suds around its rim. Mother had won: she realised it now. And, what was worse, she had let her. She thought she'd escaped when she'd gone off to uni, when she'd met Ian, had started building a life with him – but it was all an illusion. Mother had snapped her fingers and she'd come running, the dutiful daughter.

The steam rose from the water as she slopped it over a teabag. Mother had made her like this. Mother had made her lie down and take whatever people did to her. First her father and then Ian. Laurence. And now David, whoever he was. Or she. Was Anna right? Were that Elaine and Mickey behind everything? Anger zipped through her veins; she could feel it in her burning cheeks, in the thump of her heart. No. No more. She wasn't going to lie down for anyone again.

She sank into a chair and re-read the message she'd typed on her laptop, almost without seeing the words.

I am going to the police. We are close to finding you. But they have the resources to find you even quicker. Wire the money to my bank account by 5 p.m. tomorrow or I'm going to the police, you lying, cheating bastard.

The sound of footsteps outside made her look up. Why hadn't the outside light come on? Moving quickly, she tried to reach the back door, lock it before it opened. Too late.

'You shouldn't leave the back door open. Anyone could walk in,' Laurence said.

'Anyone just did.' Denise slammed down the laptop lid. 'What are you doing here?'

'Peace offering?' He held out a bottle of wine. 'For the other night. I was out of order. But, really, Denise, you need to get the money back into the charity's account. Before anyone finds out.'

'I don't want to talk about it.'

He smiled at her, not a genuine smile, not one that reached up to his eyes, more of a leer. Was that how he'd been looking at her all this time? Had his offers of help, his visits to Mother, simply been a ruse to get into her knickers?

'I'm just going to bed.'

'Oh, darling, you are a tease.'

The anger rose in her again. She hadn't realised she had the capacity to feel so much hate, so much loathing.

273

'You need to go.' She moved towards him, tried to steer him back towards the open door. 'Now.'

And yet Laurence stood firm, his arms crossed, pot belly pushed proudly out. 'Come on now, darling. Don't say you didn't enjoy it, what we did. A woman like you, she has needs. I can see it in your eyes, Denise. Don't deny it.'

Her face was less than a foot away from his. The stink of pine aftershave, of sour alcohol, filled her head, while saliva filled her mouth. She wanted to retch, to throw up all over his beige jumper.

'Get out.'

She thought he was going to go, she really did. Thought he was taking a step back, that he would turn and walk to the door. But he didn't. He put the bottle on the side slowly.

'What are you—'

She didn't have time to get the rest of the question out. He lunged for her, grabbing her arms, pinching the fat, pushing her back onto the table, his tongue, his breath, his yellow eyes, the dark hairy mole on his chin, looming over her. He pinned her down with the weight of his belly, her arms scrabbling, fighting, trying to push, to pull him off her. And then his hands were reaching down, tugging at her skirt.

No, she wanted to scream, *no*. *No*. But the words wouldn't come out.

She could feel the hardness of him against her thigh, feel his long fingernails scrabbling for her knickers.

Mother, she thought. Mother. You have done this to

me. You have invited this monster into our house. You. You. You.

She brought her knee up like a jackhammer. Laurence screamed out, lurched to the side. Freeing her elbow, she swung it to the left, heard the contact of bone against bone. And then bone against wood as his head hit the chair. There was a groan, a gurgling sound, a splutter and then silence.

Her breath came in short wheezes. Spots danced across her eyelids. She opened her eyes, levered herself up. Untangled her feet from his legs. Stood over him, staring down at him.

Laurence wasn't moving. His eyes were closed.

She knew she should bend down, check for a pulse, make sure he was breathing. Call an ambulance. Get help. She should do all those things and yet she didn't. She pulled her pants back up, slipped her feet into her sandals, grabbed her holdall and ran out of the door.

CHAPTER 29

'Pet?' Sam's head appeared around the door.

Petra looked up from her laptop.

'Dinner in ten. Okay?'

She nodded. He seemed about to say something else but he closed the door softly behind him instead.

Not long now. She pulled her laptop towards her. Just play the game, pretend everything was all right and everything would be. Only things had become more difficult recently. Was Sam beginning to see through the pretence? They had started to make love last night but she had pulled away. She hadn't been able to get David out of her mind, how he'd seemed like the answer to everything, how he was going to make everything okay. She put her hand to her stomach. He wasn't though, was he? She thought of Elaine, of Mickey, of Anna's idea that they were behind everything.

The words stood there, black against white. She stared at the message, so different from David's previous one.

You'll never find me, bitch. No one ever will. If you go to the police, I'll kill your beloved dog and then I'll kill you.

She felt the spasm in her leg again, the iciness in her fingers. Fear.

It had been Denise's idea. They hadn't spoken at first when they'd left Anna standing on the pavement after their visit to Elaine. Squeezing her lips together to stop the laughter inside her from escaping, Petra had seen Anna in her rear-view mirror, waiting, watching to see if they'd turn around. Did she really think they would go back? Petra couldn't imagine Anna knew the words to form an apology; it just wasn't in her. How could it be? She thought of one person and one person alone: herself. And Denise had finally seen it. And while Petra had kept her opinions to herself, Denise had let those words spew out.

Anna had had Denise's outburst coming, Petra knew that. Her little jibes, the words that showed she thought she was so much better than them, the way her eyes scanned their bodies from top to toe, how she struggled to contain a smirk when they talked about David.

Denise's anger had filled the car as she'd driven her home. But when she'd finally spoken, Petra had been surprised that Anna was no longer on her mind.

'I think we should go to the police.'

Petra's knee had jerked and it had taken all her energy to stop herself from doing an emergency stop. If Denise went to the police, they would launch an investigation, they would want to interview her. Sam would find out what she'd been doing, what she'd been planning to do.

She'd turned to the woman next to her. 'We can't. We'd look so stupid.'

'I don't care. I need that money back.'

She'd squeezed Petra's arm and, for the first time, Petra hadn't flinched. Had enjoyed the warmth of Denise's hand – it had taken away some of the chill coursing through her veins.

Petra had smiled at her. 'Let's threaten him with the police first. If we both do it, maybe he'll see we're not messing.'

A crashing sound came from the kitchen. Sam swore, loudly.

Petra studied the new message. It seemed she had been right: the threat had been enough.

Her eyes scanned to the start of it:

The money will be in your account tomorrow.

She thought of Denise's relief. She was relieved too, of course she was, that the situation with the money was sorted. But, for her, this whole David Kingfisher business had never been about the money. For Petra, it had been all about saving her marriage to Sam.

'You okay?'

Sam's hand reached over the table, his fingers enveloping hers. Such a strong hand. Long fingers, a smattering of fine dark hair. Warm.

'Fine.'

'You've hardly touched a thing.' He pushed a lone

prawn to the other side of his plate. 'It's not great, is it? I followed the recipe this time as well.'

All she could manage was a weak smile. The food was fine, she just didn't have the appetite for it.

'Last night—'

Her head shot up. 'I'm sorry. The consultant said—'

He brushed his hand through his hair. 'I know what he said, you need time to get over what happened, we should take our time, it's just that—'

'What?'

'Nothing.'

He stood up, pulling her plate towards him, scraping the few bits he'd left onto her mound of food. 'This is all my fault.'

'Yes.' It was important to hurt him; she wanted to see it on his face, needed him to feel it the way she did. There was a pain under her ribs, filling her mind, making her clench and unclench her fists, the muscles in her leg on fire. He was right. This was all his fault.

He shook his head and left the room.

She stood up, snatching up the plates from the table and scraping hers into the bin, before yanking open the dishwasher door, all the time listening for the sound of his footsteps coming back into the room. But the only noise was the crash of crockery being slammed into the dishwasher, and the howl trapped inside her, roaring in her head.

She was wiping the sides down, wringing the cloth out, when he came into the kitchen.

Her need to look at him, see the face she knew deep down she loved, consumed her, and yet she ignored him. He would have to make the first move.

'Pet?'

She carried on wiping, her arm moving in ever wider arcs, scrubbing, her other hand spraying, spritzing. The acrid tang of bleach filled the air.

'Pet. Pet?'

The hob was gleaming before she turned to him. 'What?'

And then she saw it. The bag she'd bought him for his birthday last year. A soft leather holdall for all the business trips he was having to make.

'No,' she said. 'No.'

'I'm going to Jacko's. Just for a bit. We need some space. To get over things. We haven't been the same since we lost the baby.'

'No.' Her leg jumped, pulsed with anger. 'No.'

She ran towards the kitchen door to block his exit but he was too quick for her, his hand reaching for the bag, socked feet skidding on the floor.

His shoes. He had to put on his shoes. In the hallway she grabbed at his arm but he shook her off. 'Petra, no.'

But she reached for him again. She couldn't let him leave her. Wouldn't. 'I'm sorry. I'm sorry. It isn't your fault. It isn't.'

He turned to her, a sad look on his face. She'd done it. That was all it took: those two words to win him over. He pulled her towards him, put those strong arms

281

around her. She let herself be held, pushed her face into the softness of his shirt, breathing him in, listening to the beat of his heart.

And then his hands were on her shoulders, his face tilted towards hers. 'We have to move on from what happened, Pet. You have to move on. We can't keep using it as an excuse.'

She pushed him away. 'An excuse? How can you call our baby an excuse?'

He bent down, his fingers fumbling with the laces of his shoes. 'I didn't mean that.'

She began to cry. The tears she thought would never come, that she'd been holding for so long, started to stream down her face. 'Don't leave me, Sam. Don't leave me. I will get pregnant. It will happen. It will.'

He stood up, took her in his arms again. And this time she squeezed him with everything she had in her. 'I'm not leaving. It's just a bit of space. We both need it.' A kiss on the top of her head and then he was gone, striding to his car, opening the door, flinging the holdall onto the back seat.

For once, her leg didn't jerk, her voice wouldn't come. But then, as the engine roared into life, she rushed towards the car, her hand touching the boot, fleetingly, before the car moved, before Sam moved away from her.

Jude pushed his nose into her leg. Bending down, pulling him towards her, she put her face to his fur, her words tumbling over themselves. 'Sam. No. No. Please. Sam.' And suddenly Jude was tugging away from her, as if he'd heard what she'd said, as if he, too, didn't want Sam to go. He bounded across the lawn, yapping, tried to jump up at the car. '*Jude.*' The scream was locked in her head. As the car swung round to the right, the wheels hit his thin body, knocking him to the floor.

'No. Sam!' He couldn't have seen what he'd done. He couldn't have, or he would have stopped.

She ran along the driveway, skidded onto her knees, leaning over Jude. But it was too late. Lifting her head, she saw her husband's car, wondered whether its speed showed the rush he was in to get away from her or his desire to get to where he was going. She put her head on the hot tarmac, next to Jude's, and wished she could howl like Jude had just done, David Kingfisher's words about killing the dog coming back to haunt her.

CHAPTER 30

Silly cow, leaving the door unlocked. No one around apart from a yowling cat. I glance up before I go in, expecting to see the dark sky above pinpricked with the stars of my childhood, but there is nothing, just blackness.

Inside is dark, too. But no need for the torch, I know this place intimately; its rooms are etched onto my memory. I creep along the hallway and then realise what I'm doing. I'm David Kingfisher. David Kingfisher doesn't creep. And anyway, why bother? She's dead to the world – I can hear her snoring from here.

The bedroom door is open wide, the curtains hanging off the rail, drawn to haphazardly.

She disgusts me. Always did. A whining, snivelling child that became a whining, snivelling adult. I can't call her a woman. A woman wouldn't be lying there like that, waiting for what was to come.

The laptop. I must remember to take it. Dirty bitch. What secrets does she have on there? What lies? She thinks she'll catch me out with it. Thinks she has me sussed.

I mustn't forget the laptop.

A laugh starts to bubble up inside me. What's taken her so long? She never did have a brain. Slow. That's what they called her. Slow. And so, when she made the accusations, when she told what she thought she'd seen, no one believed her. Slow. Stupid. Stupid girl. Stupid woman.

Like most women. So eager to please, flatter, to get laid, they don't use that grey matter in their head. They so want to believe in the fairy tale, that their prince will come, that someone will take them away from their mundane lives, from themselves. They deny it, of course. They're independent. Survivors. They don't need a man. That's why the internet dating sites are full of them, pouting and preening, tanned and false nails, doe-eyed and desperate. They all want a man. Any man. And they'll do whatever it takes to get him. Money. Nude photos. Nothing will stand in their way. A wife? A wife is the least of their worries. One flick of the hair, a parting of the legs, and they know he'll never resist. That he'll be working late, or away on a conference, or out for a drink with his mates. No, nothing will stop them. Not even the fact that the man they've fallen in love with doesn't exist.

I flick on my torch, angle it away from her eyes. Wait for her eyelids to flicker. Nothing. Just a loud snore. She's like a pig. No, not *like* one. She is one.

I open my pocket and take it out. The syringe is so

light in my hand that for a second I think it's not going to do the job I need it to do. I shake the thought away; of course it is. I was always ready for this, wasn't I? I have it down to a tee.

And yet I pause. There's a glass of Coke on the side, dark brown, the bubbles long gone. I could pinch her nose, open her mouth, watch her gasping, struggling for breath. Watch her lungs filling, that body convulsing.

No. This time I will hold back. I am so close to the final outcome that nothing can mess it up. I will do as I planned.

I allow myself one small gesture though, something to redeem her soul. I dip my finger into the glass and mark a cross with the sticky sweet liquid onto her creased forehead.

And then I take her arm, pinch together her flesh and stick the needle in, pushing the plunger down, waiting, waiting, until she snores no more.

CHAPTER 31

Three days later

'What are you doing here?'

A blush spread across Anna's cheeks. She went over to the classroom window, tried to turn the handle to push it open but it was locked. The room was stifling; the sweat of hormone-filled teenagers still hung in the air, despite their two weeks' absence.

But now the room was filled with another smell: a sharp tang of cheap deodorant.

'The courier was at the gate.' Tyler held a box in his hand. 'I was just passing.'

She looked at him, looked at the package. How could he just be passing? He lived on the other side of town. Was he following her? The heat continued to rise in her cheeks. She couldn't carry on giving him private lessons. Wouldn't. She must find some excuse to give Benson.

'It's for you.' He held out the box. She took it from

him, trying not to notice the swell of his muscles under his T-shirt.

'Aren't you going to open it?'

It would be some books she'd ordered and forgotten about. Box files perhaps. She'd asked Jenny who organised the stationery to make sure she had some for the new school year – perhaps they'd been sent directly to her. She put the parcel down on her desk.

'You shouldn't be on school premises.' It was hardly a gracious way of saying thank you, but she didn't want him here, near her.

She picked up the world map she'd found in the pound shop and clambered onto a chair.

'My mate was giving me a driving lesson. I saw your car. Do you need a hand?'

'I'm fine, thanks. You get on. You'll be stuck in here soon and then dying to get out.'

She didn't look down but she could sense Tyler near her. Why had she worn shorts? His gaze was sure to be in line with her crotch. She so wanted to say she was okay, that she had it, but embarrassment made her jump down and drop the poster onto the table.

Lifting it up, he pushed its edges to the wall, his height letting him reach the Blu Tack she'd already stuck there. The sun had bleached his sandy hair, covering it with streaks of gold. A smile lit his face as he turned to her.

She tried again: 'You shouldn't be on school premises.'

Tyler shrugged, perched on a desk. 'No one's going to tell, are they?'

Her mouth opened but no words came out. A trickle of sweat dripped between her breasts.

Tyler fancied her. It was as plain as the freckles on his face. When she thought back, he'd made it obvious from the start: his concern when they'd been on the university visit, how he'd waited behind for her when all the other students had filed away after Robbo. She'd known it and had chosen to ignore it, thinking it was a crush, an adolescent fantasy.

Twenty years, that was the age gap. She should have been appalled and yet she was flattered, and at the same time horrified she felt that way. What was wrong with her?

'Do you want that one putting up too?' He pointed at a poster lying on her desk.

'No, I can manage it.' And to show she could, she whipped the poster off the table and took it to the back of the room.

'Won't you need this?' He came up behind her, handed her the Blu Tack. His fingers touched hers. Soft, unblemished by work. She jumped at the feel of them, of him.

'Anna.'

He stepped towards her.

She tried to move back but the wall was behind her. He put his hand under her chin, lifted her face to his.

Incredible blue eyes stared at her. Into her.

'What are you doing?' The words, so strong in her head, came out as a whisper.

He laughed. Not an embarrassed laugh, as if he'd been caught doing something he shouldn't, but rather a laugh of amusement. Was this all just a game to him?

'Come on,' he said. 'Don't tell me you don't feel it too.'

Where had he got these words? They were the adult clichés of TV dramas, of bonkbuster novels, words that normal people didn't say.

'I don't know what you're talking about.' This time her voice came out louder. 'You'd better go.'

His hand was on her arm. She tried to shrug him off but he was too strong for her, pulling her towards him, his hand on the back of her head, his lips moving towards hers.

'No.' She pushed him away with such force he banged into a chair, sending it toppling.

The amused expression on his face had disappeared. 'But I thought… that night—'

That night? And then it came back to her. He had tried to kiss her in the pub beer garden and she had let him. Just for a second. But a second too long.

'I was drunk. It was nothing.'

'Nothing? How can you say that? It was everything.'

Was it? She tried to remember. She had pushed him away, of that she was sure. But after? A man had been in her bed. Had it been him? She started to shake. Was that what he was saying? That it was him? Please, God, no.

'Anna.'

'Stop calling me that.'

He swiped at a chair, pushing it over. 'You can't do this.' He was still a child, petulant, needy.

Should she ask him? Should she admit she couldn't remember? No, that would only make it worse.

'I was drunk. I'm sorry. Just go.'

As he righted the chair, she allowed herself to breathe out a fraction. It would be all right. He would go. She would pretend this hadn't happened. Would tell herself it hadn't. She had been so stupid. If anyone found out…

Instead of leaving, he sat down on the chair. 'Are you sure?'

'What? Yes.' She returned to the front of the classroom, started to gather her things.

'I don't think it would go down well with old Benson.'

She stopped moving. Her mind stilled. The air in the room was thick, cloying. There was hardly enough to fill her lungs.

'What you did. Isn't that a sackable offence?'

You wouldn't, she wanted to say. But she could tell by the look on his face he would.

'I love you.' The words came flying at her across the room. 'I love you, Anna.'

This time it was she who laughed, at the absurdity of what he was saying. 'Love. This isn't *love*. This is some silly crush. I'm twenty years older than you. You need someone young, a girl your own age. You're going off to uni next year—'

'I'll stay here. With you.'

'Tyler, I'm with someone.'

'You're not. Don't lie.' He stood up. 'A one-night stand? That means nothing.'

What? Had he been watching her? Was it him she'd

293

seen standing under the lamp post? Was it him who'd sent the message? It couldn't be. And then another thought came to her, one so terrible she had to hold onto the edge of her desk to stop herself from falling: this boy in front of her, could *he* be David?

'You led me on. You told me you loved me.'

'No.' She wouldn't have said those words, no matter how much she'd had to drink.

A car door banged. They both turned, looked out of the window. Richard was getting a box out of his boot.

'You have to go. Now.'

'This isn't the end, Anna.' Yet more words from a drama. 'I won't let you do this to me.'

'Go,' she said, urging him out of the door. 'Go.'

Her eyes scanned the room. All done. It was a nice room, large, windows on both sides, but she'd never felt settled there. Not really. Posh kids weren't her thing. While they could be as badly behaved and as childish as the kids from the comp, they had an air of arrogance about them, a sense of entitlement, believing life was going to give them everything on a plate. Maybe it would. Maybe that's what she didn't like. They would fall into good universities, good careers, meet good partners, have good children. She'd once thought that would happen for her too. Her career was the only thing that had worked out and even that she could have done better at. She should be head of a school by now, not just a department.

Her chair creaked as she lowered herself into it.

Would she have been happier if she'd made head though? She picked up a pen, twirled it around her fingers. Or would she still feel this empty inside?

Maybe she didn't want to be happy. Had she sabotaged herself, knowing deep down it was wrong to follow Robbo, to try to win him back? Maybe she was addicted to failing, to emptiness; comfort blankets that shrouded the pain of loneliness.

She had messed things up. It would be impossible to stay here, in this town, to work here. Tyler could kick off at any moment, tell his friends: text messages, social media, spreading until everyone heard what she'd done. She would lose her job, be banned from teaching. Her fingers stopped twirling the pen. She might even go to prison. And the photos. If David made those photos public... It didn't bear thinking about. She would drive out to Bickley, catch Elaine unawares, fight her for that bloody laptop if she had to.

The pen fell from her grasp and rolled onto the desk, butting up against the parcel Tyler had dropped off. She pulled it towards her. Her name was written in felt-tip, a childish scrawl not a typed label – unusual for a stationery delivery.

The wrapping came off easily, revealing a mass of bubble wrap. She resisted the urge to pop the bubbles, pushing the plastic aside, letting it float to the floor.

She stared at the black underside of a laptop. Hers had been new back in January. This was obviously for someone else. There had been a mix-up. She turned it over. It slipped from her fingers, clattering onto the desk. Or had she thrown it down? Wiping her hands on her skirt, she looked at what lay in front of her. No, it couldn't be. She blinked and stood up. Fresh air. That's what she needed. Everything was getting to her. Tyler had started it off. She was imagining things, that was all.

She picked up her bag, but her eyes kept sliding back to her desk.

Pink sparkly stickers, butterflies, fairies had been stuck to the lid in a haphazard fashion. She'd seen this before.

Why had Elaine sent her her laptop?

She hadn't wanted to let it go when they'd visited her, clutching it with fat hands to her stomach. Why would she send it?

The heat in the room was stifling. Anna tried to push back her fringe but it was plastered to her forehead.

She lifted the lid.

Her finger hovered over the power button. She didn't need to switch it on, she guessed what she would find, and yet she pressed down, needing to know for sure.

There was no password. Just a single folder that said, *Open me*. What was this? Yet another game?

She selected the folder. Five Jpegs. Images. Ones that were etched in her memory, photos she didn't need to see again, and yet she still clicked on them, opened them up.

It was her. Her lips. Her buttocks. Fingers teasing a nipple. Legs wide open.

'Fancy a drink?'

'What?' Anna slammed down the laptop lid. Richard, wearing a smug grin and raised eyebrows, was leaning against the door jamb.

'You look like you've seen a ghost. Sorry, shouldn't have crept up on you like that.'

'No.' Anna could hardly get the word out. She glanced at the laptop. Denise had been right. It wasn't Tyler. Elaine had done this. How dare she? That fat, monstrous lump who preyed on people. Anna would go to the police, to hell if Denise and Petra didn't like it. She would tell them everything, tell them that this sick pervert of a woman was insane, needed locking up.

But then it would all come out. Be in the papers perhaps. People would know. And she couldn't risk that. No, far better to go back to Bickley, confront this vile excuse for a woman, have it out with the monster. She wasn't afraid of her, after all; how could you be afraid of someone who couldn't drag themselves out of bed? No, Elaine's body didn't scare her. But, her mind, this sick mind that had led them on, that had pretended to be a man? Perhaps she should be afraid of someone with a mind like that.

'So, do you want that drink? Reckon we deserve one.' Richard had moved from the door and was wandering around the room. 'You've done a great job. I could have given you a hand. You've got my number, haven't you?'

'I—' She'd been about to say that Tyler had helped her. She clamped her mouth shut, bit down hard on her lip when he said:

'I bumped into Tyler James on the way in. He hasn't

297

been bothering you, has he? Think he's got a bit of a crush on you. Can't say I blame him though.' He winked at her.

Anna stood up, picked the laptop up and pushed it into her bag. She didn't care what Richard thought. She just had to get out of the classroom. Had to decide what to do.

'Sorry, I have to go.'

'You can't keep running off like this, you know.'

'I have things to do.'

Suddenly he was standing beside her. 'Don't you think we have unfinished business, sweetheart?'

She could smell the coffee on his breath, see a dark line of sweat around the collar of his polo shirt.

He moved away from her and sat on the edge of the desk. 'That night in The Vaults? I know you were drunk but, come on, you weren't that drunk. I'd be mightily offended if you were. Doesn't do much for the old ego, does it?'

Anna picked up her bag. 'I have to go.' Was it him? Had he been the one she'd taken home to her bed? Acid shot into her throat. That would almost be worse than it having been Tyler. She wouldn't have sunk so low, would she? Even if she had been drunk.

'I think Tyler was a bit miffed that night.' He laughed, a snort shooting out from his nose. 'As if he stood a chance. I did see you out in the beer garden with him though. Seemed quite cosy. Naughty Miss Farrow.'

'He wanted some advice.' The words sounded lame. 'He's not sure which uni to apply for.'

He laughed again. 'I can't see Benson falling for that one. We had a chap here once who was giving a year ten girl "advice". Someone should have given him some.'

Anna hoisted her bag onto her shoulder.

'Knocked her up, didn't he? That's taking advice a bit too far, don't you think?'

She made to move past him but Richard stood up, blocking her way. 'So, how about that drink?'

The room seemed to close in on her. A high-pitched buzzing started in her ears. She had to get out of here. Her stomach lurched. Her mouth watered. She was going to vomit.

'Anna?'

'Go to hell, Richard,' she said, pushing past him, the laptop banging into him as she ran from the room.

CHAPTER 32

Denise took a gulp of wine. And then another. A bigger gulp. It felt good. As she lifted the glass to her lips again, she tried to put out of her mind what had happened the last time she'd had a drink. How could she have been so stupid? She set down the glass and upended a bag of nuts into her mouth. She wouldn't think about Laurence now. She wouldn't let him spoil her evening. And, anyway, hopefully that business was over. She hadn't seen him since the night he'd banged his head. It had been his fault. If he hadn't lunged at her, then none of it would have happened. And yet a small part of her was still worrying that he was lying somewhere in a ditch, passed out, unconscious. Dead even. At least she'd checked all around her garden, searching for his light tan slip-ons poking out from under a hedge. But there was nothing.

Mother had been livid, of course. Not at what he'd tried to do – no, Denise would never tell her about that – but at the fact they hadn't seen hide nor hair of him since that night.

She blamed Denise, of course. 'You must have driven him away. Who would want to come around here with that miserable face staring at them? Jealousy. That's what it is. You couldn't have him so you didn't want me to have him either.'

Denise had shaken her head and left the room. But on the landing, her feet had stopped moving. She'd looked up at the fringed dusky pink lampshade that had hung there for as long as she could remember, before turning around and retracing her steps.

'What now?' Mother shot the words at her, not shifting her eyes from the flickering TV screen. 'Spit it out then.'

She drew a breath so deep she felt as if her lungs would burst. And then the words flew out of her in a torrent: 'Maybe he was sick of *you*, Mother. Have you thought about that? Maybe he was sick of your vile, sneering comments, the way you suck all the joy out of people, dragging everyone down into this black pit of your own misery. Maybe that's why he doesn't come around any longer, eh?'

Denise hadn't stopped to see Mother's face. On shaky legs, she left the bedroom, slamming the door behind her.

Denise downed the last of her drink. Finally, after all these years of caring for Mother, of having it all thrown back in her face, she'd told her what she thought of her. Relief washed over her. Happiness. And yet there was still a sliver of fear hiding underneath the joy and bravado.

302

Denise picked up the bag of nuts and tipped them into her mouth again, pushing the feeling away. It didn't matter what Mother said to her, she wouldn't stand for it. And, what's more, she would see about putting her in a home. She would write a list tomorrow of what she needed to do, a plan. She took a large swig of her drink. No, no list, no plan, she would just do it. A care home. Somewhere where someone else could deal with her.

The man at the table opposite scowled at her and stood up, pushing his newspaper under his arm before picking up his pint and stalking off. What was wrong with him? And then she realised what had probably scared him off: she'd been grinning like a Cheshire cat. And why not? The world had suddenly opened up to her. With Mother gone she could finally go and start her own life. She would get herself an accounts job in an office, make friends. She'd find herself someone like Ian, someone she could love and who would love her back. She didn't need a man but she wanted one. This was the next chapter in her life.

And it was all thanks to the emails she and Petra had sent to David. Thank God the threats had been enough. The money had been wired to her the next day and was now back in the charity's bank account. She would put the whole thing behind her. She needed to. The words David had written in his last message continued to hover at the edge of her mind: Forget me or you'll be sorry.

Warmth flashed across her face as she filled her glass. She looked around her. Was he here now, watching her?

Was that him sitting on his own, pretending to read the paper? Or what about the man by the bar, the one who had been nursing a half ever since she'd arrived? She took a deep breath. Of course not. And, anyway, they weren't even sure that David was a man. But what did it matter anyway? David Kingfisher was a fraudster, that was all. A fraudster who hadn't had the bottle to go through with it when she'd mentioned the police. She had nothing to worry about. Nothing mattered now except moving on.

'I got a bottle. I thought we might need it,' Anna said, her gaze flicking towards the half-empty bottle on the table. 'See you've already started then.'

'I've had a good day.'

'I haven't.' Anna scowled and sat down.

Denise had told herself that, in her new life, there would be no more caring about people when they obviously didn't care about her.

'Oh, why's that?' she asked, instead of *can I do anything to help?*

'Let's wait for Petra.' Anna unscrewed the bottle. 'I don't want to have to tell it twice.' She filled her own glass and pushed the bottle towards Denise. 'You think they'd give you an ice bucket, wouldn't you? Couldn't we have met somewhere else? The Vaults is such a dump.'

'I think it's lovely. It's better than Wetherspoons.'

Anna rolled her eyes.

'Ah, here she is.' From across the room, Denise spied Petra weaving in and out of the crowd of people.

'I can't be long.' Petra pulled over a stool and perched on it.

Denise looked at her friend, at the dark circles under puffy eyes. All this David Kingfisher business had taken its toll on her. She reached over, patted her arm. 'Late surgery?'

Petra nodded.

'Here, I got you a glass of tonic water. No ice.' Denise said.

Anna held the bottle of wine out to Petra. 'You might need something stronger after you've heard what I've got to say.'

Whatever it was, it didn't seem like it would be good news. Denise had the sudden urge to put her hands over her ears; she didn't want anything bringing her down today.

Anna took a deep breath. She seemed to be enjoying dragging the moment out. 'I know who David Kingfisher is.'

This time Denise's hands did move towards her ears. She didn't want to know. She was done with it. She had the money back. Enough was enough.

Petra gently grabbed hold of the elbow nearest to her and pushed Denise's arm down, keeping her hand there. Denise took in the square nails, felt the coldness of her skin, wanted to cover the fingers with her own. This had been a terrible situation, just awful, but one good thing had come of it: she'd made a friend for life.

'I think we should hear what she has to say,' Petra said.

'I don't—'

But it was too late, the words were already flowing out of Anna's mouth. 'It's Elaine.'

The silence stretched between them, tempered by the clink of glasses, chatter, laughter, tinny music from a far-off speaker.

'Are you sure?'

Anna sighed. Really, how thick were these two? She didn't want to go over the story again. 'She sent me her laptop.'

'Are you sure it was hers?'

'Pink.' She counted on her fingers. 'Butterflies, fairies, love hearts.'

'It could be one that looks like hers.'

Anna topped up her glass. What was wrong with Denise? Didn't she want to know who David Kingfisher was? Didn't she want her money back?

'Maybe she just thought you could do with a laptop.' Petra got a bottle of hand sanitiser out of the front pocket of her rucksack, started rubbing it over her hands. 'Recycling maybe? Everyone knows schools are struggling for equipment.'

'But how would she know I was a teacher unless she was David?' Ha, that had shut her up, the sullen little elf.

'Good point.'

'Did you find his profile? Her profile? Did you see the messages?' Denise said.

Anna smoothed down her skirt. How could she convince them without telling them about the photos? It had been bad enough that that monstrosity of a woman had seen them. She shuddered. Why had Elaine wanted them? What had she done when she'd got them? It didn't bear thinking about.

Anna had been sick when she left the classroom earlier. She'd only just made it to the ladies and into a cubicle in time. Not that there was much to throw up. Her toast had been thrown into the bin that morning. Was it a bug or was it pure disgust about what that monster had done?

'So you think it was Mickey who made the calls?'

Anna shrugged. 'I've done a bit of research. You can get these apps on your phone that change your voice. It could have been either of them.'

Denise smiled. 'I really need to get with it. I only joined Facebook a few months ago.'

They were all silent as they remembered the post about David Kingfisher that Denise had put on the site.

'So, did you see the messages?' Petra asked, breaking the silence.

Anna nodded, trying not to shift her gaze, or put her hand to her mouth, both signs she knew were a sure-fire way of showing you were lying. 'All of them.'

Denise glared at her. 'You didn't read my messages, did you?'

'Of course not.'

'Look me in the eye and say it.'

A blush spread across Anna's cheeks. 'I am looking you in the eye.'

'Now I've got my money back the whole world could read them for all I care,' Denise said.

'What?' Anna said. 'What?'

Denise took a long swig of her drink and then leant forward, her breasts nearly falling out of the low-cut top she was wearing. Was that new? Was she updating herself? And she had perfume on. Chanel No. 5, if Anna wasn't mistaken. What was going on? And what was Denise on about?

'We've got our money back.' Denise held her glass aloft. 'Cheers.'

'What?'

Petra clinked glasses with Denise, leant back in her chair. 'We both sent him an email, said we'd go to the police if he didn't transfer the money back.'

'Why didn't you tell me?'

'I thought he hadn't taken any money from you?'

'He hasn't. She hasn't.'

Petra stared at her. 'But he, she, must have had something from you? You were as keen to find him as we were.'

'Yes, come on. What was it?' Denise said.

Anna sighed. Should she tell them? She had the photos back now.

Denise slapped a hand to her mouth. 'Oh, it wasn't photos, was it? You know, naked ones,' she said, whispering the last two words.

Anna swallowed. It was as if she'd read her thoughts.

'You didn't, did you?' Denise took a swig of wine. 'He never asked me for any. The cheek of him. What about you, Pet?'

As Anna waited for Petra to reply, a strange feeling

came over her. Although she knew David Kingfisher wasn't real, that it was all that mad woman Elaine's doing, she still wanted it to just be her who had been asked for the photos.

Petra nodded. 'Sorry,' she said to Denise.

'Well, you kept that quiet.' Denise stuck her nose in the air. 'I could be offended but, now we know who David Kingfisher is, perhaps I'm not.'

Anna took a swig of her drink. 'Aren't you the lucky one.'

'Hang on though. You know what this means? It's the end. She's returned our money. She's sent you the photos. Even the laptop to show she's not going to keep copies. Maybe she's had enough of leading people astray.'

Anna tried to swallow but her mouth was dry. Was Denise right? Was it the end? Elaine had given them their money back and sent her the photos. Had they scared her by going there the other day? Suddenly it all made sense. The photos weren't to threaten her, they were being returned to her. The hard drive as well. This was Elaine's way of telling her she wouldn't copy them. It seemed like Denise and Petra's threat to call in the police had worked. Anna let out a long breath and washed down the acid at the back of her throat with a mouthful of wine. It was going to be all right.

'Denise,' she said. 'I think you're right. I think it's over.'

CHAPTER 33

How stupid can they be? These bitches think they've got it all sussed out, that they know who I am. They don't know me at all, have no idea what it's like to be me. There is a rage inside me, burning my insides, corroding me, working its way up into my brain.

Of course it's all her fault. She's the one who started it. Things were fine, no, more than fine before her. She has filled my head, filled it so it's fit to burst.

I don't want them to know who I am. Things are wrapping themselves up like a neat birthday present. The past and the present are sorting themselves out so that I can think about my future.

They will leave me alone, now they think they have found me. They will go on with their own lives. And yet *her* life will butt up against mine as she wreaks her havoc. I'm sure of that. She just has that air of selfishness, that everything must be about her.

They see me and yet they haven't seen me.

I pick my drink up, drink it so quickly the bubbles

shoot up my nose. I want to do this to her. To see the bubbles coming out of *her* nose. To push her under the water and hold her there, her arms flailing, her body bucking. As I lift her head from the water she will see that I have done her the greatest favour of all: I have cleansed her. I have saved her. She can repent all her sins. In that moment, she will see what she has done and she will beg forgiveness. Will I forgive her? All I know is I will push her back under the water, hold her head while the bubbles rise, until her arms flail no more.

CHAPTER 34

The bus slowed to a stop. Denise weaved her way to the front, gripping onto handrails, the backs of seats. The last time she'd been on a bus, she'd been on her way to meet Petra and Anna for the first time. Had it really been only a few weeks ago? So much had happened in that time. She'd learnt a lot. About trust. Trusting herself. About making herself happy. True, she was still lonely, still had that feeling of incompleteness swishing through her veins. But she also had the sense it was going to be all right. That her life wasn't over and that she didn't just have a sea of nothingness in front of her. There were things she could do to fill the vacuum, the void inside. And if someone came along who she could share her life with, then that would be an added bonus.

Shielding her eyes from the sun, she turned her gaze to the left. It was a good mile walk at least and all uphill. But she needed to do it. That's why she had come here.

She hadn't told the others. They were getting on with their lives. Anna was moving away, going back down south, and Petra didn't seem interested in why Elaine had done this. Denise had tried discussing it with her but Petra had fobbed her off, saying she had to get back to the surgery, and, anyway, they should let it be. They would never know why Elaine had done it. And what did it matter anyway? They had their money back. They should put David Kingfisher behind them. Move on.

'But we'll still be friends, won't we?' Denise had hated the pleading note to her voice, the way her hand shook as she lifted her wine glass to her lips.

'Of course we will,' Petra had said.

Denise couldn't move on. All night she had lain awake, going over it in her mind. What made someone do that? Pushed a person to behave like that, to lie and cheat? Untangling herself from the thin sheet, she realised she had done the same. And then it came to her. Elaine was lonely, just like she was. Had lost two people, just like she had. Was eating herself to death. Denise ignored the decision she'd made earlier: that she would only think of herself from now on, only help herself. In another life, she could have been Elaine. She had to help her, show her there was a way forward. And, more than that, forgiveness was important. Hadn't Father drummed that into her every Sunday when they'd stood in church? She had to forgive Mother, and herself. But she had to start with Elaine.

* * *

'Helloo.'

The front door was ajar but Denise didn't like to push it open. Unlike last time, there was only silence, no thumping music. Elaine must be able to hear her. Unless she was out? But then why would the door be open?

'Hello,' she shouted again. 'Hello.'

Nothing. Perhaps she was asleep. Or engrossed in messaging her friends. Denise shuddered and stepped into the hallway.

'Hello.' She picked her way through the detritus of a forgotten family's life. 'It's only me. Denise.'

No answer.

She poked her head into the kitchen. Flies buzzed around dirty dishes, the noise almost deafening. She pulled the door to behind her. She would suggest Elaine got a cleaner in. If things were a bit tidier, a bit brighter, maybe she'd have some motivation to get out of bed. It was a lovely house, after all. Walking past the living room, ignoring the clutter piled on the floor, on sofas, strewn across a sideboard, she concentrated on the view through the patio doors: rolling hills, sheep grazing in the distance.

This was the sort of house she and Ian had dreamt about. They were both keen walkers, liked getting out into the fresh air, enjoyed their own company. They had visited houses like this, made plans, talked about the furniture they might buy. Denise stared around the room. She would put a leather sofa to one side of the open fire, a tartan-clad one to the other, a huge oak coffee table between them. There would be thick brocade curtains, candles, pictures of landscapes, photos of her and Ian, holding each other close.

She swallowed. What was she doing? The past was the past. There was no Ian. But there might be someone else. And there might be another house. She wouldn't give up on her dreams, and she wouldn't settle for anything less. She would *raise her expectations* and keep raising them until she was happy.

The corridor in front of her was dark. 'Hello,' she tried again, this time her voice quieter. Elaine was in the house; she could feel a presence. Someone was there, waiting for her.

She straightened herself up. She would not be scared. After all, she'd done nothing wrong. This was just another one of Elaine's games. Her twisted ways of getting at people. Why did she do it? That's what she was here to find out.

The bedroom door was closed. Denise pushed her hair back, put her ear to it. A noise came from within. But that wasn't Elaine, for surely a person couldn't make that noise? She took a step back, the beat of her heart thudding in her ears. It reminded her of a cat, like the cat Denise had had as a girl. The ginger Tom, Clementine, that she'd held every time she heard the shouting coming from downstairs. The sound from Elaine's room reminded her of Clementine the day she'd got home and he had been hanging from the handle of her bedroom door, his collar caught, his legs cycling wildly, his eyes bulging. Yowling. It had been too late, but she had still unhooked him, gathered him in her arms. She'd run down to the living room where Mother sat, staring out of the window, an ashtray full of butt ends on the arm of the chair, while the cat's warmth seeped out of him and into Denise. 'Didn't you hear him?' she had repeated over and over. But Mother had just shrugged, while shaking another cigarette out of the packet. 'Get it out of here. It stinks.'

The yowling from behind Elaine's bedroom door had grown louder.

Denise grasped the door handle and pushed. There was no weight to it, and the door flung wide open.

The breath she'd been holding escaped her in a whoosh. It wasn't a cat. It was a man. Or was it a boy? His shoulders were thin, his unkempt hair fighting against the tight edges of a baseball cap. He was kneeling on the floor next to the bed, his hands gripping Elaine's arm, his head pushed into the duvet, his shoulders heaving up and down. The yowling was coming from him.

Denise dragged her gaze away from the man to Elaine. What was going on? And then she saw what she'd probably known all along, the whisper that had been floating around the edge of her mind since she'd heard the sound: Elaine was dead.

Wide-open eyes, bulbous, glassy, stared at the ceiling as if she were transfixed by something there. Her skin had lost its rough redness, been replaced by a grey creamy sheen. Her mouth was gaping, her white-coated tongue flopping out to one side.

Denise yelped. The man stopped his keening, turned his head slowly to one side.

'Who are yer?' He jumped up so quickly Denise didn't have time to step back. 'Yer've done this,' he hissed, raising his fist. 'She's dead.'

'Me? No.' Denise flattened herself against the wall as he towered over her, the sour smell emanating from him making her breathe through her mouth.

He stepped back. Looked her up and down. 'Yer were here before. I seen yer.'

'Yes, that's right.' Her common sense suddenly kicked in: 'It's Mickey, isn't it? Have you called for an ambulance?' She made herself move towards the body, her feet taking one step in front of the other until she was standing by the bed.

'An ambulance? She's dead.'

Denise put her hands to the fat of Elaine's wrist, pushing down, trying to find a pulse. There wasn't one.

'You need to call someone. The police then.'

'No. No police. They'll think it was me.' He slumped onto the edge of the bed, took his cap off, rubbed at his hair and then put it back on. 'They always think it's me.'

'You? But it was probably just a heart attack. A stroke even. In her condition...' Her words tailed away.

Denise moved away from Elaine. She had to get away from here. If the police came, and surely they would, they would ask her what she was doing here, and then the whole story about David Kingfisher would come out. Explanations would be demanded. The money was back in the charity's account but she would probably still be prosecuted. She wouldn't get away with it. She stepped towards the door.

'Yer know, don't yer?'

Denise stopped. 'Know?'

'Who done this.' Mickey picked up Elaine's hand, started stroking it slowly.

Sweat dripped down Denise's back. What was he talking about? Was he simple? 'It was probably a heart attack, wasn't it?'

Mickey shook his head. 'No. Just like Davy and Susie were no accidents. Me and Elaine worked it out, you see. She was going to go to the police but I said no, what use is that, yer need to sort this out yerself. And now look.'

'What? What are you talking about?'

Mickey placed Elaine's hand gently back down onto the filthy eiderdown and stood up, moving to the bedside cabinet, his hands scrabbling through some photos until he found the one he wanted.

'Look.' He thrust a Polaroid snap at Denise.

Taking it from him, she held it under the light of the lamp.

'Look,' he said again. 'Standing between Davy and Susie.' He jabbed his finger at the photo. 'This is who done this.'

Denise closed her eyes and opened them slowly, hoping she was mistaken, that the image in front of her was merely a figment of her imagination, conjured up by the mess she'd walked into. But the face in the photo was unmistakeable. She knew exactly who it was.

CHAPTER 35

Petra put the shopping bags into the boot of the car. She fished the list out of her jeans pocket and scanned down it, ticking the items off in her head. Just one more thing to get. She walked over to a bin, scrunched the piece of paper into a ball and dropped it in.

The town centre was busy. She'd spotted her boss, Harry, but had managed to avoid him – he would know something was up with her, he was perceptive like that. She looked around. Why were people out here in this heat? Scorching sun had been replaced by a humid fug. Petra swallowed. It was so close, she could hardly breathe. She took a bottle of water out of her rucksack, flipped back the lid, rubbed at the top with a tissue and put it to her lips.

'I thought it was you. What have you done to your hair?' A heavy hand on her shoulder made her jump, her hand jerk, the bottle hitting her front teeth, water splashing down her T-shirt.

'Wet T-shirt competition. Bring it on.' Jacko laughed.

Petra put the top back on the bottle without taking a drink and scowled at him.

'Is that glare for the water,' he said, nodding down at her chest, 'or because I offered your husband a bed?'

'Both.' She started to move away from him. There wasn't time to talk to Jacko, even if she wanted to, which she didn't. His smugness had always irritated her, now even more so. Sam confided in him, she knew that. The thought of them discussing her marriage, her, caused goose bumps to sprinkle along her arms, despite the heat.

'Hey.' He caught hold of her arm. 'He's my brother.'

She shrugged him off but he took her by the elbow, steering her into a narrow passageway between two shops. 'You look like crap.'

'Always the charmer, hey, Jacko?'

'Why did you cut your hair?'

'What's it to you?'

'It doesn't suit you,' he said.

She scowled at him again.

'Just say it as it is, don't I?'

She started to turn away but he put his arm out to stop her. 'Which is why I'm saying it'll all be fine, this falling-out, whatever it is, I'm sure it'll be fine. It's been tough for the two of you, with the baby and all. Everyone needs space now and again.'

'Is that what you call leaving someone? Space?'

'He loves you, you know that.'

Tears welled at the back of her throat. What was wrong with her these days? She never used to be so bloody emotional. She swallowed, pushing them down. Was Jacko right? Did Sam love her? Would he come back? He had to.

'I'm meeting him at twelve in the square. Why don't you come along, pretend it's a coincidence bumping into him? I can then slope off and you two can have a chat. What do you say?'

Petra didn't say anything. That smile might melt many a woman's heart, but not hers. She crossed her arms tightly across her chest and walked away.

'So, have you decided?'

'The violet, I think.'

'Good choice.'

The girl with orange make-up and spiky false eyelashes sat down opposite her. Anna laid her hands on the rest in front of her and closed her eyes.

'Long week?'

She sighed. It had been. The headmaster hadn't been happy when she'd handed in her notice. 'You've rather left us in the lurch,' he'd said.

'It's my father, he's not well,' she'd replied. Benson wasn't to know she wouldn't have gone to help her father if he wasn't well, even if he were dying; she wasn't one to forgive and forget. He had never stood up to their stepmother, not even when she'd thrashed their legs with a wooden ruler or pushed their heads under the running tap in the sink. 'I have to go back to Exeter,' she'd told the headmaster. He didn't believe her but she didn't care. She should never have come here; Lisa had been right. She'd had nothing but trouble since moving here. She still hadn't confided in Lisa about what had really happened with David. She'd just said she'd decided he wasn't the man for her. She would tell her all about it one day, but not now.

'They say it's going to pee it down later.'

'What?' Anna opened her eyes.

The girl, a pink tongue sticking out of the corner of her mouth, didn't look up. 'Torrential rain. Floods. The lot. Still, we can't complain, can we? After the summer we've had.'

Anna murmured a 'Yes' and glanced out of the window. Siobhan was crossing the square, a hessian bag swinging from her hand. Was she heading this way? Anna hoped she hadn't spotted her; she'd managed to avoid her so far during the summer holidays, despite Siobhan texting her every other day, begging to meet up. But, no, as she watched, she saw the other woman wave at someone. Anna leant as far as she could to the side without moving the hand that was being worked on. It was no use. She couldn't see who Siobhan was meeting. Anyway, what did she care?

The sky was still blue but there was a haze to it that hadn't been there before. And it was so humid. Here, inside the nail salon, it was ice cold, the hum of the air-conditioning unit competing with the blare of the radio, but out there it was like wading through water. Water. She thought of Elaine. Of the brother and sister she'd lost. Drowned. Both of them. No wonder Elaine couldn't accept it as a coincidence. How could that happen? And how could someone be so unlucky as to lose two people like that? No wonder it had warped her mind, turned her into a twisted person, made her do what she'd done.

Anna stared across the town square. There was no market today and yet the centre of town was packed: people standing by the fountain, shrieking toddlers being dipped into it, their waists gripped tightly by their parents, teenage girls in crop tops and barely-there shorts, lads with their T-shirts tied around their waists pretending not to notice them, pensioners holding hands and licking at cornets. And then, past the throngs of people, she saw them.

'Hey, what are you doing?'

Anna stood up so fast the technician dropped the bottle of nail varnish she was dipping her brush into.

'Sorry, sorry.' She grabbed her bag, not caring she was smudging the nails of her right hand on the leather strap, and ran from the salon.

Denise admired the dress in the mirror, twirling this way and that.

'You look gorgeous. It could have been made for you.'

The shop assistant was right, the dress was gorgeous.

'Do you think it's a bit tight?' She twirled around so the woman could see her bottom.

'No, not at all. Perfect.'

'I tried the size fourteen but that was too big. Do they make them a bit bigger, this range?'

The woman smiled, shook her head. 'If anything, they're a bit on the smaller side.'

'Oh.' Denise had weighed herself that morning. Despite the lack of sleep, the missed meals here and there, she hadn't lost any weight. 'I'll take it.'

She glanced at her watch. Five to twelve. The bus was at quarter past. She really needed to learn to drive. Yes, that was the first thing she would do when she got a proper job. Learn to drive and then buy herself a little car, nothing flash.

With her dress carefully wrapped, she walked quickly through the department store. What had happened yesterday had kept her awake most of the night. She'd sat on the bus back from Bickley, terrified. Had anyone seen her going into the house? Would Mickey call the police? Tell them she'd been there? Would he show them the photo? She'd thought about the photo all the way back on the bus. An hour and a half to think, to wonder what it all meant. If it meant anything at all. If it had been who she thought it was. And yet, deep down, there was no doubt at all – she'd recognise those eyes anywhere. But there had to be an explanation for all of it, there had to be. None of it made any sense.

Denise stepped out of the chill of the department store into the dripping humidity of the street. She pushed the thoughts of what had happened to the back of her mind. She had something else to sort out first before she dealt with that. The care home she'd found online was ten miles out of town. It would mean a bus ride into town and then changing to catch another bus when she made her weekly visit. Until she got her car, of course.

A man walked out of the bank, head down, pushing fat notes into an equally fat wallet.

'Sorry,' Denise said, her posh designer carrier bag banging into his legs. They both looked up at the same time, both saying, 'You' at the same time.

Laurence. Of all the people she didn't want to see. Not today, not ever again. What would he say if he found out where she was going? Would he care? Would he offer to move in with Mother so she didn't have to go into a home? Where would Denise live then? But of course he wouldn't move in. He'd never had any intention of doing so. He'd made it perfectly clear he only thought of himself. Of himself and what he wanted. She shuddered.

'Denise.'

'Laurence.' She looked at his face, expecting to see a bump, but there were just beads of sweat glistening on his freckled bald head. 'Are you okay?' The words were out of her mouth before she could stop them.

He nodded. 'Despite you trying to kill me.'

'Laurence, I—'

'It doesn't matter, I probably deserved it.' He took a step towards her. 'I am sorry, you know.'

She put her hand to her mouth. She was going to laugh. He was sorry. He thought all he had to do was utter that word and she would forgive him?

'You're laughing at me?' The slightly abashed look on his face darkened. He took a beige handkerchief out of his shorts pocket and wiped his forehead.

She tried to move her mouth into a frown but it refused to give up its grin.

'There's nothing to say, Laurence.'

His brown eyes glinted at her. 'I could say a lot if I wanted to, Denise. A lot.'

She cocked her head to one side.

'Like the charity money.' His eyes swivelled towards the bank and then back to her. 'What do you think I've just been doing? Smart move, changing the password on the online account. I'm still the treasurer though.' He patted the satchel hanging by his side. 'Thought I should avail myself of printed copies of the bank statements before the AGM next week. Now they do make for interesting reading. Very interesting.' He wiped his forehead again, smiled at her. 'Where did you get the money from, Denise? You know I would have given it to you. I'm sure we could have come to some agreement.'

'Tell me, Laurence,' she said, pushing her hands down to her sides to stop them flying up towards his smug face, 'did you ever love Mother?'

The question caught him off guard for a second. 'Of course I did.'

She raised an eyebrow.

'You can't expect me to lead a life like that, though, Denise. I have needs. I know you think I'm old but I have urges like everyone else. Just like you.' He took a step closer to her. 'Don't tell me you didn't enjoy it, darling.' He lunged towards her, putting his hand on the back of her head, planting his lips firmly onto hers before she could close them, sticking his tongue into her mouth, his hand cupping her breast, squeezing hard.

'Get off, get off,' she screamed, trying to push him away.

'What's going on here? Sir, please step back from the lady.'

Laurence let her go and she staggered backwards.

'He assaulted me.'

A policeman had his hand in front of Laurence's chest, warning him to stay back.

'I did no such thing. Just a lovers' tiff, officer.'

'He assaulted me,' Denise said again, not caring that shoppers had stopped, that people were watching.

'Now, now, darling.' Laurence rubbed at the mole on his chin. 'You were enjoying it.'

Tears of anger welled in her eyes. 'He kissed me and touched my breast. We're not together. He's lying. He forced himself on me.'

Laurence rolled his eyes at the policeman, motioned to those people who had stopped to watch. 'Did anyone here see me assault this lady?'

People put their heads down, moved off.

'Come on now, Denise, you kissed me first.'

'I think you'd better come with me, sir.' The officer gestured towards a police car parked on the other side of the high street.

'On what grounds? It's her word against mine.'

The policeman looked up above the portico of the bank to where a camera was trained right on the spot where they were standing. 'I think that might clear things up, don't you, sir?'

Denise wiped at her eyes. She couldn't help feeling a tiny flutter of triumph as the officer took her name and asked her to come down to the station in an hour, before he led a fuming Laurence away.

Petra could feel the anger rising in her. 'When are you coming back?'

She willed Sam to say something, anything, but he just brushed his fingers through his hair, scuffed at the floor with the front of his shoe.

'How's Jude?' he said.

He didn't know. She opened her mouth to tell him, to tell him he'd killed his beloved dog, just like he was killing her.

She closed her mouth, turned, tears blinding her eyes, her leg jerking, propelling her forwards.

She could still hear him calling her as she ran through the crowds of people, as she stopped in an alleyway around the corner to catch her breath, as she wiped away the tears from her eyes, her fist slamming into the brick wall, over and over again.

'Whoa, slow down, miss.'

Tyler and Richard stood in front of her, blocking her path. 'Why didn't you tell me you were leaving? Mum told me.'

'Your mum?'

'She's started seeing Richard.'

Richard smirked.

Anna didn't have time for this but the need to get at him made her open her mouth. 'What about Siobhan?'

Richard shrugged. 'What about her?'

'I thought you and she were an item.'

'Miss Doherty?' Tyler turned to look at him, the scowl she'd come to know creasing his forehead. 'Hey, you're not messing my mum about, are you? Not when things are going so well for her.' He turned back to her, not waiting for an answer. 'She's in remission and the NHS has agreed to give Kai the operation he needs. We don't need to send him to America now.'

'America?' She peered past them to where she'd seen Robbo standing. He'd gone. She scanned the crowds of people but he was nowhere to be seen. Had she conjured him up?

'That's what I needed the money for. That's why I was working in The Vaults. The operation is his only chance, you see.' He must have remembered Richard was standing next to him. 'You're not two-timing my mum, are you?'

'What? No.' Richard scowled at Anna. 'Me and Siobhan were never a thing, it was all in her head. You know what she's like.'

'You weren't going to tell me then?' Tyler said. Anna had thought Tyler such a lovely looking lad and, yes, been flattered by his attentions. But the scowl. It was more than a frown, it etched his whole forehead into a mass of anger that was bubbling under the surface, fighting to get out. Had he told his new best mate,

Richard, about what she'd done? Had Letchy Leeky asked him? It was Richard, after all, who'd hinted he'd seen something in the beer garden. What was going on? Were they plotting something together? Handing her notice in had been the right thing to do; she had to get away from here – things were crowding in on her, threatening to unravel her.

The ground suddenly lurched into view, the people around her slid to one side.

'Hey, Anna. Anna? Are you okay?'

There was a strange buzzing noise in her ears. The laughter, chatter, cries of children, suddenly seemed far away as if she were swimming underwater. Grey dots popped and fizzed in front of her. She reached out for the nearest thing to steady herself: Richard's arm.

'Here, sit down.' He led her to the steps in front of the town hall, only ten feet away, but it seemed like a mile to Anna.

Lowering herself onto the warm stone, she put her head between her knees. What was wrong with her?

'Go and get her some water.' Richard pushed some money at Tyler who darted off to a nearby ice-cream stand.

He sat down on the steps, put his arm around her shoulders. She shrugged him off. 'I'm okay.'

'You don't seem okay.'

Slowly she raised her head, blinked a few times to test her vision. 'I'm fine.' She didn't feel fine though. She looked around the square but, if it had been Robbo, he'd disappeared. Maybe she'd imagined it.

'All this been too much for you, eh?'

She swivelled her gaze to him, so quickly that, for a moment, she felt disorientated again.

'All what?'

'This David Kingfisher business.' He emphasised the last word, drawing it out slowly, a smirk on his face.

'What do you know about—'

'Will Vimto do?' Tyler stood in front of them, holding out a plastic bottle of water. 'Only joking,' he said, but his tone didn't match the words.

After a long slug, she sprinkled some water onto her hand and ran it along the back of her neck.

'Better?' Tyler stood with his back to the sun. The anger was still there, in fact, he seemed furious. 'So, you weren't going to tell us?'

'No, you weren't going to tell us?' Richard echoed. 'Benson told me. The place won't be the same without you. Will you miss us?'

'Miss, will you miss us?'

Anna stood up, slowly. She still felt unsteady but she hadn't the patience for this any longer. 'I couldn't care less if I never saw either of you again,' she said, before striding off as quickly as she could on shaking legs, her eyes searching the crowd for Robbo and his companion.

Don't look, I urge myself, for fear runs through my blood, the hairs on the back of my neck standing to attention. Everything is telling me not to look and yet the need in me to know the truth makes me turn my head.

The pain hits me like a thundering train, making me stagger backwards. I want to drop down onto my knees on the hot tarmac and howl like an injured animal.

The disgusting silly cow. She thinks she can do this to me, out here in the street, where anyone can see? She has no shame. I see what I always knew, everything coming into focus as the pain throbs through me. I try to breathe, gasping at the air, drinking in the suffocating heat.

Get a grip, I tell myself, get a grip. This is no surprise. I've always known what she's like. No shame at all. As the words leave my lips, I realise they are my father's, whispered to me when I saw what he'd done.

I close my eyes and then open them. Look over at them. No, she has no shame at all. And now I see what I must do. The time has come.

I take a few deep breaths. I've thought about it before, of course I have, but it's only been a fantasy, something I've let myself indulge in. That's what I've told myself anyway. Maybe I realised all along it would come to this. Had the idea been there the day I logged on and set up the account? David Kingfisher. I shouldn't have chosen that name. That was my mistake, I see that now. But the name was always there living within me. Perhaps I sensed things would come to this, perhaps I already had it in mind to tie the past and the present together. Even when I was telling myself I was going to let her get away with it, walk away. Forgive and forget. I know a lot about forgiveness, know how the words can flow from your mouth, the idea make sense in your head.

But the anger stays buried inside you, just needing a simple trigger to come rushing out.

She has ripped my life apart, will continue to, if I let her. And I won't. Why should someone take what is mine? My father taught me that. And, as he pushed Mother under the water, the fight completely gone from her, I sort of understood what he meant, why he was doing it. To a six-year-old everything is black and white, good and bad. And Mother was bad.

Keep close what is yours. Don't let people take things from you. I could see why Mother wanted to go, could even see the attraction in that salesman. He made Mother laugh when all we had at home was silence, and he bought her shiny things, a bangle, and a ring that was too big for her and slipped off her finger. It was red-coloured, not a ruby – looking back, I don't think he made that much money – but it shone and sparkled in contrast to the thin gold band my father had given her. And he made her happy, the salesman. I heard them. Often. When my father was in the village, they would go into the spare room. Shrieks and giggles would float down the stairs. I had walked in on my parents having sex once. My father had been lying on top of my mother, shoving. That's the only way I can describe it. Shoving. In silence.

My father was an angry man, an evil man, for sure, but he wasn't stupid. Added to that, he had a pride without limits. And, on top of that, his faith. He had once cleansed me for coveting a Game Boy the cleaner's son had. As my nose had filled with water, as I'd gasped for breath, his thin fingers pushing me under the water, renouncing my sin, I'd promised myself that one day I would buy myself one. I never did. I came to realise it was a sin to covet what your neighbour had.

It was no surprise that when Mother broke the most important commandment of all, he wouldn't let her get away with it. Wouldn't turn a blind eye. Compassion? Kindness? Love? My father's Christian views didn't extend to those virtues. So when I saw him leaning over her in the bath, the veins on the side of his neck like worms burrowing out of his skin, I didn't blink an eye. She was being cleansed, just like I was on a daily basis. Did I know then what he was doing? Should I have stopped him? Although I hated my father with a passion, a lot of his values were mine too. And on that day I learnt another: don't let someone else take what is yours.

CHAPTER 36

'Where have you been? Netty's been gone an hour. Barney needed feeding. I'm parched. Old people can die of dehydration. It's not Netty's job to look after me, you know.'

Denise ignored the cup Mother was holding aloft with her good hand.

'It's not mine either.'

At first Denise thought Mother hadn't heard her. Had she whispered the words, said them in her own head perhaps? But then the cup was flying across the room, whizzing past Denise's left ear.

'You spiteful fat bitch. I'm your mother. After all I've done for you. Too much is it for you? Can't cope. Poor little Denise. No wonder Ivan left you. You're useless. Hopeless. You treat your own mother like this. You should be ashamed, Denise.'

'Ian. His name was Ian.'

Mother grabbed her hand before she had time to move it, her nails digging into exactly the same spot

337

where she had drawn blood before. 'Ian, Ivan. Whatever. He didn't want you, did he?'

The anger ignited in Denise's chest. With her free arm, she swung at the hand that was clamped around hers, knocking it away.

'You hit me.' Shock lit Mother's face, etched the frown lines even deeper.

Denise opened her mouth but the words were stuck in her throat. It was like she was being strangled.

The next words from Mother were quiet. Slow. 'He didn't want you, did he, Denise? Just like your father didn't. Why do you think he left?'

Denise's legs moved her closer towards the bed. She was wrong. Her father had loved her. She lowered her face so she was inches away from the wrinkles, the dry mouth of her mother.

'He left because he didn't want you. You drove him away with your misery. Just as you've done with Laurence.'

'Laurence? How dare you? You took him away from me. Fluttering your eyelashes at him. Don't think I don't know what you've been up to.'

'Nothing. I've been up to nothing.'

'Liar. I've got proof. Meeting up with him. In that rough bar in town. In the town centre. Kissing. Where everyone can see. It's disgusting. He's my fiancé, *mine*. How could you do that to your own mother?'

'What are you on about? I've done nothing.'

'Don't lie. I've had you followed.'

'Followed?' Denise shook her head as if she were hearing things. 'You had me followed? By who?'

'What does it matter?'

'I don't believe you.'

'Ask Netty. She helped me set it up.'

She was lying. Netty wouldn't do that. But then Denise remembered the last time she'd seen her mother's friend, how she'd told Denise to go and get her own life. And there'd been that time when she'd come home to find them looking at her laptop.

'How could you do that to me?' Is this what her life had come to? She could trust no one. Denise straightened up, moved backwards. 'I can't waste another second on you. I've found you a room in a care home. You go next week.'

Denise hesitated as the woman who had manipulated her all these years sank back into her pillows, her mouth slack, the brightness seeping from her eyes.

'You can't do that. I won't go. I won't.'

'Then I will. And you'll have no one to care for you. Your choice.'

Denise picked up the plastic cup that had rolled under the dressing table. 'Tea?' she said as she made for the door. 'I'll put plenty of sugar in it, it's good for shock.'

'I'm sorry.' Tears started to fall from Mother's eyes, her good hand reaching out to Denise. 'I'm sorry, I am.'

Denise glanced at her hand and then turned away from her. Mother wasn't sorry. Mother would never admit what she'd done to her over the years, how she'd eroded her confidence, telling her she was fat, useless, hopeless, telling her lies until she'd believed them herself. Well, no more. She wouldn't believe those lies any longer.

Denise filled the kettle and put it on the hob to boil. Her head was pounding. Was it any wonder, after the twenty-four hours she'd had? Mother had gone mad. That was the only answer to all this. Just as Laurence probably had when he'd been told he was being charged with sexual assault. After three hours waiting around to give a statement, she'd been told that the CCTV footage from the bank confirmed her story.

She was getting things sorted, moving on, moving forwards. Mother, tick. Laurence, tick. She looked around her. The house was in her name. Mother thought she didn't know that but she'd found some papers when she'd been searching for her birth certificate a few years ago. It was the only home she'd ever really known but she would sell it, get rid of the furniture, her stuff, clothes, childhood crap, books, especially the self-help books. She would start afresh somewhere else.

There was only one final thing she had left to do: get what she'd learnt in Bickley out into the open. She shut the door against Mother's screams carrying down the stairs from her bedroom, picked up the phone from its stand and began to dial, rubbing her stinging hand against her skirt as she did so.

CHAPTER 37

Anna almost didn't pick up the phone. She hadn't stopped being sick since she got in. Was it gastroenteritis? Saliva shot into the back of her throat. She wiped her mouth on the back of her hand. 'Hello?'

'I said I didn't want to be disturbed.' Alex sighed as the receptionist told him the caller had said it was urgent, of a personal nature, that it really was a matter of life and death. Probably some patient wanting to get themselves to the top of the list, he thought, as he pressed the button to accept the call.

Laurence was on his third whiskey, a bottle he'd been saving, a special blend bought on a golfing holiday to Ireland. It wasn't sitting well on the three pints he'd downed earlier. He'd never been to Wetherspoons before. But it was the first pub he'd come to after he'd left the police station. The things that bitch had said. She thought she was so clever, but he'd make her pay. He nearly knocked the phone off its stand as he reached for it, its ring piercing his ears, making his headache thump even louder.

The man looked at himself in the mirror. Should he put on a different shirt? It was important he wasn't spotted. Especially by her. He pouted at himself, admiring what he saw. No, the kingfisher blue suited him. As he snipped at his beard, wincing as the point of the scissors nicked his skin, his mobile started to ring.

Sam stood staring at his phone. He should ring her, really he should. Should explain. He lay back on the bed. She had been so mad today, had screamed at him in the street. He'd wanted to laugh. Her anger showed him she still loved him, that he still loved her. His finger hovered over the contacts list just as the phone buzzed into life.

Petra was cleaning the bathroom when the phone rang. She wanted a shower, wanted to wash everything off her that had happened today. But she couldn't get into a dirty shower, even if it seemed clean; there were bugs everywhere, bugs you couldn't see. She stripped off her rubber gloves and picked up the receiver. 'Hello?'

'My stomach thinks my throat's been cut,' Richard said to Tyler as they stared at some quiz show on TV that neither of them was watching. When a ringtone started to blast out into the living room, they both reached into their jeans' pockets, ignoring the shouts from Lorraine that tea was on the table.

Siobhan was halfway through a set of one hundred sit-ups when the phone rang. Pressing *pause* on the YouTube video that was shouting at her to keep going, she reached over for her mobile, frowning at the number she didn't recognise.

Harry had just flipped the sign to 'Closed' when his mobile rang. He hoped it wasn't his wife. It had been a long day, with five routine operations and a lifesaving one on a Labrador that had been mown down by a bus. Only it hadn't been lifesaving; the dog hadn't made it. He reached in his pocket, pulled out his mobile and breathed out a weary 'Hello.'

Mickey had washed her hair and dressed her in her best outfit. It hadn't been an easy job, in fact he'd ripped the blouse at the back, trying to get it down past her shoulders, but no one would see that as she was lying down. He stood back and admired her. He had always loved her, always, but now it was time to let her go. The phone rang in the other room.

Denise took a deep breath. She hadn't wanted to face up to the facts that were staring her in the face and yet she had to find out, she had to. Spots of blood dripped onto the floor from the cuts Mother had made in her palm. Closing her eyes, she gripped the phone harder, hoping to stem the flow, and took a deep breath:

'It's you, isn't it? All this has been you.'

CHAPTER 38

Road closed. I ignore the sign, swerving the car around it. For once, my timing is perfect. There'll be no cars out near the quarry tonight; the heatwave has finally broken, rain pounding at the dusty ground like the end of the world has come.

'Aren't we going the wrong way?'

'I just need to pick something up en route.' I've said I'll take her to a new restaurant in Manchester. My treat. She has on a new dress which suits her. The burnt-amber colour matches her eyes. 'Lovely dress.'

'I almost couldn't squeeze into it,' she says. 'I'm such a lump.'

'You are not. You're gorgeous. Stop putting yourself down all the time.'

She smiles.

'Go on, say it.'

She goes bright red. 'I'm gorgeous,' she whispers and turns to me. 'What time's the table booked for? We won't be late, will we?'

'No, we won't be late.'

Satisfied with the answer, she leans back into the seat, turns the volume up on the radio. 'Hearts and Bones', my favourite Paul Simon song, fills the car.

'Ian loved this song.' She starts to hum along.

'Ian?'

'He was The One. We were going to be married but then, well, I made the wrong choice. And you can't go back, can you? "The past is the past." That's what all my self-help books say.'

'You don't read that shit, do you?'

She laughs. 'Not any more. I don't think they have the answers.'

That's been her downfall, of course, wanting answers, wanting to know the reason 'why'. I've never wondered about the 'why'. When someone has betrayed you, they've betrayed you. It's as clear as if they were sticking two fingers up at you. I'm not interested in why they've done it. Let's face it, they probably don't even know, their brains too tiny to understand why they did what they did. And, anyway, it all comes down to the same things in the end: lust, pride, envy. Loneliness.

Loneliness. It will be her undoing. It was almost mine. I think I've convinced her I had nothing to do with Elaine's death, with little Davy Kingfisher's, with Susie's. Me? Behind all of this? A murderer? That's ridiculous. I'm not David Kingfisher. It was Elaine all along. And the photo Mickey showed her? Well, there might have been a resemblance to me but I'd grown up in Devon, by the coast, hadn't I ever told her that? And he's not all there anyway, that Mickey – anyone can see that, he lives in a world of his own. And she wants to believe me, she wants to be convinced, doesn't she? She wants to believe we're friends, that I would never do this. Why else would she get in the car with me? She trusts me.

'Let's just put it all behind us,' she said, when I picked her up. 'Just forget about the whole thing.'

I'd nodded, grabbed her hand, squeezed it. She'd smiled and squeezed mine back. I so want her to forget about it, about her suspicions, about what Mickey told her, and I know she'll try to. But I'm not sure she'll be able to. I'll always have a tiny sliver of doubt, there when I open my eyes each morning, there when I go to bed, that one day, months from now, years maybe, she might just put two and two together and make four. And she likes to talk. Who knows who she'll blurt out her suspicions to? I've convinced her tonight it's not me, I'm not David Kingfisher, there's no way I could be, but will I be able to carry on convincing her? And will I be able to convince anyone else if she blabs?

I turn the car along the road leading to the quarry, push the windscreen wipers to their full speed to try and clear the driving rain. I didn't want it to come to this. I like her. She's one of life's good people, someone you can rely on. Which is why she's in this mess. If only she hadn't messaged me. If only she hadn't thought David Kingfisher was The One, she wouldn't be here now. We would never have met. She would forget Ian, get married, have a child, be loved. And not be lonely any more.

We soon reach the quarry. We've passed no other cars. There's just open countryside, not a house for miles around.

I stop the car. Her singing peters out. 'What are we doing here?'

And in that moment, I see it in her eyes: she knows it's me.

She looks down – not frightened, I think, just trying to get her head around what her brain is telling her. That I have done this to her. I'm the person who not only took money from her but also took the little glimmer of hope that someone, anyone, loved her.

I do it before I change my mind. My fingers scrabble in the door well until they find the cloth I'd put there earlier.

'Hey, it's okay,' I say, peeling her hand away from her face. She stares at me, eyes full of hope, and – for a second – my stomach lurches and I hesitate. But then I focus on what needs to be done, on getting her out of the way so I can see the game to the end. I lift my arm quickly up and across, pushing the cloth over her face. She's so shocked she doesn't react at first. But then her fight reflexes kick in and her arms fly out, her legs jump, but it's too late, the chloroform is already having an effect.

As soon as she stops moving, I take the cloth from her face. I unclip her seatbelt, get out of the car and go around to the passenger side. I pull her by the arms and she falls face forward into the mud, her legs still in the car. Grabbing her by the elbows I heave until her legs smack onto the ground followed by the rest of her body as I let her drop. Her dress is ruined. The edge of the quarry side is fifteen feet away. Bit by bit, slowly, my chest burning, my arms shaking, my eyes stinging from the rain, I pull her to the cliff side.

I sprint back to the car and open the boot, hauling out the sleeping bag. I run back, lay it on the ground so it's nearly touching her and then roll her into it before returning to the car. The rocks from my garden are heavy. I stagger with them, one by one, across the mud, placing them around her. There are too many so I choose a few of the larger ones. That will be enough.

And then a sound, a whimper: she's coming around. I wrench up the zip on the sleeping bag. Just as I'm getting to her head, she opens her eyes, wide. The fear in them frightens me. She opens her mouth and I brace myself for a scream, but there's just a whisper.

I drop my head down towards hers. 'What?'

'I'm glad it was you. I'm glad David Kingfisher was you,' she says.

A moment's hesitation and then I zip the sleeping bag all the way around, over her head.

And then I get down on my knees in the mud and push and push. And finally, just when I think I'm not going to be able to do it, that the rocks are too heavy, I feel her body move. But it's her who's moving it, not me – she's kicking and punching. And then she rolls, first towards me, and then the other way.

Straight off the cliff.

And, as she falls, I swear I hear her call out something. At first, I think it's 'David', but then I realise it's my name. She calls it again and again. And then there's a splash and the sky lights up and I imagine her lungs gasping for air, the water filling her up, making her complete, cleansing her. And, it might just be in my head, but I'm sure I hear my name echoing around the steep sides of the quarry, Denise's voice bouncing back and forth, *Petra, Petra*, before a boom of thunder drowns it out.

CHAPTER 39

I sit and watch, my hands gripping the steering wheel so tightly I'm sure I won't be able to remove them. An hour and a half, he's been in there. Ninety minutes for the rage to build in my veins, to make me open the car door, retch onto the road, my vomit, the bile, washed away by the rain as my whole body jerks, shudders. *No, no, no,* is screaming through my head. *No.* I won't let her do this to me. To us. I won't let her take him away from me.

I didn't let that silly bitch Susie take what was mine. Susie with her long red hair, her baby-blue eyes, laughing at his jokes, whimpering. We were supposed to be friends. We'd pricked our thumbs with a penknife, pushed them to each other, blood sisters. Some sister. Some friend. She thought I didn't know, thought I hadn't seen them. But I was a lot like my father. Clever. Watchful. She should have known that.

She said she had to babysit the twins, he'd said he was staying in, wanted to finish his biology homework. My gut told me something was wrong. Since he'd arrived

351

in the village, there wasn't a night we hadn't spent together, walking, talking, kissing. So I'd sat on the bench, waited until the light had gone off in his bedroom window, until the front door had opened quietly and he'd slipped out. It wasn't hard to follow him. Susie was waiting at the kissing gate. Funny, eh? A howl built inside me as she put her lips to his, as they lay down on the grass, as his hand burrowed its way up under her T-shirt, as his head moved down, his body up. I listened to their moaning, their giggles. It reminded me of Mother and the salesman. He was mine. Mine. And she, the silly little slag, she'd bewitched him with her open legs, something I couldn't do, for it was a sin, sex before marriage, my father had told me that.

So it was her own fault, you see. Her own fault. She didn't like water but I tempted her in, splashing her a bit, making her wade out until her feet could no longer touch the bottom of the quarry lake. 'I can swim,' she'd shouted. 'I can swim.' But she was no match for me. Water and I were as one. 'I can swim, Nell,' she'd said, bobbing up and down in front of me. And then I'd reached up, put my hands on her head, my fingers tangling in that long red hair, and pushed her under. Pushing, pushing, batting her thrashing arms out of the way, holding her until she didn't thrash any longer. And then I turned and looked up at the quarry edge and saw little Davy, little David Kingfisher. And understood that he would have to be next.

Anna smiles as she hears the doorbell ring. He can't keep away. That's what he'd said to her when he'd seen her earlier in town, when she'd gone up to him: 'I can't keep away from you and I don't want to.' Maybe he wants to make love to her again, to feather kisses over her eyes, her face, every inch of skin. To hold her, his arms wrapped around her, clinging like a man who fears, if he lets go, he'll drown.

A throb pulses between her legs. Make love. That's what they'd done. It hadn't been the throwaway sex of the past, riding on top of men who weren't him, trying to get herself into it, moaning in the right places, urging them on so it could be over. No, this was different. Robbo loved her. Always had done. He'd kissed the words into her. Always would. She had never felt so happy. And then he explained why he'd pushed her away. All those years ago and last year. She'd held him as he'd cried, had put her arms around him and told him it would be okay, even though she knew then that it wouldn't be.

She glances at her reflection in the hall mirror as she passes it. The lines on her forehead are relaxed, her skin is a blush of pink, the whites of her eyes shine. She looks alive. Glowing. And, for once, it's nothing to do with the expensive creams and lotions that litter her dressing table.

'Have you forgotten some—' She pulls open the door, stopping mid-sentence when she sees who it is. 'Oh, it's you.' Great. This is all she needs. Tightening her dressing gown around her, she pushes the door until it's open only six inches, her face in the gap. 'What do you want?' She knows she doesn't sound friendly, but they'd hardly parted on good terms last time so why should she bother being nice now?

'I've come to say sorry.' Tyler looks up at her from under his floppy fringe. 'I've been a dick.'

She can't deny that, so she says nothing.

'Can I come in?'

'It's not convenient.'

But he's already pushing past her. She follows him, wishing her bra and knickers, the dress she'd had on earlier, weren't lying over the back of the sofa.

He spots them straightaway. 'What's been going on?'

She wants to deny it, but why should she? This is her home, her life. It has nothing to do with a silly seventeen-year-old and his stupid crush. And anyway, the scent of sex is still heavy in the room, hanging over everything.

'So?'

How dare he? Who is he to question her like this? 'I think you'd better go. It's late and I—'

He raises his arm and, for a second, she thinks he's going to hit her, but he just pushes his fringe back with his fingers.

'You're a slag, aren't you? Got your best undies out for him, did you? I prefer the red set myself, the thong with the butterfly.'

The words hang in the air between them for a second but then anger fizzes in her stomach. It was him. She was right. Someone *had* been in her flat. 'Get out.'

He rummages in his pocket and pulls out a key. 'I can get in at any—'

'Where did you get that?' She lunges for it but he jerks his arm away, dangling it over her head, teasing her.

'You should be more careful of your things. You went to the toilet in the library, and I, well, borrowed it and it only took ten minutes to get a copy. I went to get my cap when we were in the café. Remember?'

She thinks back to the woman in the library who'd been scowling at them. Had she seen Tyler rooting through her bag? Why hadn't she said anything?

'I'll call the police.'

'No, you won't. Why would they believe an old slag like you? I'll tell them you gave it to me, we were having an affair. Letchy Leeky was right. You lead men on, get what you want from them and—'

'Get out. Get out. How dare you come into my house? Give it to me.' She walks over to him, trying to usher him towards the door, before standing on her tiptoes, straining to reach the key.

'You're a slag.' He swipes at her dressing gown, pulling one side away from her, exposing her right breast. His eyes light up as he sees her nipple.

She pulls the dressing gown back around her, pushes him. 'Get out. Get out.'

He grabs her by the shoulders. 'You're going to fucking pay, Anna. You're going to fucking pay.'

He pushes her and she stumbles back, landing on the sofa. He's on top of her, his hands pulling at her dressing gown, his fingers moving for his zip, the freckles she'd once admired so close. Too close.

No, Anna wants to scream but her lips are fused together, the word stuck in her head, swirling around. He prises her legs apart with his knee. And then suddenly there's a huge bellow and an umbrella is swinging through the air, its tip catching him on the temple.

'Get off her, you animal. Get off.'

Tyler lets out a yowl, scrabbles to his feet, pulls up the zip of his jeans. 'Who the fuck are you?'

The tip of the umbrella prods his chest. 'Go. Go.'

He hesitates, glowers at Anna. And then he goes.

They wait until they hear the door bang.

'Are you okay?'

Anna nods although she's not sure she is. What has happened to Tyler? She knew he had a crush on her, but this? He's turned into a monster. Is it Richard, filling his head with spite, hate?

'The door was open and I heard you shouting.'

Anna looks up at Petra. What is she doing here? She must have grabbed the umbrella from the hallway. It's a golfing one, borrowed from school and never returned.

'Thank you. Thanks.' She pulls the dressing gown around her, pushes her hair back, wipes away the tears she didn't even realise had fallen.

'You need tea. Plenty of sugar.'

She does – every part of her is shaking. She needs a bath too, needs to scrub away every last trace of what has just happened. She will have her tea and then get rid of Petra.

'Will you check the door is shut? And the bolt is across?' Anna hates sounding feeble, especially in front of Petra. Out of the three of them, she's always been the strongest. She will have to call a locksmith as soon as she's gone. What if Tyler comes back?

Petra leaves the room. Anna hears the scrape of the bolt, the jangle of the safety chain, the kettle boiling and then she's standing in front of her. 'Here, drink this.'

Anna takes the mug, curls her legs under her. She has to do something about Tyler. This has all gone too far now. She'll report him to Benson in the morning. Maybe she'll even ask for the police to be called in. But what if he tells them about the kiss in the beer garden? What if Richard backs him up? She'll lose her new job. She might never be able to teach again. And she thought it had all been over when Elaine had sent her the laptop. She finds a tissue in her dressing gown pocket, blows her nose. She'll call Lisa as soon as Petra has gone; her sister will know what to do.

Petra sits down on the chair opposite her. 'Should I not ask what all that was about? You and him, you're not...?' She nods to the back of the sofa where Anna's dress and underwear still lie.

'No, no, of course not. He's a pupil.' Is that what Petra thinks of her, that she would betray her integrity, stoop so low? And yet she had kissed Tyler, that time in the pub garden, if only for a second. Robbo had confirmed her memory. 'You were so drunk.' She'd thought he'd be mad, but he'd just laughed. 'It's a good job I was there to see you home.' So, it had been him, the man she'd slept with. How could she not have known? But then, despite her drunken fugue, perhaps she'd always known.

'Drink your tea.'

Anna does what Petra says. It feels good, the hot liquid, soothing, the sweetness of it comforting.

'New boyfriend then?'

Reaching over, Anna pushes the clothes so that they drop down over the back of the sofa. 'Old one.'

'Oh?'

'You remember I told you about that man, my Mr Right?'

Petra's mug is halfway to her lips. 'I thought he didn't want you?'

Anna suddenly feels sorry for the woman in front of her. Petra with her sallow face, her wet hair plastered to her head, the pinched demeanour that says she knows no man will ever be interested in her, is jealous.

'Seems like he still does.'

'What was stopping him before?'

Anna puts her mug down and yawns. Her eyelids start to flutter. A bath and bed. That's what she needs. She'll feel better in the morning. Then she can decide what to do about Tyler.

'His wife,' she says.

'What?' The word hardly makes a sound. But it's out of my mouth before I can stop it. And I wanted to stop it. Wanted to grab onto it as I grab onto my leg now, want to push it down, away from me, to stop it from escaping. I don't want to know.

358

A howl builds inside me, the howl that has always been there. It was there when my father shoved my head under the water every day, saying he was offering me redemption. *You are cleansed, Petronella. You are cleansed.* The upstanding vicar, the one who was supposed to be the beacon of light, who took delight in my suffering. The one who killed my mother. It was there when I'd seen Susie kissing Sam. It was always just Sam and me, we had always been together, were meant to be together. Why could no one understand that? I barely suppressed that howl when I'd followed Sam on one of his trips away last year, knowing there was something wrong, not wanting to believe it, until I'd seen him walk into the arms of another woman. This woman. Anna. The one he'd nearly left me for, all those years ago at university. But I wouldn't let him go, had persuaded him to go to America, to take me with him, to forget all about the stupid girl with the strawberry-blonde hair. I've never forgotten her. I'd seen a photo, taken at graduation day, and the image of her, her beauty, the face that had seduced Sam, had stayed with me, always hovering at the edge of my mind. I've tried to push it away over the years, forget about it, but I've realised these past few months that there is only one way to get rid of it forever.

'When did it start again?'

'You remember when we went to Bickley and I had a massive hangover?'

I know all right. I remember the reek of alcohol seeping from the woman sitting next to me. But, more than that, I remember my own fear: Sam hadn't come home till the early hours of the morning. He'd climbed into bed next to me and I could smell the stench of her on him. I'd known it then. Known it had started up again. Despite Sam's reassurances it wouldn't, that his mistake the year before had been just that: a mistake.

A grey hotel in Birmingham last September. I was hiding under my umbrella, the rain lashing down, feeling like it was soaking my bones. He hadn't seen me, was too wrapped up in her, his hand on the small of her back, his lips touching hers. Five minutes, ten? An hour? I had no idea how long I'd stood there, the rain soaking me through, mingling with my tears. Should I have confronted them? Would things be different now if I had, if I'd hared up the thick-carpeted steps, run up to their room, banged on the door? And yet, in the days, the weeks that followed, I thought I'd made the right choice: ignore it and carry on. Pretend it had never happened.

But while I could do that, Sam couldn't. A night out with Miranda and Jacko late last year, beer, followed by wine, then brandy, a taxi called for them, and then it had all come out. He'd met someone else. There were tears – not from me, I'd cried all mine that day in the rain in Birmingham – but they poured out of him. He didn't know what to do, he was in love with two women, he needed time to think. I gave him a week and at the end of it I told him I was pregnant.

He stayed. Of course he stayed. Three failed IVF attempts and then I was pregnant naturally.

Would he have stayed, without the baby? Had he chosen me over this other woman? It was a question I tormented myself with, rubbed away at, let infect me. But he stayed, I told myself. And that was the most important thing. And although the terror of him leaving never subsided, and the forgiveness refused to flow, I had learnt to live, to exist, side by side with him.

Until the other woman had come back four months later. And this time there was no baby to keep him.

He'd told me the very day he'd seen Anna again, about how shocked he'd been that she was there, at the university where he worked, standing in the lecture theatre. He'd told her to keep away from him. And anyway, he'd shouted, she wasn't interested in him, she was internet dating. And that's when the plan had formed. Could I find her, this woman who had taken my husband away from me? Could I find her and make her fall in love with someone else so that she would leave my Sam alone?

It had been simple. She was on the second dating site I visited. And it had been easy to haul her in. What better way than choosing someone who had a passing resemblance to 'her' Robbo? Jacko, his half-brother, the perfect fit. Alex Michaels.

It was a game at first, trying to see if I could get her to fall for David Kingfisher. I wanted her to be so in love with him that she would forget all about Sam. But I wanted to hurt her too. I wanted her to feel that stab of rejection when he let her down, to understand she wasn't as loveable as she might think. The photos had been a stroke of genius on my part. Would I have shown them to the school, got her sacked? Yes, that was my initial plan. But I wanted to see what she was like too, see how her body was different than mine, see what had tempted Sam. I didn't want to look at them, but I had. And it just made me hate her even more, this woman with her curves, her soft skin, her tarty underwear – she was nothing like me. She had something I didn't and something Sam wanted. And I knew then I would have to kill her.

Denise was an unfortunate victim in all this. I don't know why I started chatting to her. Perhaps I sensed her loneliness. Perhaps I, too, needed a friend. And we did become friends. She adored me. And adoration can be addictive. I started to like her. I didn't want her to die, I really didn't, but she had to. I had come so far I couldn't let anything get in the way of my life with Sam. And she would have talked, she wouldn't have been able to stop herself. She threatened to go to the police, didn't she? That's why I sent her the money back, the money I was going to use to pay for the IVF. I didn't want any paper thread leading back to me.

Anna lets out a huge yawn. 'I bumped into him. In The Vaults of all places, can you believe that? Anyway, well, he came back here and…' She shrugs.

I nod, very slowly. My head feels like it's too heavy for my neck. Is the pain etched on my face? Would Anna, wrapped up in her selfishness, notice if it was?

She must sense something, for she says: 'Things will work out for you too, Petra. You do know that, don't you? You'll meet someone. You'll have a baby.'

So much concern. So much concern for me now, when really she has none at all. And she's right, I could have a baby, I could find a man on a dating site, someone like David Kingfisher. I could preen and fuss over him and open my legs and let him impregnate me. But far better to go to a clinic, to rely on a professional and another man's sperm. Sam would never know, just as he hadn't known I was lying about being pregnant last year. As I'd shown him the positive test, I'd thanked God that Kirsty had had that scare, that know-it-all Jane had told us about the evaporation line – a positive result when there was no baby at all.

'You must be nervous, after what happened.' She puts her hand to her stomach and in that second I look at her and I know. And I wonder if she even knows it yet herself. The howl rises in my chest. The consultant's words are loud in my head, as if he were in the room with us. 'Even with your low sperm count, Sam, miracles do happen. But I do have to tell you that sometimes, biologically, you just aren't a match.'

I lean towards her, this slut, this woman who biologically matches my husband, my Sam. My words are slow as if I'm talking to someone stupid. 'I was never pregnant. I made it up. My husband was going to leave me.'

'Oh.' Is that a flicker of understanding in Anna's eyes? If so, she rubs it away as her hand moves over her face. 'Oh,' she says again. 'I didn't know you were married.'

'I still am.' I hold out my left hand, the wedding band I'd always stuffed in my jeans pocket whenever I'd met her standing proud, dwarfing my thin finger.

'Oh,' she repeats once more, stretching her legs out along the sofa, leaning to the side, supporting her head with her hand. 'Maybe you could try again? Or try for the first time? It might bring you closer together?'

The words are so hard to get out, the howl filling my mouth. But I won't let it out, not yet. 'Sam and I couldn't be closer.'

For a second, Anna's eyes focus. 'Sam? Talk about coincidences. That's Robbo's first name. But I always call him Robbo.'

I move quickly, so quickly Anna doesn't realise what's happening. Grabbing her by the shoulders, I shake her, the words spitting out of me: 'He's not Robbo, he's Sam, and he's mine, you stupid bitch. Mine. Sam Robertson is my husband.'

The scent of lavender fills the room. I've put in far too much bubble bath but I don't care. It's not like she'll need it again, is it?

She's heavier than she looks, although there's nothing to her.

I grab her under the armpits and heave her top half into the bath. I'm careful not to bang her head. We don't want any tell-tale signs, do we? I lift her legs and bum and push. She's lying on her side, at an awkward angle. That won't do. The water makes it easier to move her. I pull her till she's lying flat on her back. Her breasts are perfect, full, the nipples large.

She's murmuring. Is the sedative wearing off? I hope

so. I want her to be at least a little bit awake when I do it.

I sit on the toilet seat, trying to calm my jumping leg. Her head begins to slip under the water and suddenly her arms start moving. I rush over and grab her under the chin, lifting her up. She opens her eyes and her mouth, those eyes that have gazed at my husband, those lips that have kissed his.

'No.'

'Yes,' I say. 'Yes.'

I grab a chunk of her hair, those beautiful, glossy locks, and push down hard on her head before dragging her back up.

'He's mine,' I say as she surfaces, suddenly noticing the necklace, the same one Sam bought me, the one Denise had pointed at the first time we met in the pub. I snatch at it, breaking the chain, the silver heart disappearing under the bubbles. 'Mine.' And then I push her head back under the water and move the lavender bubbles aside so that I can see when the air has finished escaping her lungs.

Her glassy eyes stare at me. *You could have cleansed me*, they seem to be saying. *You could have forgiven me.*

I put my head down close to the water, so close I'm nearly touching her, only an inch of water separating us.

'No, Anna,' I whisper. 'No, I couldn't.'

CHAPTER 40

He's there when I get back, the television on low, a beer in his hand. 'Hey,' he says as I walk through the door. 'You look like a drowned rat.' I shake myself, just like Jude used to do. She's even taken my dog from me. Sam was probably on his way to see her when he ran him over.

'Do you want me to bath him?' He peers around me, expecting to see Jude shaking himself.

'He's at the vet's. Nothing to worry about,' I say when I see the alarm in his face. 'A tummy bug. Harry wants to monitor him overnight.' I decide not to tell him, about how, in his eagerness to get away from me, he killed our dog. I don't want anything spoiling his first night back.

I take off my sopping coat. 'Throw you out, did he, then? Jacko?'

He smiles and I smile back. With any luck Jacko will get hauled in for questioning when they find her body. Maybe it was stupid picking someone so close to us, but what better person could there be? Alex Michaels,

Jacko to his friends, in honour of his surname and once attempting to moonwalk on a drunken night out. Jacko, top surgeon, Mr Gorgeous, made the perfect David Kingfisher. And it's his own fault; he should never have covered up for Sam last year when he was messing about with her. I must admit I was nervous when Denise found him but God, the very same God my father blessed and threatened me with, must have been looking down on me because Anna and Denise never mentioned my name when they went to see him.

'I need a shower.' I head upstairs, peel off my wet clothes and step into the thundering water, trying to wash away every trace of her from me, from our lives.

And then I fall into bed, waiting two, three hours until he crawls into the empty space next to me. And when I'm sure he's asleep, when his snores fill the silence, I snuggle up behind him, breathe him in, whisper into his back that nothing will part us ever again.

Sam puts down the newspaper. I reach for his arm. Give it a squeeze. 'It's good to have you back,' I say.

'Pet, I need—'

'Sit down. It's nearly ready.' I've cooked him a huge fry-up, sausage, bacon, two eggs, mushrooms, baked beans, fried bread, the works. He's going to need something to line his stomach.

I slip the fried eggs onto the plate and put it down in front of him. 'Eat up.'

He smiles his thanks at me. I have to keep him busy, have to stop him from saying those words, that he's going to leave me, leave me for her. But there is no her. And once he realises that, he'll stay.

I sit opposite him, sip at my chamomile tea, nibble at the corner of my toast. How long will it take to find her? How long must I stop him saying those words?

He puts down his fork. 'I need to tell you something.'

I get up, turn on the TV screen that hangs on the wall. It's just before ten. The local news will be on in a minute. I hum along to 'Walking on Sunshine', the backing track for an advert, as I pile the pans into the sink. It's still throwing it down outside; the scorching summer seems like it never happened.

'The top story today is that one woman has been found dead and another seriously injured in separate incidents, both in suspicious circumstances.' We both turn towards the TV. A reporter who looks like he still should be at school is standing at the entrance to the quarry. 'A local dog walker spotted what he thought was a body on the shore of the quarry lake. He assumed she was dead, but the woman was still breathing. She's being treated at the university hospital. I spoke to a doctor there earlier who said she's in a coma but they're certain she'll pull through.'

She's survived? Denise has survived? But she won't make it, will she? A coma, the reporter said. I'll go and visit her later, go and make sure she'll never wake up. I am her friend, after all, that's the least I can do: put her out of her misery.

Sam turns away, picks up his fork and spears a sausage with it.

The reporter turns to a man to his left. His face is familiar, or is it the shirt he's wearing? A kingfisher-blue one. I'm sure I've seen him somewhere before. 'This is Guy Hardy, a private investigator. I believe you saw the woman last night, Mr Hardy?'

The man nods. 'I'd been paid to follow her, by her mother.' He turns, nods at the camera. 'Only Mrs Crowley wouldn't pay what she owed me so I followed her daughter into town, thinking I might tell her what had been going on.'

'And you last saw her where?'

'Standing outside Picasso's.'

The reporter thanks him, turns back to the camera. 'The police are asking anyone who saw the woman to contact them urgently.'

Sam is mopping his plate with a hunk of fried bread.

'The other woman was found in a block of flats on Trent Road, close to the hospital.'

I wonder if Sam has heard, for he carries on mopping. But then he drops the bread, gets off his stool and goes over to the TV.

'The woman has not yet been formally identified but locals have named her as Anna Farrow, a teacher at St Edward's. According to locals she was found by a teenager who called around for a private lesson.'

So, I think, that lad did go back. I say a silent thank you, for suspicion will surely fall on him. Of course, he may tell them I was there but how will they trace me, how can they link me to her? The only person who knows that I knew her is Denise. And I've nothing to fear from her. There's Jonathan and JC, I suppose, but they were heading off on a tour of Australia the day after we visited them; it's big news for where we live but it won't reach them.

And, anyway, it's suicide. I'd taken Elaine's laptop from Anna's flat last night, posted the images on social media sites from Elaine's account. Anna was a teacher, respected. She couldn't live with the shame of what she'd done. That's what everyone will think.

Sam is staring at the screen.

The reporter taps his earpiece. 'And news just in, an unnamed source tells us that the woman was pregnant.'

I cleaned up well. My OCD tendencies have come in useful after all. As did the antibacterial spray from the vet's. Harry won't miss it. Or if he does, he won't ask, he knows what I'm like. I gave Anna's flat a much more thorough going-over than I did Elaine's hovel of a house. That would have taken me a week. Elaine. If only she'd let it rest. Did she recognise me that day? No, I don't think so, she could hardly see out between the folds of fat surrounding her eyes. And I'd changed my hair. I'm a lot thinner than I used to be. And there was my name. I'd changed it when I left Bickley. Nell was the child, Petra the woman.

But Mickey. I don't think he recognised me at first, that day when we knocked on his granddad's door. I perhaps looked familiar to him then, but it wasn't until he saw me at Elaine's that I think he realised who I was. And he told Elaine, of course he did. And I knew she'd call me, and that I'd have to get rid of her. But I have no worries about Mickey now. He's slow, has been in trouble with the police; they will never believe him.

Sam has gone to bed with a headache. That's what he says. I've checked on him twice and he's just lying there, his eyes open, staring at the ceiling.

I go in for the third time, get on the bed next to him, lie down, reach for his hand. It's then I realise that the fusty smell in the room has gone and I wonder if I'd been imagining it all along, if the smell was her, invading my thoughts, my mind, every part of me.

'It's going to be okay, Sam.'

He starts to cry, great wracking sobs that reverberate along his whole body. I hold him and shush him and tell him everything will be all right, that he's mine and I will never leave him.

'She didn't want me,' he says. His words are so soft I can hardly hear them. 'I loved her but she didn't want me. I'd lied to her. That's what she said. A baby. My baby.' He looks up at me then. 'I love her.'

I wrap my arms around him, pull his head onto my chest. 'You love me, Sam. You love me.' The anger that has coursed through me this past year, the anger that made me shout and hit, that made him sometimes cower in front of me, has gone. There is nothing to fear any longer. She has gone. And Sam will love me.

It's dark when I wake. I turn over but the bed is empty next to me. The red numbers on the digital clock blink

372

at me: five. I can't remember the last time I slept for so long. I stare out of the window. The storm seems to be sitting right over the top of the house; trees are thrashing back and to, the rain is thundering onto the window.

I open the bottom drawer of the bedside cabinet, my fingers reaching for the vodka bottle.

I go downstairs, empty the liquid down the sink, shove the bottle to the bottom of the recycling bin. I get the burner phone, the one with the voice-changing app on, and my Kindle, and go out into the garden, digging a hole and pushing them in, stamping on the ground.

I go back inside, suddenly hungry for the first time in months.

'Sam,' I call, looking into the living room.

'Sam?' I walk into the kitchen. The newspaper is where he left it, the TV is still on. I go over to switch it off, glance through the window, hear the crunch of gravel as a police car swings onto the drive. And then I see it, propped up against the kettle, an envelope with my name on.

I rip it open. And then it finally comes. The howl that's been building inside me all these years, the howl tearing at my insides, waiting to come out, roars from me, drowning out the hammering of the fists at the door.

Acknowledgements

Just Another Liar wouldn't exist without the help and encouragement of many, many people.

Firstly, a huge thank you to my wonderful agent, Bill Goodall, for taking a chance on me and this novel.

Secondly, another huge thank you to Phoebe Morgan for acquiring the rights to the book. Yes, I am still pinching myself!

The Avon Books team has been just brilliant. Tilda McDonald helped me knock the story into shape (I have to admit you were right about cutting the gangster!), Katie Loughnane stepped in when Tilda moved to pastures new and Lucy Frederick, my brilliant editor, brought everything together. Sabah Khan got me a mention in – amongst other places – *The Bookseller* (a dream come true!) and Becci Mansell, Ellie Pilcher and El Slater have worked tirelessly to promote the novel. Thanks are also due to Avon's assistant Elisha Lundin, and if you're reading this, then the sales team will also have done a brilliant job, so a big thank you to them.

I'm so grateful to everyone who has bought this book. I hope it hasn't put you off internet dating. It can and often does help you to find 'The One' – see below!

I started this novel on a Faber Academy writing course in 2016. Mark McNay, who tutored the course, helped me to shape the first 15,000 words and my fellow students, especially Fran Benson, Katie Mork, Louise Guest, Colleen Goth and Lorna Taylor, gave me the encouragement and honest feedback I needed. Thank you.

At the time of writing, I am currently a creative writing MA student at UEA. I'm indebted to Henry Sutton, Tom Benn, Nathan Ashman and Julia Crouch, for helping and pushing me. My fellow students have become firm friends: Sharon Bale, Katherine Black, Libby Brookes, Hannah Brown, Virginia Cole, Alan Jackson, Denise Kuehl, Lynne McEwan, Simon Margrave, Pat Page, Sue Thomas. As well as being a great bunch of people, they're also fantastic writers. I look forward to celebrating your successes with you all!

My friends have always cheered me on and believed in me: Jac Dale, Rach Cooper, Kaz Wright, Rachel Wright, Isabelle Killicoat, Amy Clowes, Julie Brazier, Katie Armitt, Barrie Eyden, Joe Eyden, Luisa Plaja, Fran Benson and Kevin Ryan – about time we had a party to celebrate!

I'm grateful to everyone who read the novel at its various stages: Fran Benson, Dan Minchin, Luisa Plaja, Rich Parkinson and Roz Watkins. And a big thumbs up to Jane Shepherd for lending me both her name and the name of her Irish terrier, Barney.

Thanks must go to the Parkinsons – Bob and Anne, Tom and Sharon, and Ben, Katie and Charlotte – for welcoming me into their lovely family.

I have been blessed to have three wonderful children (now teenagers!) in my life over the past few years. Emma, Sam and Beth – thank you for always asking me how the writing is going.

My parents have always been there for me. Mum and Dad, I'm so grateful to have your support and love. My sister, Nicola, is the best sister I could ever have asked for. And her husband, Paul, is a great brother-in-law.

Finally, I wouldn't be sitting here and writing these acknowledgements if it wasn't for Rich (proof, if anyone does need it, that internet dating can work!). Thank you for everything, Rich. I'm so happy we found each other.